The Yonker

Lost Treasure of Esopus Creek

The Devar-Garrison Historical Mystery Series

IV

A novel by

Curt Ench

Published by Alexander-Ench Press
First published in 2025 (USA)

Illustrated maps by Curt Ench; cover design by David Fischer

ISBN: 979-8-9922831-1-2 (e-book)
ISBN: 979-8-9922831-2-9 (paperback)

Printed in the United States of America

Alexander Ench
PRESS

To those who defend "Freedom of Conscience"

The Yonker

(Jonk Herr - Dutch for Young Gentleman)

Acknowledgments

I would like to express my gratitude to the following people who provided help, expertise, and encouragement for this novel

* * *

Ann Kovara, David Burkhead, Carol Steffgen, David Fischer, and Don Walters, my early readers for their indispensable knowledge, input, and unwavering support

* * *

David Fischer for his contagious enthusiasm throughout the project, and his expertise and skill designing the book cover for *The Yonker - Lost Treasure of Esopus Creek*

* * *

And Mary Alexander, my partner and creative collaborator in all things, without whom this book would not exist

Prologue

(Loevestein Castle – 1621)

The abrupt stop made his head bump into the side of his crude wooden prison. Constructed of planks, he tried not to dwell on the coffin-like appearance of the crate he hid in.

Terrified, sweat stung his eyes and his breathing became shallow. For the first time he faced the possibility that each moment could be his last. The urge to claw his way out became unbearable, but he couldn't risk moving. The slightest shift in weight could cause his discovery, and as an escapee, the guards would be quick to run him through with razor sharp swords.

Another quick jostle and they were moving again, downward this time. The muffled sound of the guards grunting under the weight of the crate filtered through the gaps in the rough wooden planks as they lugged him down a time worn stone staircase.

They entered the cold night air of the central courtyard, and the temperature inside the wooden crate began to fall. Mind racing, he was barely aware of the guards' voices arguing among themselves before unceremoniously dropping the crate onto the stone pavement.

The impact cracked several of the dry wooden planks, threatening to expose the crate's contents. Cold winter air poured through the gaps.

An uncontrollable shiver passed through him as the frozen night penetrated his thin coat, and the fear of being discovered chilled him to the bone. He was desperate to see his wife who had risked everything to arrange his escape, knowing they would both be executed should he be discovered.

Moving once again, he found he was able to see through the widened cracks in the crate. He was focused on the drawbridge and main gate when the angry words of a guard caught his attention.

"I'm tired of lugging books to and from this heretic's cell. He should suffer the same fate as his heretical mentor."

"We could send his head back to Delft as a warning to the rest of the Armenians, but for now, I'd settle for tossing this crate into the moat," a gruff voice replied.

He struggled to control his panic as the smell of stagnant water seeped through the cracks. The sound of boots marching on wooden planks confirmed they were crossing the drawbridge over the inner moat. After rounding the north side of the castle nearest the river, they turned toward the second drawbridge at the outer moat.

He focused on the plan his wife had described to him. He was to be loaded onto old Stoffelsen's cart once beyond the second moat, but something was wrong.

Terror gripped him as they turned toward the Waal River and marched down the pier to a waiting barge. There would be no cart for him tonight.

His thoughts began to tumble out of control. Had their escape plan been discovered? Was he destined for the bottom of the river?

He was certain they heard him gasp as the crate was dropped on the foredeck of the river barge, but they had not.

Unmoored, the strong current soon had the barge gliding down the main channel. Each minute seemed like an eternity. Then the soft sloshing of the river against the hull was interrupted by the sound of boots approaching.

His heart quickened as the shrill sound of the crate lid being pried loose pierced his ears. He held his breath, fighting an instinct to recoil like a caged animal, when a strange calm came over him.

Mustering the courage to accept his fate, Hugo Grotius opened his eyes and looked up through the steamy clouds of his own breath into the clear night sky.

Part One
(Present Day - Brooklyn, New York)

Chapter 1

Brooklyn Museum – Special Exhibit Gallery

"You look amazing. Your gown is perfect for the opening."

"Thanks, but it's the exhibit that needs to look amazing," Annah replied, with a trace of anxiety in her eyes that had developed over the last several weeks of preparation.

Although pleased with the professional presentation of the Cheshme Shafa exhibit and its prominent placement in the main gallery, she was equally nervous and emotional about the speech she planned to give honoring her dead brother Thomma's contribution to the discovery.

"I see the sapphire is where it was meant to be," he said, eyes following the contours of her neck to the exquisite star sapphire pendant they discovered in Palmyra, Syria. Although she declared and catalogued the find, she had also negotiated a lifetime custodianship with the Brooklyn Museum, satisfying her powerful desire to possess it. Wearing it at the opening was part of the deal.

Feeling the movement of his eyes on her skin, Annah whispered, "Shouldn't you be focused on your presentation?"

"Your gown is making it more difficult than you think," Will countered with a grin.

Looking over his left shoulder, Annah made a face that said, *Someone is right behind you…*

"Director de Boer," Will said tactfully as he turned around, "It's a thrill presenting our work here tonight."

When necessary, he could be amazingly gracious in a formal setting, an ability that always tickled Annah, as this was in direct contrast to the basic and somewhat goofy man she had come to love.

"Please call me Beatrix. You both are now family."

"Thank you for all your encouragement and support," Annah added.

"And you two for this amazing exhibition. It's going to be a huge draw for us."

Turning directly to Annah, Beatrix took her hand and added, "You've done right by your brother. He would be so proud of you."

Getting back to the business at hand, the director continued, "I came over to tell you that Governor Tess Hendriksen is making a surprise visit to the opening of your exhibit tonight. She is a good friend of Riley Spaulding's mother from their college days, and I'd love to introduce you to her."

Will Garrison's college sweetheart, Riley was on the staff of the Brooklyn Museum where she was murdered in connection with the artifacts he had brought back from Afghanistan.

"Governor Hendriksen," Will repeated, surprised and excited about her appearance. "You can be sure there will be a special mention of Riley's contribution in my presentation."

* * *

Annah had a deep fondness for Special Agent Johanna Martin, and an abiding trust that had developed in the wake of their harrowing experience with the Mandate, a murderous ring of religious artifact smugglers. It was a great comfort to see her enter the museum lobby. Tonight was a celebration, and Martin looked stunning in a formal gown, a look Annah had not seen before. It was quite a contrast to her usual black pants and hip length blazer.

Accompanied by a distinguished and very British gentleman, the striking couple strolled to the reception desk and picked up their guest badges. Tonight was a private event on the eve of the official public opening, and dozens of large donors and dignitaries had already arrived.

Annah caught the attention of Sydney, one of the museum interns who had volunteered to take candid photos of the event. Seeing Annah tip her head to the right, along with a mock frame and finger click, Sydney focused her camera on Martin and Albert.

As they were about to be absorbed into the crowd milling about the exhibit teasers in the main lobby, Annah took Martin by the arm and guided the couple over to Will, who was standing across the lobby near the exhibit entry in front of an enormous map of the Silk Road and the ancient sea routes between India and the Mediterranean.

Albert, always delighted to see his nephew, narrowed his eyes as they approached Will, silently reminding him to skip the Uncle Albert routine. He was, after all, thirty something and dressed in a tuxedo.

Will caught the look in his eye as he started to greet them. "Uh, Albert, I am so pleased to see you here tonight. You and Martin truly are two of the heroes in this story. You really deserve to be recognized."

With a hint of a smile, Albert peered over his glasses and whispered to Will, "Remember, no names. That goes for Martin as well."

"I know, I know," Will whispered back as he ushered them to the VIP area just in time to catch the timely arrival of a waiter with a tray of champaign glasses.

With glasses in hand, they made a toast to the evening's success. Annah felt that simply staying alive in Afghanistan and Syria was enough to celebrate, but her desire to give recognition to Thomma was her main focus this evening. She silently willed herself to get through her tribute without crying, and honor her beloved brother for his part in the discovery, for which he gave his life.

The light conversation with Martin and Albert distracted Annah from her nerves and buoyed her spirits.

Martin tried to steer the conversation toward their personal life, curious about their plans as a couple, but Annah skillfully directed the conversation back to archeology and their plans to restore Will's small farm in the Catskills. Will had recently acquired a large portion of the original farm acreage that had been sold off years before by his great grandparents. He was deeply grateful to his parents for establishing a trust to maintain the property, which had now produced sufficient excess funds to make the land purchase.

Annah smiled to herself, knowing that Martin was equally coy about her relationship with Albert. With a glance, they silently agreed to table discussions of a romantic nature for the evening. It was, however, no mystery how Martin felt about her British gentleman.

About to make a toast, Albert raised his glass just as a hush washed over the lobby. Governor Hendriksen and U.S. Senator Torres of New York entered the museum lobby, accompanied by their senior aids and security entourage.

* * *

Annah took advantage of the governor's surprise visit and skillfully maneuvered her into cutting the ribbon at the entry to the exhibit.

As the crowd poured into the large exhibit gallery, Will recognized Anika Spaulding, Riley's mother, walking arm and arm with Tess Hendriksen, deep in conversation.

Aware that his presence could stir deep emotions he hesitated before approaching them. Although cleared of all wrongdoing in the murder of Riley, he still held the guilt of knowing that he had inadvertently led the killers to her place of work at the museum, something he would forever regret.

Will had not seen Anika since Riley's funeral when she had been in deep mourning. She came to the event tonight knowing her daughter would receive recognition from him, so as uncomfortable as he was, he knew it would be inappropriate not to greet her.

Annah saw his painful hesitation and quickly linked her arm with his as he started to walk across the room. Above all else, they were a team.

"Anika, I'm so glad you could be here tonight," Will said with a warmth in his voice that made Annah pay attention.

When he first arrived at the dig site in Karala, India, Will kept his emotions hidden. Learning of his childhood trauma and later, the accidental death of both parents, Annah began to understand the courage it took for him to reveal his real feelings. She had watched him become less guarded and more genuine in the few years she had known him, and tonight she saw an openness and compassion that made her proud.

Anika looked down for a quick moment, then lifted her eyes to meet Will's. She knew how close Will had been to her daughter and began to see that he, too, must be suffering deeply from her loss. She stepped forward and wrapped her arms around him in a warm embrace.

As she gently pulled away, she turned and said, "Have you met the governor?"

Will unconsciously stood a bit straighter. "I'm very pleased to meet you Governor Hendriksen," Will said in a formal voice, as if she might be royalty. "Let me introduce you to my partner in life, and science, Annah Devar."

Annah, following suit, nearly bowed, then blushed as she shook her hand.

"Call me Tess."

A loud hum coming from the governor's camel hair jacket distracted her.

"Excuse me while I respond to this text from my partner," she said looking up from her phone.

A moment later she explained. "Seems as though his event ended early so he's on his way here to make a quick visit before we head over to the Manhattan campaign rally."

Turning to her aide, she said in a low voice, "Have them bring the limo around so Senator Torres can go ahead to the rally. I'll catch a lift from Geoffrey after he does a quick tour of the exhibit."

"Sorry for the interruption. I was about to say that Anika has told me so much about this exhibit and some of your incredible exploits that I've been looking forward to meeting both of you. A manhunt directed at you, Will, and the horrible circumstances around your kidnapping, Ms. Devar. What an amazing journey you've been on."

"Please, call me Annah."

"Well Annah, I hope this presentation affords you some comfort, and gives both you and Will the professional recognition you deserve."

"A bit too much recognition at times, I'm afraid," Annah said wryly.

"I know the feeling," Tess replied, glancing at the security team hovering conspicuously nearby.

"As a woman traveling through the war-torn backwaters of Asia, weren't you terrified?"

Annah glanced up at Will, "Well, I had an amazing partn . . .

Stopping mid-sentence, a chill ran up her spine. Annah turned to look over her shoulder an instant before the large glass windows of the museum entrance exploded, sending shattered glass and shrapnel flying across the lobby.

Chapter 2

Brooklyn Museum Lobby

Engulfed in acrid, black smoke, they maneuvered through broken glass and the ghostly dark forms of panicked guests. Encircled by her security team, Governor Hendrickson followed Will and Annah as they were rushed toward a secure back room, with Martin in the lead.

Intent on protecting her charges, Martin barely had time to worry about Albert, or the possibility that an attack or a second explosion could happen at any moment. Doing a quick assessment to ensure no one had life threatening injuries, she left them in the room, locking the door behind her.

Martin found her way back to the lobby, breathing a sigh of relief when she saw Albert was still in one piece. He had taken charge and was directing disoriented and injured guests into the now dark gallery. Jumping in to help, she guided them into the large space and had them line up with their backs against the stone wall furthest from the lobby.

* * *

Annah felt like she was floating over her body. Everything happened so quickly that it took several minutes to remember the moment before the explosion.

She had been visiting with the governor when she felt a cold chill run up her spine. A split second later, the force of the deafening explosion knocked her off her feet and into Will, who pulled her into his arms and protectively turned her away from the blast.

Annah had experienced premonitions from an early age, but nothing this visceral or immediate. If she had been paying attention, could she have known what was about to happen? Could she have stopped it?

Her fractured thoughts were interrupted by the chime of a text. She mindlessly reached for the phone in her beaded purse and saw that it was from Kaizad. Glancing at his message, she quickly read his wishes for a successful opening, and his excitement about bringing the exhibit to Mumbai the following year. Tucking her phone back into her small bag without replying, she turned to Will to tell him about her premonition, but stopped when she saw him. His face was white and withdrawn. She scooted closer to him and took his hand in hers.

* * *

Martin stood in the corner of the large, dark gallery and called Agent Obsharski' s cell. When he didn't pick up, she quickly dialed the Brooklyn office of the FBI and asked to be put through to his office.

"Sharky, answer your god damned cell when I call. Get the FBI terror response team to the Brooklyn Museum immediately. We may have an active terror attack in progress. There was a huge explosion near the south lobby entrance and we have a large number of injured visitors. Keep in touch with me directly."

Within two minutes, Sharky called back. "Got word that the governor's limousine was blown to pieces near the south entry. The NYPD is searching for her and Senator Torres, who they believe was with her."

"The governor wasn't in the limo. Let them know we have her secured here," Martin replied. "She's okay, but we have nothing on the senator at this time."

Martin found Albert in the far corner of the dark gallery and had a quick conversation. He headed for the secure room, while she headed for the lobby, and the tangled pile of metal that used to be the governor's limousine.

* * *

Still reeling from the news that her limousine had been the source of the explosion, the governor had a delayed and horrific realization.

"Oh my god, Senator Torres!" she cried. "He was going to catch a ride in my limo!"

Gathering her emotions, Tess finished another quick conversation with her husband who was safe and enroute, and walked across the small room eerily lit by emergency lights. She sat down next to Albert, hoping to get more information. Instantly drawn to his calm demeanor and charming British accent, she felt safe for the first time since the horrifying explosion.

"My limo, were they after me? What if they find us?"

Albert reached out and took her hand. "There's been no gunfire, no more explosions, so I think it unlikely that there's more to come. Martin should be back shortly with an update."

"I didn't think much of it when we pulled up to the museum entry. The limo was surrounded by protestors wearing death masks. My security attachment had to back them off."

"It felt like they knew we were coming."

Her words rattled around in the back of Albert's head. He had learned to pay attention to odd details that were often less about paranoia and more about intuition.

Careful not to amplify her anxiety, he responded quietly, "They're likely not the bombers, but you should mention them to the investigators."

"You seem to know a lot about this kind of thing."

"Let just say I've had my share of first-hand experience with this sort of thing."

"In America?"

He nodded. "And Britain before that."

* * *

Martin entered the room followed by the governor's Chief of Security and several state troopers.

The steel in Martin's eyes softened as she came to a stop in front of the governor. "I'm so sorry, but we have confirmation that Senator Torres was in the limousine when it blew."

Chapter 3

Catskill Mountains – Esopus Creek

A deafening roar came from the east as the jets appeared on the horizon just above the tree line. They were coming directly at him. He turned and looked across the barnyard and saw the fear in the horses' eyes as they kicked at the gate. As he reached for the latch to set them free, a blinding white-hot flash erased his world.

Will bolted upright in bed. Soaked in sweat, he tried to slow his breathing and vanquish his memory of Kosovo, when his first teenage love had been incinerated by a Serbian air strike. After a reprieve of more than a year, the PTSD driven nightmare had returned with a vengeance.

Just after the car bomb exploded at the Brooklyn Museum, Annah was able to see the impact that earsplitting second of terror had had on Will. With Martin's help, they were able to give their statements to the police and FBI quickly, and as soon as they were taken, she whisked Will back to his farmhouse in the Catskills.

But as she feared, the night terrors were back. She grabbed him some dry pajamas, changed the bedding, and put a kettle on for tea. Spiced chai helped in almost every situation. It wasn't long before Will was settled back in bed.

* * *

Will's family farm was west of Kingston, New York, along the Esopus

Creek. The creek was named after the Esopus tribe, a branch of the Lenape, one of the scores of tribes the Dutch colonists called the *Wilden*.

The house and surrounding farmland had been under the care of a Mohawk Indian named Kariwase for many years. In return, he had the use of the land for his crops and livestock.

Annah and Kari knew each other casually, and she had found an article Will's mother had saved about one of his horses who was trained in equine assisted therapy. She thought it may be worth a visit to their neighbor to see if he could help Will with his current struggle.

After a simple breakfast, Annah put on her hiking boots and followed a trail through the woods that surrounded the old farmhouse, over to the small pasture where Kari kept his horses and alpaca.

The trail eventually opened onto an idyllic forest meadow with a small creek meandering through it on the far side. Patches of morning mist still hung over the glistening grass, and half a dozen horses and alpaca had their grazing spots staked out. They didn't seem to mind her presence.

Tucked into the forest on the other side of the meadow was a weathered corral next to an old wooden stable. Annah spotted Kari's truck parked on the dirt road behind the corral and picked up her pace.

She found him in the small tack room working on one of several saddles. Annah smiled to see his total focus as he lovingly treated the aged leather with saddle soap.

"Kari," she called from a distance, trying not to startle him.

"Miss Devar," he said looking up from his work. "How pleasant to see you. What brings you to the woods this early in the morning?"

"I hope you don't mind, but I wanted to talk to you about Will. He's been pretty shaken since the bombing at the museum."

"Yes, I read about it in the paper. I am glad neither of you were seriously injured."

"Perhaps not physically, but it's revived some old trauma for Will. When he was in his teens, he witnessed an aerial bomb in Kosovo. The blast killed his friend and her family, and devastated their barn. It was full of horses."

"I am so sorry. I did not know this," Kari said solemnly.

"He's started having reoccurring nightmares about the explosion again, particularly about the horses."

"Not to get all Indian about it," Kari added, "but those memories possess their own existence, like dark spirits. It is like every action or non-action you have taken, while awake or in a dream state, comes back and interjects itself into your everyday reality. In Will's case, it is causing him to relive the fear and helplessness he felt in Kosovo."

"I read an article about your horse, or one of them, who was trained in equine assisted therapy."

"That would be Mary Lou. You are familiar with the song *Hello Mary Lou*? Well, she's right down there, grazing by the creek."

"I'm hoping that she may be able to help him," Annah murmured, turning her gaze toward the pasture.

* * *

Hearing a few solid raps on the heavy wooden door, Will set down his pancake ladle and hurried from the kitchen to see who it was.

His caretaker, Kari, stood a few feet away from the front porch. He had a big smile on his face and was holding a lead. At the end of the rope stood an Appaloosa mare. She had a speckled white coat from her rump to her shoulders which quickly faded into a charcoal gray under coat, and a dark tail and mane. She was majestic.

Will found himself at a loss for words, and could feel the sting of tears as he silently looked her over. He had known Kari for many years, but this was the first time he'd shown up with one of his horses.

Kari was the first to speak. "Will, I want you to meet Mary Lou."

Finding his voice, Will answered. "Hello, Mary Lou. What can I do for you two this morning?" He paused, adding, "Did I just reference an old song?"

Kari chuckled. "I believe you did. I was hoping you could look after her for a while. Maybe keep her in your barn?"

Will's eyes narrowed as he realized Annah must have something to do with this odd request. "For how long?"

"A few weeks, maybe a month," Kari answered, slightly tilting his head to the left.

"The barn, you say?" Will said as he stepped off the front veranda and slowly approached Mary Lou. She responded to his stroking of her forehead by gently putting her muzzle up to his ear.

"Her way of greeting you," Kari said. "Like a kiss."

Will could feel his resistance melting, immediately taken by this gentle creature.

As they walked back across the barnyard, Kari nonchalantly handed the lead rope to Will. Veering away, he left Will and Mary Lou to circle the yard several times.

Annah emerged from the house and stood beside Kari.

"This is a good beginning," he said. "It has already allowed a beam of light to pierce through the dark cloud over Will."

Annah smiled. "You see it too?"

Chapter 4

Catskill Mountains – Garrison Farm

"Ready to make room in the barn for Mary Lou?" Will asked, rising from the breakfast table.

Annah grinned. "Ready. Are you excited?"

"Yes, and nervous about having things ready for her. She'll be here tomorrow morning."

"We've got all day," Annah replied, popping up from the table. "The apples and cinnamon were a nice touch."

"I've got a few apples left for the girl."

The way Will's eyes lit up when he spoke of his new spotted friend lifted Annah's spirit.

* * *

After several hours of hauling out old farm equipment and raking up the dusty remnants of hay, the first of several stalls was empty. Encouraged by their progress, they pressed on. By Noon the south half of the barn was cleared out.

The north half was daunting. Their progress was obstructed by two old tractors and the heaps of inaccessible junk trapped behind them.

Annah made grilled cheese sandwiches and served them with fresh chilled pickle spears, the way Will had shown her back in the tent structure of the research lab in Kerala, which now seemed so long ago. They had been through so much since then.

After lunch and a short rest, Will found new determination to move the tractors. He returned to the barn and sized up the situation. The smaller of the two, which was closest to the open barn doors, looked to be in better condition.

He went out in the yard, now filled with piles of stuff, and retrieved the gas can still holding a few gallons of gasoline of questionable age. Even if the battery turned the engine over, the gas might not fire.

Ten minutes later, Annah maneuvered Riley's old Beetle around the house and wove her way through the junk in the barnyard toward Will, who was waiting restlessly with a pair of jumper cables.

Shaking her head, Annah thought, if he starts naming the junk like he has a habit of doing, I'll know he's on his way to recovery.

Gassed up and cables clipped on, Will crossed his fingers and hit the ignition. The old tractor had a six-volt system and he was worried he might burn out the electric system. Surprised when the old engine began to crank, he cut the ignition and jumped to the ground, remembering that the carburetors on these old motors needed a bit of primer.

Quickly disconnecting the jumper cables, he removed the air cleaner and poured the last bit of gas into the open throttle.

"Here goes nothing," Annah yelled, clipping the cables back onto the old battery terminals.

Will hit the tractor ignition one more time. Flames shot out of the carburetor and the engine fired up, followed by a thick bellow of smoke from the tall vertical exhaust pipe.

Annah disconnected the cables and moved the Bug out of the way.

Will put it in gear, backed out of the barn, then circled around the yard.

"I think I'll call her *Joan Deere,*" he hollered to Annah.

"Well, that happened quicker than I thought," Annah yelled back with an exaggerated eyeroll.

"Thought what?" Will asked distractedly. "Hey, I've got an idea. Grab that chain I saw out of one of those barrels over there."

As she searched through the barrels, Will managed to find reverse in the old gearbox and backed Joan close to the barndoors in front of the old Case tractor.

Annah was between the two tractors before Will could ask. Hitching them together, she stepped aside and gave Will two thumbs up. He put it in gear and slowly drove forward until the chain was tight. Joan was groaning with effort, but he continued forward until her wheels lost traction. He wound the engine down.

"Wait!"

Annah, who had driven tractors many times on archeological digs in India, remembered something she'd learned. Climbing up on the old Case at the other end of the taut chain, she found the gear shift lever, and with some muscle and a foot on the clutch was able to push the sticky gear box into neutral.

"Okay, now give it the gas," she yelled over the noise of the engine, beaming as her hands gripped the wheel.

He revved the engine and eased the clutch into second gear for better traction. The large ribbed iron wheels began to grip the ground and started moving.

Annah was so captivated watching the enormous wheels turn she didn't notice the heavy beam across the head of the barn doors.

"Duck!" cried Will, spotting the beam at the last second.

With quick reflexes, Annah spun around and ducked as the splintery old beam stole the cap off her head. Disaster averted.

The old Case was in the sunlight for the first time in years. It was so elegant, yet so primitive compared to modern tractors, Annah immediately considered it an object of art, an antique worthy of restoring. It was the archeologist and preservationist in her that could see the beauty of it.

She was still sitting in the molded steel tractor seat wondering what it would look like when the decades of dirt and grime had been removed when Will yelled from the barn. "You've got to see this!"

Annah hopped down and walked into the shadowy corner of the barn previously concealed by the two old tractors. Will had moved a couple of barrels that were blocking a heavily weathered sliding plank door, and was now standing in the dark interior of a shed attached to the north side of the barn. The pitch break from the main barn roof to the shed roof was on the wooded side of the barn and they had never noticed it.

Annah's eyes slowly adjusted to the darkness, lit only by a few pencil thin beams of sunlight sneaking through the old wooden shingles. Will took her by the hand and they moved to the center of the room, using his phone for illumination.

"This should appeal to the archeologist in you," he chuckled.

The room was filled with old equipment and storage crates, piled high along all four walls. It all looked to be significantly older than the tractors.

"I don't remember my parents mentioning this room."

Annah squeezed his hand. "Maybe they were never inclined to move the old Case. We need more light to see just what you've stumbled into."

* * *

Will returned with two headlamps, dust masks, and several pairs of exam gloves from their expedition gear.

"You up to date on your tetanus shot?" he asked through his mask.

Annah nodded absently, staring at the pile of wooden boxes. Intrigued, she put on a mask and one of the headlamps, then focused a tight beam.

After moving a few of the boxes, Annah almost squealed. "Will, it's an intact printing press! Eighteenth century, I'd guess."

"Or older," Will said, brushing away the remnants of a badly decomposed canvas cover.

Pointing to the heavy wooden vertical piers supporting the press head frame, Annah said, "Look at this engraved plaque. It appears to be written in German."

"Dutch," Will said leaning closer. "It's the name of the company in the Netherlands that fabricated the press."

"What's this etched at the bottom in fine print?" she quizzed.

Gemaakt voor Andres Gerritsen

The excitement in Will's voice rose. "Gerritsen was the Dutch version of my family name. This had to belong to my ancestors. I have vague memories of my grandfather's stories about them and their print shop. I thought they were tall tales like the ones my Uncle Dan used to tell me on our visits to his home in Kingston. He always told me the same story when I was frightened by thunder, that it was Heinrich Hudson and his men playing ninepins in the nearby Catskill Mountains."

"Back up a second. Your ancestors were printers, and used this press? How fantastic! Do you see a date anywhere?"

"Here, in Roman numerals" he said, bringing his flashlight closer to the numbers etched into the metal. "MDCLIV."

As Will was trying to decipher the Roman letters, Annah blurted out, "1654. This press is almost 400 years old!"

"How did you do that so fast?"

"You're the language guy. Didn't you take Latin in primary school?"

Will snorted, ignoring her comment. He knew the Roman numerals, more or less. He just found them tedious, atypical for the efficiency driven Romans.

* * *

After a thorough inspection, they were surprised by the condition of the printing press. Having been stored on large stone blocks, it was spared from termites. Not so for the mice, who considered the space beneath the lower platen a hotel. They found countless nests in the debris.

Will pulled on the screw drive lever and the upper platen began to move down. Out of caution that the old mechanism might be damaged, he stopped after it dropped a few millimeters.

Barely holding back his excitement, he whispered, "I think this thing may still work. We'll give it a real try after a complete cleaning and conditioning of its moving parts."

Annah's face was beaming with the excitement of such an unexpected discovery, tied directly to Will's ancestors no less. It was like history coming back to life. "Let's see what else is in these boxes."

Will fetched a hammer and a large rusty screwdriver from the old Case tool box, and began prying open one of the boxes that was sitting on the press. The wood, still firm, held the rusty forged nails tight. Prying with the screwdriver loosened the lid enough to grab the nails with the hammer claw.

The box contained neatly stacked galley trays filled with carefully arranged lead type, although with the typeface upside down and written in a language that clearly wasn't English, it made the words indecipherable to both of them.

The next box held printed sheets of what appeared to be public proclamations and legal announcements. Will lowered another crate from the galley carriage extension. This one was filled with ledger books and leather-bound files.

With meticulous care, Will untied the binding cord around the first file and proceeded to peel back the leather wrapping.

"I think this is written in Dutch. That makes sense with the family heritage. But I can only make out a couple of words, like this name at the bottom, *Van der Donck*."

The name rattled something loose in Annah's memory. "I remember reading about someone with that name in a condensed history of New York while waiting for you in the museum gift shop, something about a sawmill. These records are certain to have significant historic value."

"I wrote a paper about the origin of our Bill of Rights, in which Adriaen van der Donck played an important role. He fought the corporate overlords in the high courts of Holland to establish the full rights of colonists to be the same as those of citizens back in the Netherlands. Those rights established in New Amsterdam later became a cornerstone of the U.S. constitution.

"We seriously need to get this stuff into the Brooklyn Museum."

* * *

Kari arrived towing his horse trailer behind his GMC Sierra late in the afternoon. As he led Mary Lou down the trailer ramp, he was intrigued with the machinery and organized piles of boxes he could see through the open barn doors. He had lots of questions, but they would have to wait.

"Will, come and greet Mary Lou," he called from the yard.

"Hello Mary Lou," Will crooned, happily torturing the old rock-a-billy song by Ricky Nelson as he walked out of the barn.

"Take the lead," Kari said, handing him the rope.

Lead in hand Will took a few steps, pausing as Mary Lou gently nuzzled against the side of his head. With the hint of a smile, he guided her to her new temporary home. She entered the stable, gracefully turned around, and then pawed at the bare ground.

Will looked up to see Kari unloading several large bails of fine wood chip bedding. The fragrance of the white pine chips was a welcome substitute for the musty hay they'd been raking all day. Mary Lou generously stepped out of their way until they were finished covering the stable floor, then turned a few times before curling up on the fresh bedding.

Will was taken by the horse's grace and keen empathy, almost doglike in the best sense of the word. He joined Kari in unloading bails of alfalfa, sacks of oats, and bags of wood chips, more than enough for the next few weeks. Kari handed him a clipboard with a schedule of her care and feeding, and an outline of her social skills and riding behaviors, along with notes on how to manage them. Will hung it from a large rusted spike in the wood support post nearest the large stall, intent on following his instructions to the letter.

"Use that shovel and wheelbarrow to clean her stall. There's a pile over by the woods where you can dump it," Kari said with a grin as he got back into his truck.

As Kari drove off, Will guided his new friend on a short walk to the edge of the woods, then back to the barn. After he filled her feed and water buckets, Mary Lou returned to the stall on her own, then turned to face Will.

He'd seen those eyes before. Empathetic dark orbs that held the entire universe. Something deep inside him began to shift.

Chapter 5

Midtown Manhattan Office of the Governor

An early morning thunderstorm had not deterred the rabid crowd of protestors gathered outside the governor's New York City offices. She planned to call a press conference later that day to present more details about her proposed new policies concerning the involvement of religious organizations in politics and their tax-exempt status.

She understood that her expanded policy regarding the separation of church and state, and its tax issues was going to create a strong reaction. Even so, the crowd was surprisingly large that morning considering her trip down from Albany had not been not made public.

Riding in her second limo, they turned the corner of her office building on Lexington Avenue in midtown Manhattan, and slowly approached the secure underground parking garage entry. She recognized among the protestors lining the sidewalk some of the same masks worn by the crowd the night of the Brooklyn Museum bombing. That event, too, had been an unannounced and unscheduled stop.

The limo began its descent down the dark car ramp, and Governor Hendriksen gripped the armrest, subconsciously bracing for an explosion as a shot of adrenalin pumped through her veins.

She wondered where the protesters were getting advance notice of her itinerary. The only other thing she could think of was the possibility that they were permanently camped outside all of her offices, all the time. It was a creepy speculation, but less likely.

* * *

As had been prearranged with the FBI Brooklyn command, Special Agent Martin was there to meet Governor Hendriksen backstage at the large meeting room on the Mezzanine level of her office tower. After the bombing, Tess had requested Martin be made special liaison between the FBI and her security division of the New York State Police.

"Agent Martin, we meet again under much better circumstances."

"Madame Governor, it is an honor to work with you."

"Please call me Tess. I suspect we'll be working together quite a bit. I also have a few discreet investigations I'd like you to add to your duties."

Martin had been concerned this assignment might turn into a huge babysitting operation, so she was relieved by this new development. She had a distaste for bullies, for people who were greedy or used hatred as a divisive tool, and investigating was something she was good at. She was determined to bring the bad guys to justice.

"Governor…Tess, you can count on my discretion as long as what we do is legal. I'm not insinuating you would condone anything that is illegal, it's just in my experience, everything isn't always black and white."

"You have my assurance everything will be above board, and speaking of discretion, I'd like you to get in contact with Albert Harding for me. I have growing suspicions about my staff and members of my own security detail. I'm no longer certain who I can trust. I need someone completely on the outside, someone trustworthy. Someone like Albert."

Tess made it clear she had done her own off-the-books background check on each of them. Although Albert's file was thin and mostly *Confidential*, Martin's held numerous commendations from her superiors for work requiring high levels of security and covert action. But it was ultimately Martin's close relationship with Albert that convinced her of his merit.

"My plan to involve Albert is to be kept secret from everyone inside my administration and campaign, no matter how close they are to me."

* * *

One by one the press passed through the metal detectors at the security checkpoint, filling all available seats and most of the standing room. Before the governor took the podium, Martin moved inconspicuously through the room, assessing the governor's security preparations and looking for anything suspicious or out of place. With a spiral note pad and bogus press pass, she neatly disappeared into the crowd. She had images of all invited press on her phone, so crosschecking anyone who raised an eyebrow was relatively easy. She realized that a good number of the legitimate press always looked suspicious to her. Perhaps it was an occupational hazard for someone in the business of being suspicious. Much like herself.

* * *

The crowd stood as Governor Hendriksen emerged from behind the curtain and took the podium, an elegantly crafted piece of furniture made of walnut and glass with the gubernatorial seal prominently etched into its face.

She tapped the microphone for sound check, then adjusted it for her height. The governor was tall and fit, and although in her fifties, had the endurance of a woman half her age. With an open, intelligent face, she wore her dark hair long, her clothes tailored, and didn't apologize for being a strong, compassionate woman.

"It's good to see so many guardians of facts here today," she began to a brief applause. "I'm hopeful that what I say today won't be taken out of context or released in soundbites that are meant to twist my words into lies, but I'm not naive."

There was a tentative laugh from the group, however, Martin saw more than a handful of journalists squirm in their seats. She was quick to make note of them.

Over the years, the governor had come to see that the growing financial influence of an extreme religious minority was at odds with the electorate and the will of the majority. She intended to strike a blow against it that afternoon and set her reform plan into motion.

Recent investigations of the extreme right and their religious operations revealed a huge amount of dark money going into the campaigns of their selected candidates, not to mention the graft that went into the pockets of several preachers who openly advocated for a religious state from their pulpits. It was these flagrant violations of election laws that had to end, given the reality of an ever-growing diversity of citizens and their belief systems. Moreover, the coordination between the candidates and church officials was spilling over into the realm of criminal conspiracy.

"However, I intend to make my position crystal clear today, even if I have to repeat myself. I'll take questions only after I complete my presentation, so relax and get ready to enjoy a bit of history."

"Our laws in New York regarding religious freedom are based on the right to Freedom of Conscience as passed down from the Dutch colony of New Netherlands, to the British in the Articles of Capitulation presented by Pieter Stuyvesant, director of the colony, to British Admiral Nicolls, representative of the Duke of York and Albany, and younger brother of King Charles II, later to be crowned King James II of England."

"So according to Dutch law, now the law of New York, an individual is to be treated equally regardless of what, if anything, they hold to be divine. I'm sure we can all agree on that.

"Now consider the foundation of the United States in the Declaration of Independence. Allow me to read from my notes to be precise.

We hold these truths to be self-evident, that all men are created equal, that they are endowed by their Creator with certain unalienable Rights, that among these are Life, Liberty and the pursuit of Happiness. That to secure these rights, Governments are instituted among Men, deriving their just powers from the consent of the governed.

"This document makes it unambiguous that *We the People*, that being the government, are responsible for securing *Life, Liberty and the pursuit of Happiness* for all of the governed. Simply, the government, represented in this case by my administration, and by all future governors of this state, shall secure the essentials of life for every individual, including food, housing, education, and healthcare; this means making sure these needs are met.

"I can see by your nods that most of you are following, although there are a few frowns that concern me."

This got another small chuckle from the room.

"Therefore, the State of New York's number one priority will be ensuring that these basic rights are provided to every citizen. Specifically, any charitable organization or person who helps lift *The People's* burden will always be welcome, as long as there is no political or religious advocacy or coercion involved."

The governor paused for a few moments to let the room catch up and to regain their full attention.

"So, what is this all leading to?

The crowd became quiet and focused.

"Essentially, any individual citizen, NGO, or other charitable organization, can receive reimbursement, equal to what they currently receive as a tax deduction, for their actual cash contributions or the fair market value of their physical efforts and donated materials. What could be more just?"

Tess saw heads nodding and a general recognition by the press of the logic being presented.

"You may be wondering *Isn't this what we already have?* The answer is no, absolutely not. This policy is based on everyone's basic needs being met, regardless of circumstances, and that meeting these needs is the principal responsibility of *We the People*. Where the combined efforts of individuals or corporate entities cannot fully satisfy a deficiency in meeting those basic needs, the government will step in and make sure the gap is taken care of.

"If the motive of current contributors is truly charitable, you should see little change. The bottom line is that the responsibility of the government can be reduced proportionately with the growth of private charity. This new policy will help weed out the pseudo-charities lurking around every tax loophole. If you are legitimate, you will find the government to be a good partner and you will be fairly compensated."

"What will not be tolerated is homelessness, starvation, unnecessary deaths due to unavailable healthcare, and a poorly educated citizenry."

"Execution of these changes will affect tax and corporate law. There will effectively be no more special tax-exempt privileges for any *Person*, as defined by the high court to include corporations as well as actual individual human beings. Corporation *Persons* will receive the exact same consideration under the law as any individual *Person*, no better or worse."

"In a parallel and related matter, religious affiliation will no longer be mingled with taxation. The 'specialness' that went hand and hand with those privileges has long been eroding our constitution. An illustration of why this no longer works is that if one person or entity should receive a tax break for being part of a special religious group, then everyone should receive the same tax break because their individual beliefs are equally special, and for that matter, their non-beliefs.

"Simply put, my proposal eliminates tax exemption provisions for charity and religion, but instead creates an application process separate from the revenue service, to review submittals for legitimate charitable acts, and return a fair portion of legitimate expenses. The help they give the government in meeting its responsibility to all of *the people* will still be indispensable."

Governor Hendriksen stepped back from the podium and took a long sip from her water bottle as she watched the press chomping at the bit to fire questions at her.

"I'll open the floor for questions about my taxation reform plan only. We are not ready to comment on the museum bombing other than to say the investigation is rapidly progressing.

"And before the questions begin, I want to be perfectly clear. We are not outlawing religion. What we are doing is performing our sacred duty to secure the essentials of *Life* for the people; food, housing, education, and healthcare, because without *Life*, there is no *Liberty*, or *Pursuit of Happiness*."

Chapter 6

Brighton Beach - Brooklyn, New York

"At least we got the senator," Nardos said entering Sofiya's second-floor office on Brighton 4th Street, just north of the elevated tracks.

"I'll tell you what you've got, you fucking moron! You've got Tess and her goddamn security forces on high alert, making it that much more difficult for us to get to her."

The beaded sweat on his bald head began to run down the side of his face. Trying to head off further beratement, he shot back, "There's no way she's getting away from me next time."

"There's not going to be a next time for you. You're dangerously close to becoming a loose end yourself. Speaking of which, have you taken care of your own loose ends from the botched bombing?"

"I've worked with these guys for years."

Sofiya paused while another passing train rattled the old wooden windows looking out on the track.

"I see. So, you'd rather join them?"

The sweat was now dripping from his chin. "No, not join them."

Her voice became low and sinister, "You're lucky I don't kill you right now."

Nardos took a step back, involuntarily recoiling from her wrath.

"Get out of my sight and clean up your mess. Then lay low and don't show your face around here unless I call you. You don't need to be a rocket scientist to know that the Feds are looking for you and your lousy bombers."

Nardos felt his knees go weak. Backing out of her office, he scurried down the stairs and rushed down the sidewalk. He didn't know how far he'd walked when he finally stopped to mop the sweat from his head.

Taking a deep breath, he turned right and headed for the station, unaware of the man in a dark hoodie following him.

* * *

Rybak returned mid-afternoon with the satisfied look of a cold-blooded killer pleased with his work. "No more loose ends."

"I'm getting a lot of heat from higher up," Sofiya stressed. "There can't be anymore screwups. We still need a Middle-Eastern fall guy for the senator. And no more fucking bombs."

"We've narrowed it down to a Palestinian grocery clerk with known family connections to Hamas."

She frowned, "A lot of people have connections to Hamas."

"My inside man doesn't like this Palestinian guy anyway. He'll appear to have blown himself up making the bomb in his place down in Bay Ridge, with plenty of evidence left of his plan to kill the senator, not the governor."

"OK, but doesn't this make your inside man another loose end?"

Rybak let out an audible groan. Leaning back in his chair, his steel gray eyes stared at her.

Sofiya wasn't concerned. He was a professional and would finish the cleanup, whether he liked it or not.

* * *

In the smokey club room of the Originalist Confederation's historic Manhattan headquarters, Bass Drexler sat in an expensive leather lounge chair nursing his scotch and soda, fully aware that he was out of his depth in a room filled with billionaires and wannabe political celebrities. With assistance from their confederates, like minded groups they helped fund like the Mandate, the reach of the Originalists was long.

Adjusting the sleeves of his shark skin jacket, he nervously played with the stylized fish charm that hung from a gold chain around his neck and rested on his form-fitting black tee. Tight black trousers, Italian shoes, and slicked back hair, along with a heavy-handed dose of cologne, completed his signature look, unaware it gave the impression he was a B grade entertainer that worked in a seedy seventies lounge.

Drexler was surprised that Grimes had suggested they meet at his exclusive club. He jumped at the offer, imagining it as a chance to move closer to the inner circle of the organization.

The burner phone in his inside jacket pocket buzzed. He did a quick scan of the room, and seeing no one within hearing distance, he lowered his voice and answered.

"I appreciate your prompt reply to my call."

"We're joined at the hip on this one," Sofiya replied, barely hiding her defiance. She considered herself an equal, but of late harbored serious doubts about her place in the operation. Was she actually on the inside, or was she another disposable asset?

"We can't afford to make any more mistakes," he growled. "We got you the intel on the governor's planned public appearances weeks ago, directly from an inside asset. This should have been handled before she went public with her reform agenda. The last thing we need is to make her a sympathetic figure, or even worse, a martyr."

An awkward silence followed before the man continued.

"We'll be in contact. Meanwhile, stay put and don't talk to anyone."

He cut off the call and dropped his cell into his jacket pocket.

* * *

Garson Grimes, a large balding man wearing overly large glasses that highlighted the dark circles under his eyes, approached carrying two drinks and set them on the low table. Bass Drexler rose and shook his sweaty hand, resisting the urge to wipe his hand on the back of his pants.

Noticeably put off by the overpowering scent of Drexler's cologne, Grimes retreated to the lounge chair on the opposite side of the table.

After dabbing his forehead with an eternally damp embroidered handkerchief, Grimes leaned closer and lowered his voice, "We just got word of a large explosion down in Brighton Beach. I think a toast is in order."

Chapter 7
Governor's Manhattan Offices

Albert entered the lobby of the governor's Lexington Avenue office suite for an appointment arranged by Martin. There to greet him, Martin barely recognized the nerdy man in a brown plaid sportscoat, thick glasses, and slicked back hair who walked through the door.

"Wow," she whispered as she took his arm and guided him through security. "You look like the professor in my first-year psychology class. Tortured any small furry animals today?"

"The day is still short," he muttered, his normal British accent toned down a bit.

"Where did you get that jacket? It's going to attract attention, or even better, force people to look away."

Even though he reminded her of her first-year psychology professor, she had to restrain herself from nibbling at his ear.

* * *

Closing the door behind Albert, Martin said, "Madame Governor, please let me introduce you to Everett Pendrake."

"No need for introductions. We met briefly at a literary function several years ago," she said rising to her feet and coming around the desk to shake his hand. "It's good to see you again."

"Yes, and under much better circumstances," he added, with a hint of a wink.

"Shall I stay," Martin asked, "or leave you two to your writing?"

"No need for you to stay. I happen to know you're busy."

"Then I'll let you two get on with it. By the way, I've assigned my second in command on the FBI taskforce, Special Agent Obsharski, to give your security chief periodic updates on the taskforce process, without giving him any important details of our investigation. Keeping him completely out of the loop would only foster suspicion."

Closing the door behind her, Martin walked toward the elevator, mentally going over details of the bombing that needed follow-up. By the time she pushed the down button, however, she was thinking of how much fun it was going to be to spend the night with the nerd who reminded her of her psych professor.

* * *

Everett Pendrake was a well-known ghost writer and co-author of more than a dozen memoirs of well-known celebrities and political figures, according to various on-line articles and websites planted by a couple of old friends at British Intelligence. Everett remained British, as everyone involved agreed there was no way to rid Albert of his Cornish accent. The back story was simple. Governor Hendriksen and Everett Pendrake met at a literacy conference near London years before. Impressed with his work, the governor agreed to give him co-authorship of her new biography, due to come out in the summer.

Ironically, Albert was an accomplished author in his own right, having written more than a dozen books published under the penname Edgar Penrose. International espionage, unsurprisingly, was his specialty.

"Albert…shit. I'm sorry, let me start again. Everett, I'm sure Martin has filled you in on my situation. I'm finding it hard to trust anyone in my administration, including my security detail, and suspect there may be a traitor in my inner circle. I realize this may be paranoia induced by the museum bombing, but I'm finding it nearly impossible to schedule events or meet anyone in public."

"I presume you're getting threats."

"Yes, a lot more than usual."

"I've noticed the headlines in certain outlets about you *outlawing religion*."

"I know. And isn't that ironic, coming from people who tried to ban Muslims."

"It would be safest if I scan your security files from your laptop right here in your office. Then there is no way to trace it to me."

"Good idea, but can't my IT and Security team track all of my network and internet activity?"

"Not to worry. My covert programs are state of the art. They'll never know I was here," Albert said, inserting his thumb drive into her laptop.

"They seem to know our movements, even the location of unadvertised events like the one at the Brooklyn Museum. And how did they get a bomb under my limousine when it's always under guard?"

* * *

While Albert combed through the limousine maintenance files and surveillance videos of protestors at the museum and at her Manhattan office, Governor Hendriksen received a call from Dell Thatcher, her chief of security.

"Governor, a suspected terrorist blew himself up in his Bay Ridge apartment, apparently while making a bomb. Authorities have found evidence that links him and the museum car bombing to a plot to kill the senator."

When she hung up, Tess's face was white. Turning to Albert, she restated her conversation.

"Convenient," he said without looking up from the monitor.

"Convenient? Dammit, you think he's a patsy. I was looking forward to feeling safe again."

"Sorry. It follows a typical pattern of throwing investigators off the trail, while moving the attention away from you to Senator Torres."

* * *

Martin caught up with Albert later that night at her Brooklyn apartment.

"I just got word of a professional hit on two Belarusians down in Brighton Beach. One had been suspected of being part of the metro bombing in Minsk but was never indicted by Interpol."

"And the other one?"

"Nothing yet. I've got my bud over at ATF digging into the second guy."

"The chances of the explosion in Bay Ridge and this hit in Brighton Beach not being related are zero," Albert said. "The trail to whomever is actually behind this is drying up fast."

"What did you learn from your visit with Tess?"

Albert took a moment to reply. "I've just scratched the surface, although I've got a huge download on my thumb drive. I believe her suspicions are well founded. Some of the protestors at the museum were also at her Lexington Avenue offices. Both times the protestors arrived at unannounced stops at the same time, approximately half an hour before the governor."

"No chance that's a coincidence?"

"None. We need to check the phone records of the men in Brighton to see who they've been talking to."

"And the bomb maker in Bay Ridge," Martin added, "although we never recovered his phone."

"Not surprising."

Chapter 8

Annah was impressed by the exceptional Indian restaurants in Prospect Heights, several within a few blocks of their apartment on Saint Marks Avenue. She had a couple of favorites on Vanderbilt, ones she passed every day on her walk to the Brooklyn Museum.

Their consulting agreement with the museum had been extended at the director's request, and she and Will were immersed in the continued translation and documentation of the Cheshme Shafa and Palmyra artifacts. Additionally, they were excited about their new agreement to exhibit items from their recent discovery at Will's family home in the Catskills.

To help facilitate their work on the recent exhibit, they rented the first floor of a lovely three story brownstone within a fifteen-minute walk of the museum. In spite of the bombing incident, Annah felt at home in Brooklyn, surprising after their past tribulations with the Mandate.

Annah was less than comforted when the Feds released Rayne Ashcroft to home arrest, while she appealed her murder and antiquities smuggling convictions. The former director of a ruthless international criminal enterprise of religious zealots known as the Mandate, needed to remain locked up as far as Annah was concerned. She was disgusted how money and influence protected the guilty.

* * *

To assist with the translation of the handwritten files and printed materials discovered in Will's barn, the curator of the Colonial American history collection at the Brooklyn Museum secured the services of Kai Theron, a direct descendant of the Dutch who arrived in Cape Town, South Africa, in the 1650's. His expertise was in the original Dutch dialect spoken during the early colonial period of South Africa and the Afrikaans language that evolved from it. As these languages branched off from mainstream Dutch during the same historic time period as did the Dutch spoken in the New Netherlands, he had a unique understanding of the subtleties and references contained in the Old Dutch of early America.

He was comfortably familiar with the work of the New Netherlands Project, often corresponding with Director Gehring about his groundbreaking translation work. When he learned of the Gerritsen printing press and the cache of old documents, he spent little time considering whether to accept the consulting position offered to him in Brooklyn.

He'd arrived at JFK only a few days earlier and wasn't quite over jetlag, yet he was energized about his first meeting with Will and Annah that morning.

* * *

"What have you got for Doctor Theron this morning?" Annah asked Will, anxious to kick things into a higher gear. She'd been cleaning and cataloguing the handwritten portion of the records for several weeks without understanding a word of it, and was dying to know what they were about. Theron's translations would be more than welcome.

She was interrupted by a knock on the door of the lab. None of the museum staff knocked before entering, so it had to be their anticipated guest. Will beat Annah to the door, and pulled it open.

"Kai Theron here," the man said in near perfect English, although there was a touch of something in his accent that wasn't exactly British.

Will offered his hand, something he'd not done much of since Covid. "Pleased to meet you. I'm Will Garrison and this is Annah Devar, my partner on this project and many others."

Taking her hand, Kai spoke directly to Annah, "Miss Devar. It is my great pleasure to meet you." While he wasn't quite as smooth as Uncle Albert, he quickly had Will's attention.

"Let me show you a few of the treasures we've discovered," Annah said, guiding him across the lab to a tall item draped with a large sheet.

Will stepped up and removed the cover, revealing a finely crafted and very old printing press.

"Now that is something you don't see every day," Kai said after issuing a low whistle. "Seventeenth Century?"

"We believe that's correct," Annah confirmed, "based on this nameplate, which is still very legible."

Kai leaned closer to the heavy vertical pier and studied the nameplate neatly secured to it by small brass nails. "That makes this press nearly four hundred years old."

"These are a few print proofs of the bulletins and legal notices we found in a metal lined wooden file box," Will said as he spread them out on the press carriage extension. "My guess is these will substantially add to the established record of the New Netherlands."

"This is a significant discovery. What else did you find?"

"This way," Annah said, leading them to her work area. "I've conserved dozens of the hand written sheets from another storage box. They were in fairly good condition for having been in the barn for who knows how long. I'm grateful for the craftsmanship of those Dutch box makers."

Annah stepped over to one of her work counters covered with sheets she had already conserved. "My guess is that most of them are something like a contract or invoice, but the page layouts in this group appear to be correspondence."

"Perhaps," Kai said, leaning closer to the sheets Annah had referenced.

After a brief scan of the documents, he looked up at her. "Good guess. These are most certainly correspondence, an incredibly fortunate find as letters like these often reveal personal information that helps bring the author and their recipient back to life."

Kai pulled up a stool, pulled on his nitrile gloves, and began to examine the letters in detail.

"Not one for wasting time, I see," Annah teased.

"Not when the artifacts are as gripping as these," he murmured without looking away from the letter in his hand. "Although this collection was composed by a variety of writers, as evidenced by the different handwriting, a couple of names stand out on this one, those of *Elias and Sarah Doughty* and *Andres Gerritsen*.

"It seems as though Mister Andres Gerritsen was asking Mister Elias Doughty for his daughter's hand in marriage."

"Will's ancestors?"

"Likely so."

"This one caught my eye," Annah replied. "All I recognized was the name *Van der Donck* from a periodical I skimmed through."

He studied the letter at great length. The growing intensity of his focus was palpable. "It seems as though this letter is from one Cornelius Melyn to Adriaen Van der Donck regarding a legal matter."

"He had something to do with a sawmill," Annah recalled.

"Yes, but so much more. Adriaen Van der Donck was a brilliant lawyer and among the first settlers of the New Netherlands. He became a bit of a legend among the locals."

Part Two
(Year 1641 - Atlantic Crossing)

New Netherlands and Neighboring Colonies
(Mid Seventeenth Century)

Chapter 9

Voyage to America

The deafening blast of cannon fire startled everyone onboard. Those brave enough to venture topside were greeted by the acrid smell of black powder and smoke trailing over the first pink light of morning. The crew of *Den Eyckenboom* scrambled to deploy more sail.

Seconds later another blast came from the small frigate bearing down on them from behind, but their returned fire fell short. The aggressors were flying the flag of the Dunkirk raiders, privateers in the service of the Spanish crown, who prowled the English Channel near the Straits of Dover in search of easy prey.

The captain ordered *Den Eyckenboom* turned downwind. The added sail array snapped full and she quickly began to keep pace with the frigate. For several heart stopping minutes, the raiders drew perilously close to the range of cannon fire. Through the light haze along the south English coast, the flags of a Dutch warship came into view on the eastern horizon. Wanting to avoid a sea battle, the Dunkirkers abandoned their attack and turned back toward the Flemish Coast.

* * *

The captain was pleased with the performance of his crew. Commending them for a job well done, he directed them to bring the ship back to her original course and rigging. The crew, still jubilant about avoiding a bloody fight, made short work of the sails and set the ship back on course toward the capes of Brittany.

He was equally pleased by the performance of his ship, *Den Eyckenboom*, impressed that she was able to match speeds with the smaller frigate. Like her name in English, *The Oak Tree*, she was a sturdy and seaworthy vessel, fully loaded with immigrants, tools, provisions, and livestock, bound for the colony of New Netherlands in the Americas. Designed in the Dutch fashion of efficiency, each of her lower decks was organized by necessity and sanitation, animals being on the bottom deck.

* * *

The sound of the cannon fire still echoed in Adriaen's head, adding to his nausea from the tossing seas. Never a good sailor and still hung over from his late-night celebration over too much Dutch beer, he made another dash above decks to the nearest gunwale railing.

Stomach empty, Adriaen returned to his cramped semiprivate cabin on the passenger deck, looking drawn and perhaps, a few shades of green. He barely remembered boarding the ship on the midnight high tide. If it had not been for his friend Jurre, a fellow graduate of the Leiden Law School, he would still be lying on a crate quayside in the Port of Amsterdam.

As Adriaen entered his cabin, a tall gentleman rose to his feet from the wooden deck where he'd been sitting with his wife and seven children. The children were quiet and well behaved, all but three-year-old Yzaak who was pestering his older brother Abraham.

After filling a tin cup with a dark liquid from his flask, he approached Adriaen.

"I'm Cornelius Melyn," he said offering the cup. "You look like you could use a remedy."

The thought of more alcohol made Adriaen recoil. "No more drink," he said, waving Melyn away.

"Trust me, this will do you some good."

Adriaen cautiously took the cup, mostly out of a strong Dutch sense of politeness. He braced himself for another round of retching as he tentatively took a sip.

The thick blackberry brandy brought welcome relief. He could feel his stomach unclench with each small sip.

"Careful, not too fast," Melyn cautioned.

When Adriaen felt well enough, he stood and properly introduced himself to Melyn and his family.

"I am Adriaen van der Donck, esquire, bound for the private estate of Rensselaerswyck, a large patroonship in the province of New Netherlands. I've been hired on as a schout by Killien van Rensselaer, a position that combines the duties of both sheriff and judge, to bring law and justice to the tenant farmers on his vast estate up the North River."

Cornelius responded in kind, "My family and I are bound for the port of New Amsterdam, where I have secured the patroonship of Staten Island across the Upper Bay from New Amsterdam. Many of those onboard are under contract to settle in my new colony. Forty-one souls in all."

"Farmers?"

"Mainly, but among them are many different trades, including teachers, blacksmiths, carpenters, tinkers, and of course, brewers. I chose carefully with the vision of a well-balanced community. Their tools and supplies are on the middle deck below us."

Adriaen was impressed. "If you are ever in need of legal services, you'll know where to find me."

* * *

In the late afternoon of their fifth day at sea, they rounded the Capes of Brittany on a southwesterly course for the Canary Islands. Adriaen was finally getting his sea legs and able to hold an intelligent conversation without his head swimming.

The balmy weather and pastel colors of the sky brought many of the passengers to the main deck. They had a glow about them, knowing their dreams of a new life in the vast and unknown frontier were nearing reality.

"You're looking human again," came a friendly voice across the deck.

"Melyn, your voice gives you away," Adriaen said, turning his way.

"My children have been worried about you."

"That is very kind. They are so well-mannered. How do you do it?"

"I give them ten acres of farmland for each day they are well behaved on the voyage."

"Well, they certainly understand value," Adriaen complimented.

"They're Dutch, aren't they?" Melyn laughed with obvious pride.

The pod of bottlenose dolphins that was providing entertainment for those still on deck, finally disappeared with the setting sun. The moon rising in the east was bright, casting its silver rays across the water.

* * *

Melyn and van der Donck remained on deck and like most Dutch men of the day, loaded their pipes with the finest Virginia tobacco, something Melyn intended to grow on his new farmland. He had the seed, tools, and men onboard to make that possible.

"So, tell me of your last rowdy night in Amsterdam," Melyn said.

Adriaen laughed. "I believe my stomach can now handle the telling. So, on the evening before we sailed, my classmate Jurre and I were celebrating our recent graduation from the Leiden Law College in a tavern on Dam Square in Amsterdam.

"It's not a very well-kept secret that most of the current thinking at the college aligns with the progressive ideas of Hugo Grotius and the original Remonstrants.

"I understand that after his daring escape from Loevestein Castle, by hiding in a book crate while serving a life sentence for heresy, Grotius has been living well in Paris in the service of the Swedish king as his ambassador to France."

"His writings from before and after prison are still making waves at the Leiden Law College and other legal institutions across Europe. He is considered the father of international law and the leading advocate for self-governance. His publications were my most treasured textbooks at Leiden."

"A real disciple, eh?"

"Definitely. Anyway, after a few mugs of beer, I was loudly espousing his virtues."

"This I would love to have seen," Melyn chuckled, "the indiscretions of youth."

"As it happens, Jurre is the great nephew of Johan van Oldenbarnevelt, the champion of the Remonstrant philosophy of tolerance and early mentor to Grotius. Jurre stood on a chair and loudly made a toast to his uncle.

"Unfortunately, his salute did not go unnoticed by a couple of old Gomarists sitting across the room. They wore the trappings of that devout Calvinist political group who ultimately had his Uncle Johan, hero of the wars of liberation against Spain, beheaded for heresy. Sadly, the civil and religious laws are entangled, so the charges brought against Oldenbarnevelt were not for some actual harm, but for having a different interpretation of some obscure scriptural reference."

Melyn's disdain was obvious. "We need to completely separate the state from the domination of any religious group. I know the exile proclamation against the original Remonstrants was finally lifted, and the state now allows any religious group to build establishments and hold meetings, but strict Calvinists in the Dutch Reformed Church still dominate the Dutch West India Company and other trading corporations, and rule their overseas colonies according to their religious dictates."

"I agree," Adriaen nodded emphatically. "I could see the Gomarists' agitation rising, but it did not deter me. More of a speech than a toast, I praised Grotius and the virtues of his views on natural law, emigration, tolerance, free trade, and good governance.

"As the evening progressed and more beer was consumed, things got louder and more heated. The Gomarists went beyond insults. Finally threatening violence, they rose to their feet shouting that it was intellectuals like us that needed to be struck down by the strong hand of the church, meaning of course, their church."

"I quickly rose in response to their threats, but the alcohol got the best of me and I fell over my chair. The bar tender, a Jew who had fled persecution in Spain, was not sympathetic to these would-be Christian dictators and threw them out of his bar."

"I have a vague memory of Jurre helping me to the waterfront. The next thing I remember is waking after midnight covered with dew. I found myself lying on a large wooden crate on the quayside, surrounded by tall sailing ships and a seagull gawking at me from the top of a nearby barrel."

* * *

Over the course of their voyage, Adriaen and Melyn had the occasion to speak of many things. Adriaen was impressed by the knowledge and sophistication of his new friend. Having already voyaged to *America* as they both now called it, Melyn inspired countless dreams in his younger shipmate.

They spent most evenings on the fore deck, discussing strategies for the new province. Melyn was not one to mince his words.

"The New Netherlands will not survive as a mere trading outpost under the dictates of the corporate director. We need normal governance, at minimum on par with that currently in our homeland."

With the certainty of youth, Adriaen added, "You'll get no argument from me. Even though I signed on with Rensselaer to be the law in his new colony, I firmly believe the New Netherlands will become much more than another trading outpost like those in the Caribbean and West Indies.

I expect that due to the small land area of the homeland, and the love we Dutch have for growing things, this province will become an extension of the Netherlands, with all the same rights and privileges extended to its new inhabitants."

"Optimistic," Melyn nodded, "but certainly within our reach. It will take careful navigation through the greedy straits of the West India Corporation and their current director Kieft, who fancies himself a little king. He is quick to say that his is the word final on all legal matters. Of course, I did manage to persuade him to grant Staten Island to me. But beware, he is a dishonest man, always out for a bribe and an undue share of the cargo."

Adriaen took another sip of brandy before passing it back to his new friend. "I'm sure I'll have the occasion to match wits with him."

Chapter 10
The New Netherlands

The bright beaches of Sandy Hook and Coney Island rose with the outgoing tide, flanking the mouth of Godyns Bay, the gateway to the North River estuary. The lower bay, as the locals knew it, was teaming with life. The caws of the shore birds produced a cacophony so rich it became numbing to the ears. Adriaen, always a keen observer of nature, was fascinated by the boundless number of birds and fish species flourishing in the bay.

Sailing north through the narrows named after the Italian explorer Verrazzano, into the upper bay, they were presented with the largest network of sheltered harbors and navigable waterways on the entire east coast of America. Adriaen delighted in the same views that had captivated Henry Hudson some thirty years earlier, who upon his first arrival immediately claimed the waterways and surrounding land in the name of the Dutch States. This estuary would become the beating heart of the New Netherlands.

* * *

Den Eyckenboom first set anchor on the eastern banks of Staten Island near the mouth of Kill van Kull, just south of a small neglected Dutch military observation post.

Melyn was concerned about the weak security forces of the Dutch West India Company (WIC) in the New Netherlands. First among the articles of his contract with the WIC, as it was for all other emigrees, was the company's obligation to provide for the defense of the colony and its settlers at their own expense. To date, their meager defense and security provisions had been adequate given the peaceful relations with their neighbors in the New England colonies to the east, and the aboriginal Americans surrounding them. But he was wary that this could all change in an instant.

* * *

It took all of two days to unload the passengers, livestock, and supplies needed to start a new life in Melyn's Staten Island frontier. While the passengers were being shuttled to the beach in the onboard long boat, several cargo barges for hire approached from across the bay.

The main hatch was aligned with the large hatches on each of the lower decks, allowing the spar and tackle hinged on the main mast to be lowered to a horizontal position and swung over the hatch. The crane assembly, operated by pulleys and cranks, lifted the livestock in large cargo nets above the main deck, then swung them over the gunwale and lowered them onto the waiting barge. This operation was repeated dozens of times, as it would be again when *Den Eyckenboom* reached her final destination at Rensselaerswyck.

Standing on the ground of their new home for the first time, many threw themselves down onto the soft warm sand, thankful for their safe passage. The children were already busy chasing each other through the cool surf and shore grass. Even the animals were noticeably joyful to finally have fresh grass and space to move around.

When the ship had been unloaded and organized for the new arrivals, Adriaen bid farewell to Melyn and his family. The children had grown very fond of him over the long voyage and were sorry to see him leave. The two men embraced, vowing they would one day meet again over important matters of the law and liberty.

At the edge of the deep forest, shaded faces looked on with a mixture of curiosity and impending dread.

* * *

The north shores and converging river banks of the upper bay were dotted with new settlements, but none more prominent than at the tip of Manhattan Island. From high on the forecastle of *Den Eyckenboom*, Adriaen van der Donck first laid eyes on the sprawling village that was intent on becoming a Dutch city worthy of its namesake.

His mind reeled with possibilities. The abundance of calm waters and good anchorage, combined with an endless fertile shoreline, gave promise to future growth that could not be matched anywhere in Europe. And it was located at a pivotal corner of the Atlantic trade circuit, guaranteeing a bustling port and vigorous economy. He was already fashioning a letter in his mind to his family back in Breda, encouraging them to join him across the ocean in this new land.

Adriaen's first visit to New Amsterdam, the thriving new port on the Island of Manhattan, was limited to a few hours, just long enough to ferry fresh provisions out to *Den Eyckenboom* for her journey upriver to Rensselaerswyck.

Director Kieft was unavailable to meet Captain Cornelisz, but his senior official, Cornelis van Tienhoven, was there with his hand out ready to take a bribe disguised as an import tariff. His men had crossed the bay in the guise of assisting the newcomers, and while they generously offered help unloading the ship, they quietly took inventory of the cargo and passengers. Tienhoven knew exactly how much he could squeeze out of the captain before getting Director Kieft involved. Most of it would never reach the company's coffers.

* * *

It was late summer when Adriaen aboard *Den Eyckenboom* set out from New Amsterdam on a week's long journey a hundred and fifty miles up the North River to the main fur trading post of Fort Orange, named for the Dutch royal family. The North River was broad and sailable the full distance between Manhattan and its confluence with the Mohawk River eight miles upriver from the fort.

The currents of the North River were heavily influenced by the Atlantic high tides. The raised water levels in the lower bays sent daily surges as much as six feet high upriver as far north as Fort Orange. The Mohicans named it *Mohicannittuk*, the "river that flows two ways."

This unique river flow allowed brackish water to extend upstream to the Fishkill, nearly sixty miles north of Manhattan. In his journal, Adriaen noted the vast diversity of fish life at this transition zone from brackish to fresh water. It was his intention to eventually publish his observations and discoveries in the New Netherlands as an almanac promoting emigration.

* * *

The excitement of finally being in America filled his dreams with imaginary adventures and strange new creatures, often waking him in the night. That was when the river was most enchanting, reflecting the waxing moon and the warm glow of Indian campfires scattered along the forested banks. The fireflies were out in great numbers, following the contours of the land like a blanket of sparkling stars.

This was sublime nature, barely touched by civilization. In the serene stillness of the night, his purpose for being there became crystal clear. He would be a caretaker of justice and the rights of everyone in his jurisdiction, including the native people. He revered the writings of his legal hero Grotius on natural law, and vowed to make a detailed study of how it was expressed by the local Wilden, or *Americans* as he now came to call them, before they were completely overwhelmed by the Europeans.

Chapter 11

Schout of Rensselaerswyck

Den Eyckenboom anchored by the village the settlers nicknamed Beaverwyck that had grown up around Fort Orange on the west banks of the North River. The settlement was at the center of Rensselaerswyck, the vast patroonship of Killian van Rensselaer that extended twenty-three miles down both sides of the North River, and twenty-four miles inland from both banks. Van Rensselaer owned the land under this makeshift village, and the squatters were high on the patroon's list of tasks for Adriaen to look into.

The gravelly shores soon turned to thick mud as Adriaen made his way to the fort at the base of the bluffs. Fort Nassau, built too close to the North River on Castle Island to be spared from the seasonal flooding, had recently been replaced with Fort Orange, along with a new trading post.

It was there that he first met Arent van Curler, financial officer of Rensselaerswyck, who owed his position to his great uncle, Killian van Rensselaer. Van Curler's first order of business was to assign Adriaen a tract of farmland land on Castle Island across the Normans Kill just beyond the remnants of the old fort. Ravaged by torrents of flood water, all that remained of the old fort was a sad and ghostly tangle of tree branches, rotting logs, and river debris.

Adriaen rejected his offer, immediately negotiating a tract on higher ground. For his own use, he also selected one of van Rensselaer's prized black stallions rather than the retired plow horse originally offered to him.

In van Curlers view, van der Donck's independence bordered on insolence, and was soon a regular topic in his weekly reports to his great uncle. Van Rensselaer would have considered replacing him if it wasn't close to impossible finding someone willing to go to the New Netherlands who knew anything about the law.

So began Adriaen's three-year contract and tenuous relationship with the patroon. He was given a list of settlers who were late making their contractual payments. Their debts included transport to America, the allocation of tools, seed and livestock given to them upon arrival, and their use of the land. With direct orders to force them to pay up, he found many settlers living in hovels, struggling to survive. At these, he looked the other way and kept riding.

A second list of names were those who had completely abandoned their contractual obligations and fled from van Rensselaer's colony, most of whom had sought refuge in New Amsterdam and the surrounding villages. On one of many treks downriver to New Amsterdam in search of them, he tracked down a woman who had fled the colony after her husband had died. Finding her well along in carrying a child, he suggested she remain in New Amsterdam, to return to Rensselaerswyck only after she delivered her baby and they were both fit to travel.

Killian was livid when he learned of Adriaen's lenience and issued a stern warning demanding harsh punishments, reminding him that his only purpose for being there was to look after his patroon's personal interests.

Completely at odds with Adriaen's view of the justice he was there to dispense, he soon came to see van Rensselaer's patroonship as akin to the medieval feudal estates with lords who answered to no one for their cruelty and greed.

Before long he began to dream of his own colony, founded on the principles of good governance as advocated by the likes of Grotius and his progressive instructors at the Leiden Law School. Basic human decency that sprung directly from Nature was at the heart of good governance, as it would be someday in his new colony.

* * *

Adriaen's rounds on the east side of the river always began at the Ferry House near the ruins of old Fort Nassau. The ferry shuttled passengers to the mainland on the east bank just south of the Mohican trading camp on de Laet's Island.

On one of his first visits to East Rensselaerswyck, he followed the meandering trail upstream from the Red Mill to the top of the ridge to visually survey the terrain. The view up and down the North River was spectacular. Any Netherlander he knew would love to own a piece of this seemingly endless new world, given how land was in such short supply back home.

It was on this high place that Adriaen van der Donck first met Michiel Janszen, an emigree farmer originally from the southern province of Zeeland in the Netherlands. Michiel called his allocated tract of land "de Hoogeberch", meaning "the High Hill" in Dutch, a large portion of which was too steep and rocky for proper farming.

Although not college educated like van der Donck, Janszen was well versed in many of the theories of good governance. Fleeing Zeeland to escape the same feudal attitudes Adriaen despised, he was also able to escape the wrath of Fytje Hartman's uncle for running away with his niece.

Recognizing in each other a kindred spirit, they soon formed a lifelong friendship and bond of trust. Adriaen freely offered legal advice to Michiel, particularly in his dealings with the patroon.

After Michiel was denied a fair percentage of the profit from the clear crystals being mined atop the hill on his own farmland, he had turned to illicit trading with his Mohican neighbors to the east, avoiding tariffs arbitrarily imposed by partners over imported goods. Michiel believed it made up for the poor farmland he had been allotted, and though van der Donck had his suspicions, he never pursued a legal case against him. It was never clear to Adriaen if this was simply to protect a friend, or due to his growing distain for the unchecked power of businessmen like Rensselaer.

* * *

As Schout of Rensselaerswyck, his duties as arbiter of the law included everything from investigating and prosecuting formal charges to holding court and issuing judgements. Most cases were typical bar room fights, infidelities, and petty disputes over goods and services, but it soon became clear that his employer, above all else, thought he should be recovering delinquent payments from settlers, preferably in beaver pelts.

Van Rensselaer went so far as to issue a proclamation requiring all tenants in his colony to swear an oath of loyalty to him, for themselves and their servants. Van der Donck felt that servants should not be held responsible for the deeds of those they worked for and essentially refused by simply not carrying out his orders.

Adriaen was unwilling to collaborate with most other schouts in the colony, considering them to be nothing more than extensions of the corporate greed and tyranny of their overlords back in the Netherlands. The need for good governance that supported the wellbeing and mutual interests of all inhabitants became self-evident.

Chapter 12

Friend of the "Americans"

There was an eerie hush in the deep woods. The morning fog blanketing the forest floor rose to the tops of Adriaen's riding boots as he led his horse between the trees. Except for the saddle gear, the horse was so black he was invisible in the dark.

Close ahead Agheroense of the Mohawk tribe was leading the way to the village he'd grown up in by the Mohawk River. He was going to see his elderly grandfather and had asked Adriaen to come along. Adriaen was enthralled by his good fortune, the opportunity of having a personal invitation to go inside a traditional Mohawk village.

Aghar, as his Dutch friends called him, had become close to Adriaen soon after he first arrived at Fort Orange. At the time, Aghar was living with a Dutch widow in Beaverwyck, making his way by translating for the Dutch Mohicans, and Mohawk pelt traders in the fort.

Adriaen hired Aghar to teach him to speak the Iroquois tongue of the Mohawk and the Algonquin of the Mohican. Over the months that followed, they developed a tight bond. Each knew they were at the crossroads of epic historic events that had the potential to produce good results for both of their cultures, or very bad ones in the wrong hands.

There were rumblings coming upriver of strife between the Dutch and Wilden, but Adriaen was absorbed by the countless new wonders to be found in America, and felt a world away from the trouble down south.

As the fog lifted, Aghar and Adriaen were able to remount and follow a well-worn path. The faint odor of campfire caught Adriaen's attention just as Aghar turned and raised his brows, his silent way of telling him there was something to see ahead. Adriaen came to realize that it was in Aghar's basic nature to travel as silently as possible, a good strategy for both hunting game and avoiding one's enemies.

They were now well beyond the limits of Rensselaerswyck, in the wilderness beyond the frontier. Adriaen was sure he could smell food cooking but had no idea what it was. He was hoping it was better than the half raw coney Aghar roasted at their campsite the previous night.

Most of the villagers had seen Dutch traders before, but seeing one in the company of Agheroense caused a stir. As they approached one of several longhouses, Adriaen saw an elegant structure of overlapping elm bark sheets sandwiched between a row of double four-inch vertical posts and secured in place by long horizontal battens made of sapling trees.

He estimated the longhouse to be twenty feet wide and double that in length. Beside the entry was a lodge pole garnished with items that were clearly important, but of what Adriaen had not a clue.

A tall wiry old man with long gray hair and a dark weathered face etched with wisdom emerged from the entry and paused beside the lodgepole.

Aghar had warned Adriaen that it was proper to bring a gift and hang it from the pole, especially if he intended to barter for something.

What Aghar had not told him was that his grandfather was considered a Hoyane by his people, an important chief thought to have specials gifts and mystical powers. Adriaen wisely approached the wampum pole and hung a bag full of fine flints as his offering. He returned to his position next to Aghar and remained still.

Oakwari looked deeply into Adriaen's eyes, as if looking through him. Only for a few moments, it felt like an eternity. The tension was finally broken when Oakwari reached out to take Adriaen's arm in a traditional Mohawk greeting, the way Aghar always had. He felt as though he was in the presence of royalty, but without an air of superiority or privilege.

Soon they were exchanging stories by the fire with Aghar serving as interpreter. Adriaen later learned that Oakwari knew more Dutch than he first let on. It turned out he was the one who encouraged his grandson to learn as many languages as he could, especially those of his enemies.

Known by other Iroquois Nations as the "People of the Flint" Oakwari graciously accepted Adriaen's gift. He was impressed that the young man understood the symbolic and practical significance of flint to his people.

Openly accepted by the village community, he stayed on for several weeks. Rarely seen without his notebook, they were intrigued with Adriaen's habit of writing, and then drawing everything he saw. It seemed there was nothing that did not catch his interest. Hunting and fishing, plants grown and foraged, the cooking and storing of food, medicine and cures, morality, family and marriage customs, and rules on trade. And central to his belief in natural law, he wanted to understand how their legal system functioned, as well as their concepts of the divine.

However, the time had come for Adriaen to return to Rensselaerswyck. Aghar remained behind in the village, planning to trade more stories with his grandfather, some perhaps not intended for Dutch ears.

The first snow had fallen the night before his departure and the trail back to Beaverwyck was covered with pristine snow, with only the occasional footprints of rabbit and fox. Shafts of early morning sunlight filtered through the tall trees, making the ice and snow sparkle. Soon the silence and serenity of the ancient forest swept his mundane thoughts away, and he was left only with the realization that his notes and drawings could never do justice to what he was experiencing. All he could do was look on in amazement.

* * *

Adriaen's new house on Castle Island was finally complete enough to move in. Warmed by a blazing fire in his large stone fireplace, he spent many snowbound mornings compiling his observations of New Netherlands.

Today was no exception. The overnight storm was finally beginning to let up after leaving more than a foot of snow on the ground. That was fine with him. He had a good fire going and was deep into his journal writing.

He was expanding his notes about Mohawk law, intrigued by their ability to resolve legal disputes quickly, yet without formal courts or any written rules. Their system assumed honest and ethical behavior from tribal members. Adriaen saw the social structure as a direct expression of natural law, rising from the basic goodness in people.

About to dip his quill in the inkwell, he was interrupted by several firm raps on the front door. For someone to be out in this snow it must be important. He rose to his feet and hurried to the door.

To his surprise, it was his Mohawk friend, tightly wrapped in fur.

"Aghar, come in out of the cold."

Aghar shook the snow from his coat before entering. He had observed this curious habit of the Dutch as they tried to keep puddles off their wood floors. It was something he had never thought of, as his people had earthen floors.

"It is good to see you," Adriaen said. "What brings you out in snow?"

"It is my grandfather. He had a dream vision that I must pass on to you."

"You have my attention. Please sit and we'll talk over something hot."

While Adriaen made tea, Aghar sat by the window looking out on the pristine fresh snow, disturbed only by his own footsteps.

"Dreams are like the snow," Aghar said.

"How's that?" Adriaen asked returning to the table with two steaming mugs.

"They take on the shape of the real world, then melt away leaving no trace."

"Speaking of dreams, what is this message from Oakwari?"

Pausing with his mug close to his lips, Aghar peered through the steam at Adriaen, then slowly broke a grin. "He had a dream about you."

To the Wilden, especially a Mohawk Hoyane, dreams contained important messages.

"He dreamed about me?"

"More like you entered his dream."

"This must be serious business if he sent you here in this weather."

"To grandfather, dreams are always serious business."

Over tea they talked of how similar their destinies were, both bringing the understanding of an unknown and alien world back to their own people. That was why Aghar set off as a young man to learn the language and customs of the Dutch and his neighboring tribes. And whether fully intended or not, it had become Adriaen's quest in New Netherlands. They both imagined a long and peaceful coexistence between their people.

With now empty mugs, Adriaen's curiosity got the best of him. "We've spoken of many important things, but not yet of your grandfather's vision."

"Grandfather knew you were not the typical European when you gifted him flint without any foreknowledge of its sacred meaning to the Mohawk. When I told you to bring a gift, I never mentioned flint. Why did you choose it?"

"I traded for the flint even before we spoke of going to your village. I had the idea of trying to make some kind of tool or weapon, an attempt to understand more about traditional Wilden ways."

"Grandfather thinks you walk with the ancestors in your dreams. That is how you knew about the flint. That is also how you appeared in his vision with your question."

"What question?"

Aghar paused for a moment, trying to properly translate his grandfather's words. "Your question was whether or not your people were capable of returning to natural law, and govern themselves without the use of force or threats."

Adriaen's skepticism about receiving messages from dreams was quickly erased. He leaned closer as Aghar continued.

"We have learned that your leader in New Amsterdam does not listen to his council and has made dishonorable attacks on the Wilden. This Kieft only listens to his boss across the sea, not to those he lives among in this land."

Adriaen had heard much the same and was impressed how well informed Oakwari was. His thought returned to the dream.

"And did he answer my question?"

"He said you already know the answer."

* * *

The sojourn to Aghar's village was the first of many visits into the heart of Wilden country. With Adriaen's unquenchable curiosity and Aghar's knowledge of languages, he was soon speaking the Algonquin language of the Mohicans and began crossing into their territory. As with the Mohawk, he was fascinated with their cultural traditions and way of life. Although the recent war between the Mohawk and Mohican was long and bloody, the peace between them was presently holding, with the Dutch sandwiched in between.

On one trek deep into the high country between the North and South Rivers, known to the Dutch as the Catskill Mountains, they crossed from Mohawk territory into Mohican.

Adriaen was captivated by the beautiful array of wigwams lining the upper edge of a large meadow, each nearly identical domed structure skillfully formed of arched saplings and sheets of birch bark. A mountain stream wound its way down the grassy slopes, providing irrigation water to a dozen carefully tended plots of corn. The people were cheerful and industrious by nature, busy fashioning all of the items necessary for everyday life, including their elegant buckskin clothing. Other than the youngest children, there was not an idle body amongst them.

Aghar was well received by Seconeok, who knew and respected his grandfather from their recent peace negotiations. Yet due to certain events of late, he was extremely wary of the Dutch, and kept a suspicious eye on Adriaen throughout their introduction.

With a fair understanding of the Mohican tongue, Adriaen came to learn the reason for his caution. Seconeok was first cousin to Oratam, the great sachem of the Hackensack Lenape, whose people suffered a massacre at the hands of Cornelis van Tienhoven, henchman for Director Kieft.

Adriaen had already had his own legal encounters with Tienhoven in New Amsterdam and deemed him to be a foul individual, yet one he unfortunately had to deal with. As head schout of the New Netherlands, this overblown and lecherous man often administrated court by himself, proclaiming outcomes most profitable to the West India Company regardless of the facts, as though it was his own money. Rumors spread that a good portion of it wound up in his pockets to pay his gambling debts.

At length, Adriaen was acknowledged and allowed to speak. Seconeok was impressed by his ability to speak the Mohican language, and hesitantly agreed to consider Adriaen's suggestion that not all Dutch were barbaric. After exchanging information on a wide range of topics, the chief solemnly passed him a pipe. At the end of the simple ceremony, Adriaen was given permission to learn what he could from the people of their tribe and record his findings in his book, under one condition. He could only document the truth.

As with the Mohawk, Adriaen delved into every aspect of their life.

He found the Mohicans in this remote area every bit as interesting as the Mohawk, and although they were similar in basic ways, their cultures were distinctly different. The Mohicans were more attuned to music, artistry and community life, whereas the Mohawks were excellent hunters, fierce warriors, and excelled at negotiating and forming strategic alliances.

The Catskills were a magical place to Adriaen, a place he felt he could make his permanent home. Each of the many rivers could support several villages, and the meadows would make excellent grazing land.

So full of life and possibility, it rekindled his dream of founding his own colony. The question from Oakwari's vision was never far from his mind, yet it remained unanswered.

Part Three

(Present Day - Albany, New York)

Chapter 13

Battlelines Drawn

Although a lifelong church goer, Tess Hendriksen saw the growing abuse of religious tax exemptions by massive church affiliated political action groups, blatantly using their acquired donations to espouse and encourage extreme political views.

She understood the importance of presenting her reforms to the media in a clear and concise manner. The changes to the law would be beneficial to legitimate religious communities, weeding out those who abuse the system by siphoning money away from charitable acts that actually help people meet their basic needs.

She argued that the Constitution of the United States and the Declaration of Independence held the government, *We the People*, responsible for making sure those basic needs were met for everyone. And where individual citizens or corporate persons could not fully supplement deficiencies in those basic needs, the government would step in to fill the gap.

The public argument quickly heated. Her main critics wanted the proposal killed without debate, showing up in media circles to provide counter programming filled with false accusations and fear mongering. Curiously, and without fail, the media hype exploded immediately before her scheduled presentations of the actual facts.

They were always one step ahead. It was as though they had an exact copy of her playbook. She began to face the chilling possibility that that might actually be true.

Had she been looking at the museum bombing wrong? Going back over the timing, she realized the attack wasn't about people hating her, which was not news for any politician actually attempting to govern. It was about stopping her before she could gain public support for her tax reform plan and introduce the new legislation.

As it turned out, an unexpectedly large percentage of those polled were enthusiastically in favor of getting religion out of the forefront of politics. With growing popular support, combined with her party's control of both houses of the state legislature, the laws necessary to enact her policy had quickly moved through committee and were heading for a floor vote.

The opposition launched a full-bore defamatory campaign to stop it, sparing no lie, personal attack, or veiled threat of violence. Governor Hendrikson was being portrayed by the most rabid media personalities as the *Bride of Satan*, at war with religion. Predictably, the battle spawned intense national interest.

* * *

In a historic building in lower Manhattan, purchased by the Originalist Confederation decades before to serve as their headquarters, a small clandestine group of prominent confederation members met secretly in a secluded basement room with their underground counterparts. These overpaid mercenaries who possessed an obedience like the orcs of Mordor, carried out the Confederation's covert and bloody missions.

Engraved in the granite lintel over the door was their maxim, The State Exists to Preserve Freedom, which was a convenient catchall for whatever they wanted it to mean, simply because no two people have ever agreed on what freedom actually means. And in that moment, what it meant was freedom from Tess Hendriksen.

Gaston Grimes, an obscenely wealthy broker of international currency for a handful of shady foreign partners, presided over the meeting.

Years before the revelations of Jeffrey Epstein, Grimes had failed to fully appreciate the potential criminal exposure his sexual escapades could lead to until a former Russian business associate asked him to lean a certain way on an important matter. The old photos he was handed when he hesitated confirmed the old KGB, now the FSB, was behind it, and he knew the consequences for not following their *request* would be devastating to him and his family.

As he dabbed beads of sweat from his forehead with his monogrammed handkerchief, he scanned the eyes of the men around the table. It was a habit he had developed over the years, certain he would recognize the same look he saw in his own eyes, a tell that they, too, were compromised.

Uncomfortably aware he was being watched remotely by his superiors in the organization, he pushed his large glasses up and began.

Grimes scrutinized the two operatives responsible for executing his orders. In a thin raspy voice he asked, "Has intel learned anything new from our inside source?"

Bass Drexler sat forward, and as he did, the gold fish charm he'd cleverly commissioned to signify his first name, glinted in the long, linear light that hovered over the conference table.

"She's planning a series of appearances upstate."

Turning to his left, he looked at his operational equal who was in charge of logistics. A large muscular man sporting a clean-shaven head and tattoos that were oddly circus themed, jumped in.

"We've already begun surveillance at each location, assessing her advance security measures. We have our best snipers on standby, waiting for final orders."

Drexler quickly added, "No bomb this time. We're going to use professionals."

Clay Daggert, a retired evangelical minister and senior confederation member, glared at him as he rose from his chair. "I thought you were the professionals."

"Hold on," Drexler pushed back. "Our strategy was good. The fact that the governor opted to catch another ride at the last minute could not have been predicted."

"You should have had someone tracking her husband! So much for your intel," Daggert snapped, hooking his thumbs in the pockets of his burgundy vest.

"Your inside man tried to call the Alpha Team leader as soon as he learned of the governor's change in plans, but wasn't able to get the message through in time."

"Well, who didn't answer their goddamned phone?" Daggert demanded.

"Our point person in the field, Sofiya Balashov."

Chapter 14

Loose Threads

The ring of Martin's cell phone startled her out of a nice dream. Being on-call was an occupational hazard, but getting up from her cozy spot next to Albert was not what she had planned for the morning.

"Sharky, this better be good," she whispered, stepping into her slippers as she reached for a robe with her other hand.

"Sorry boss but I'm sure you'll want to hear this."

"Hold on a second," she said entering the living room. Naked, she put her cell down long enough to pull her robe on and tie it around her waist.

"Okay, what've you got?"

"Another Russian."

"Dead?"

"You got it. This one was supposed to look like a heart attack, but the CSI guys found traces of duct tape on her wrists and ankles. They also found a tiny needle mark."

"Where did they find the body?"

"Staten Island, in her Midland Beach home," Sharky answered, "but get this. Her office is in Brighton Beach."

Martin rolled her eyes. "Coincidences never cease."

"Right? I directed our team to start checking into every contact she had. Problem is her phone and laptop are missing."

"We need to search that Brighton Beach office."

"They're already on the way with a warrant in hand."

"Excellent work, Sharky. Keep me posted."

* * *

Rubbing the sleep from his eyes, Albert found Martin in the kitchen brewing a pot of coffee.

"I was hoping that call was part of a dream, and you were still in bed beside me," he said, nuzzling the back of her neck.

"Wasn't my plan either. Sharky tracked down another murdered Russian, this one over on Staten Island."

"Eliminating the ones involved in the botched assassination attempt. Most likely starting at the bottom."

"That was my initial assessment. We need to find out everything there is to know about one Sofiya Balashov."

She turned around and held out a fresh cup of coffee. "Even though the FBI is officially taking the lead on this, I wouldn't mind some of your former associates looking into her overseas connections."

"I take it the coffee is a bribe."

"Oh no, the bribe is much better than that."

* * *

Everett Pendrake was getting accustomed to the governor's Manhattan office suite. Albert's alias had carved out a cozy work space near the large windows overlooking Lexington Avenue.

He intensified his deep dive into the governor's security concerns, everything from pre-event planning to the maintenance records on her bulletproof limousine. He started with a detailed study of the security staff. Scrutinizing everyone, from the chief to the support staff, he knew if any one of them was compromised, it would be the most direct route to the governor.

In the maintenance records there were a few unexplained instances of security chief Dell Thatcher taking the limo out for the evening. Albert immediately began to comb through his personal life. Other than his wife and two grown sons, no one else seemed very close to him, other than Margo Shrader, his liaison to the state Attorney General.

Albert used the governor's login to search the AG personnel calendars, and found that the dates and times of Thatcher's limousine excursions corresponded to Shrader's scheduled debriefings with the chief of security. Albert would have laughed if it wasn't so predictable.

Most of the other maintenance entries over the last month prior to the bombing were for typical items you would expect; wiper blade replacement, an oil change, tire rotation, and the like. At first, nothing in the vehicle's record stood out as odd, until he discovered a minor scheduling irregularity several days before the bombing. He noticed that it went in for a front-end alignment a few days before a work order for wheel and tire rebalancing and rotation. This sequence was reversed from what he knew most good mechanics would follow. The alignment almost always came second.

Going back to the previous month, he discovered that the limo had already undergone a full alignment. Turning back to the second alignment report, Albert confirmed that only one of the three mechanics assigned to the governor's motor pool was in the garage the afternoon the alignment was supposedly redone.

Digging into the personal background of all three mechanics, Hollis Marsh, the only one on duty the afternoon of the suspicious work order, raised an eyebrow. His sports gambling was eating up most of his take home pay, and his credit cards were nearly maxed out, never a good combination. Interestingly, his work reviews were always stellar, but his finances appeared to never have been reviewed.

Gambling addiction, as the data was suggesting, exposed people and made them susceptible to compromise. It simply depended on how much money you owed, and to whom.

Albert's suspicion grew further when he reviewed the entry-exit logs from the highly secure garage that day. Hollis had apparently scanned himself out midafternoon, returning to the garage just prior to the end of the regular work day where he remained for another two hours. Although overtime was not unheard of, there was nothing pressing on the governor's schedule that would require this. Albert realized a simple explanation might be that Hollis was making up time lost while on an appointment. That would be something he could easily run down.

* * *

Martin and her assassination team were being debriefed by FBI techies in her third-floor situation room at the Brooklyn field office. They had made significant progress isolating cell phone calls in the vicinity of the museum immediately before and after the bomb blast.

With state-of-the-art computer technology, they were linking the precise times of cell calls to a security video provided by the museum that showed a handful of individuals making a call or answering one. There was a margin of error in the procedure given the thousands of calls running through the nearest cell towers in Brooklyn, but it gave them serious raw material to follow up on, particularly from calls originating from or being received from burner phones. Methodically, a list was being compiled of people who needed to be interrogated.

Recognizing her customized ring for Albert, Martin paused the meeting to take the call.

"Special Agent Martin here," she answered in her most direct and professional voice.

"Should I stand at attention and click my heels," Albert asked, tongue in cheek. He imagined Martin surrounded by curious minds, perhaps placing bets on her love life.

"What do you have for me?"

"We need to keep an eye on Dell Thatcher and Hollis Marsh."

Martin took the call into her office and closed the door. "What have you got on my Chief of Security, and who is Marsh?"

"Regarding Thatcher, I suspect it may simply be cheating on his wife with Margo Shrader over at the AG's office."

"Yeh, I've met her. Some pretty extreme views. And Marsh?"

"One of the governor's limousine mechanics. Check both their phone numbers against your list of callers. We need to be very discreet. If either of them was in on the plot, I don't want to spook them anymore than they already are. Especially with people dying all over Brooklyn."

"Got it. Catch you later." He could hear her soft, alluring laugh as she hung up.

* * *

Sharky caught Martin in her office. He'd been following up on the cascading dead Russian count and had put together a few pieces of the puzzle.

"The FBI bomb lab was able to shed some light on the explosives used at the museum. As we suspected, it was a perfect match for the blast at the Palestinian bombmaker's apartment in Bay Ridge. The lab was quick to isolate the unique chemical signatures, linking both bombings."

"What kind of explosives were used?"

"American-made C4. It points toward homegrown terrorists, but the detonators used were actually Serbian from the Kosovo War era."

"Who are these people?" Martin exclaimed rising to her feet. "Grab a seat, I'm calling the bomb lab director."

Pacing with phone in hand as she had a habit of doing, she punched in his number.

"Director, Special Agent Martin here. I don't want you to release your findings about the explosives used in the museum bombing to anyone until I give you the go-ahead. *Museum bomber blows himself up* is a far too convenient wrap up for this assassination attempt. "My gut says this Palestinian was a fall guy."

There was a pause before he replied. "And if we release our findings that link him to both explosions, perhaps the real terrorists, if they exist, may relax and let down their guard."

"I'll keep that in mind, but for now keep it under wraps until I give you the word. We've got to run down this Russian connection before another attempt is made on the governor. They're showing up dead all over the city, and now we have old Serbian detonators."

"The governor? I thought the evidence at the scene pointed to the senator as the target."

"Another convenient misdirection. We think the governor was the real target. That's classified, so don't repeat it to anyone."

"Understood. I'll await your orders."

Chapter 15

The Woods

Returning Mary Lou to the barn after one of their therapy sessions, Will and Annah took a walk down a footpath that ran through the woods beside the Esopus Creek.

They came to a small clearing in the forest near a waterfall where a shaft of afternoon sunlight bathed a shallow depression in the ground. Will remembered from his childhood visits to the farm that this particular spot was said to be the burial place of a great Lenape chief. The fine green grass lining the recess was like a soft blanket, calling them closer.

The sloped edge of the spot made a perfect backrest as they lay down, arm in arm. They soon fell into a deep slumber. This kind of sudden sleepiness was not unknown in the Catskills, as memorialized in Irving's legend of *Rip van Winkle,* but this time there were no funny little men with strong liquor.

They slept for several hours, waking only when the evening dew began to settle. Something from their dreams stayed with them as they headed back to the old Garrison farmhouse. The experience left Will with the feeling that there was an important question that needed to be answered, but he was unable to bring it to mind. He could only remember bits and pieces of his dream, exploring other pathways through the forest, then walking through a city to a grand historic building he didn't recognize.

Annah looked back on the path to find that Will had stopped. He had a blank, faraway look on his face.

"Hey, where are you?"

"My dreams were weird, and very vivid."

"Yours too?"

As soon as she uttered the words, she remembered an eerie thought she'd had just before waking. It gave her a chill. "Did we just sleep on someone's grave?"

"That just might explain a few things," Will replied. "I'm guessing there's an element of truth behind a lot of these local legends."

"Yikes, what is this?"

Seeing Annah wildly waving her arm sleeves across her face, Will asked,

"You okay?"

"Sorry, it was just a spider web."

They were both on edge, and the web had added a little more tension to an already spooky day in the woods. They stepped up their pace. As they reached the barnyard, Will came to a stop and whispered to Annah, "Quiet, there might be a prowler."

They silently crossed the barnyard in the dark and approached the back of the house. Without warning, an enormous wraithlike shadow swept past their faces. Annah screamed.

"Shit," Will said, starting to laugh nervously. "It was only an owl rising up from the rim of the rain barrel next to the kitchen door."

* * *

Will was restless and saddled up Mary Lou for an early morning ride. Kari had the tack in such superb condition it fit her like a glove.

With no coaxing, Mary Lou followed Will out into the morning mist that blanketed the barnyard. Great clouds of steam billowed from her nostrils as she came to a stop and waited for Will to mount.

The sweeping sprays of fern rising up through the fog lent a fairytale quality to the woods. They rode past the burial site and followed the trail down to a small pond in the woods near Kari's stable.

In the dim morning light, Will spotted Kari standing on the opposite edge of the pond, casting his line into the water.

"Any luck?" Will shouted as he rounded the pond to join him.

Kari silenced him with a finger across his lips.

"Don't want to spook them," he whispered.

As if on cue, his pole bent under the strain of a bluegill strike. With light tackle, the fish put up an honorable fight but inevitably wound up in Karis wicker fishing creel.

* * *

Kari gathered his fishing gear and they walked down the small wooded path to the stable.

Several crows gathered on the corral fence as Kari cleaned his fish, waiting for him to toss them scraps of fish guts.

"Nothing wasted," he grinned as they dove to get their share.

"You've been training them?"

"No. They seem to have figured out that I bring fish back after I leave with my fishing pole."

"Smart birds."

"Survivors," Kari said looking up from his fillets. "So, you had a vision?"

Will didn't bother to ask how he knew.

"More like a dream, but yes, something was being revealed."

Kari carefully sealed his catch in plastic bags and placed them carefully in his cooler. After rinsing his knife in water scooped from a rain barrel, he removed his blue nitrile gloves and poured two metal cups full of coffee.

Will took a cup from Kari and hopped up on the top rail of the corral fence. Coffee always tasted better outdoors on a chilly morning, especially if you could find a shaft of sunlight to sit in. The warm rays felt good on his back as he sipped the dark steaming brew.

"What did you see?" Kari asked, perched beside him.

"Several different pathways through the forest, one that continued on to a city and a grand historic building I didn't recognize."

"Was there more?"

"I felt strongly there was an important question that needed to be answered."

"By you?"

"I presumed so."

Will's vision had a familiar ring about it. Kari quietly searched his memories for a story told to him a long time ago by his grandfather's eldest brother. At length, his silence was broken.

"You once told me that your ancestors who came to this place were Dutch."

"Yes, they came here before the English."

"I remember a tale told to me by my uncle about a Kristoni, the name given by my people to the first Dutch settlers. In our tongue, it means *Men who make metal.*

"This legend was about one of the first Kristoni to walk through these woods. He too, had questions that needed to be answered."

"Okay, now you have me a little spooked. You're not joking, are you?"

"I never joke about dreams. I hold them to be sacred, filled with messages from our ancestors, from nature's spirits and guardians, and from what many people now call their higher selves."

"You say he too, had questions."

"Yes, he wanted to build a colony here in these hills, where the Wilden and Kristoni's could live together in peace. A place of tolerance governed by natural law, where each person had the freedom of conscience to practice whatever spiritual tradition they chose, or practice none at all. As long as one refrained from harming, shaming or intimidating others for their beliefs, they would be free to follow whatever path they chose."

"Could such a place really be possible?"

"Perhaps that is the question you are trying to answer."

"Did he have a name?"

"They called him the Young Gentleman, or in the old Dutch language, the *Jonk Heer.*"

Part Four
(Year 1644 - New Amsterdam)

New Amsterdam and Vicinity

(New Netherlands - Mid Seventeenth Century)

Chapter 16

From Rensselaerswyck to New Amsterdam

After Adriaen's first visit to the Catskills, he returned several times to meet with leaders of all three nations that shared territory in those highlands; Munsee in the southwest towards the South River, Mohican in the southeast towards the North River, and Mohawk in the upper half. The chiefs were intrigued with Adriaen's ideas about a new colony based on natural law. They were also aware he might have a challenge getting approval from the West India Company.

Having reached an agreement with the tribes for a large tract in the eastern reaches of the Catskills, the next step in realizing his dream for a new colony was to get the approval of Director Kieft.

He returned to New Amsterdam as he regularly did on legal business for Rensselaerswyck, but this time he had important personal business as well. He was received at Fort Amsterdam by Kieft, along with his senior aide van Tienhoven, who was never far from his ear.

Adriaen had come this far but was reticent about presenting his plans for the Catskill colony in the presence of van Tienhoven. Having argued numerous times over legal matters in court, the man seemed to have little to no conscience. But Adriaen's distrust went much deeper than that, and he had grown to have a particular disdain for the disrespectful way he treated women.

* * *

Court in New Amsterdam was held in the stately stone structure on the waterfront of Manhattan known as the Stadt Huys. This all-purpose court house and city hall was actually the main village tavern, built by Director Kieft several years earlier.

Adriaen was in court that morning for a legal matter between Killian van Rensselaer and the Dutch West India Company, to present a petition to adjust the boundaries of Fort Orange and Beaverwyck. Against his better judgement, and driven by his enthusiasm to start a new colony, Adriaen had requested an audience with Director Kieft to hear his petition for the Catskill patroonship.

Cornelis van Tienhoven presided over the court that day as part of his duties as the provincial secretary, schout-fiscal, and principal aide to the director. He was also the person who took the van der Donck hearing request to Kieft.

The first case before the court that morning was a complaint brought by the Reverend Francis Doughty against a young Englishman. Charging slander of his eighteen-year-old daughter, he recounted the young man's ongoing attempts to humiliate Mary Doughty by singing vulgar and sexually suggestive songs about her in public.

Adriaen watched Tienhoven lustfully eye the young woman, clearly enjoying her discomfort as, at his request, the defendant sang his vulgar song before the court.

Since leaving home he had been focused on his law school studies in Leiden, and now his legal work in New Netherland, leaving him little time to think about marriage and starting a family. But those thoughts caught up with him that morning.

He felt his eyes linger on the young woman. Adriaen admired her quiet dignity and grace under such uncomfortable circumstances, and she appeared to be as self-assured as she was beautiful. He felt his face redden when she looked up and caught him gazing at her.

Found liable, the young Englishman was sentenced to be bound to the Maypole in the forecourt of Reverend Doughty's church throughout his Sunday morning services, with his neck bound and his defamatory transgression posted above his head.

When the case was settled, Adriaen rushed to introduce himself to Francis and his daughter, using his very best English. Standing face to face with Mary for the first time, he had the feeling he'd known her all of his life. Time stood still. The spell was finally broken by the extended hand of Reverend Doughty.

* * *

The property boundary amendment for Rensselaer was quickly decided, after which Adriaen was escorted to Director Kieft's office on the second floor of the four-story Stadt Huys. The sound of their heels on the wooden stairs reverberated through the vertical space.

Kieft's corner office had two large windows, bathing the room with sunlight. The views over the bustling waterfront and anchored ships along the East River toward the villages of Breukelen were most impressive.

Director Kieft was sitting behind his ornately crafted desk, confiscated from a Spanish galleon in the Caribbean by a Dutch privateer, when Adriaen entered the room. He casually rose to his feet and offered Adriaen a weak and surprisingly clammy handshake for such a cool, pleasant morning.

Kieft plainly spent more time grooming himself and tending to his clothing than most men. Unfortunately, his shifty eyes, pointed face, and slight build created a silhouette against the bright sky that looked more like a scarecrow than a man.

Tienhoven moved his chair closer to Kieft's right side, uncomfortably so from Adriaen's perspective. He assumed it was done to make whispering into his ear easier.

And as he feared, Kieft took his petition under advisement, essentially putting it on hold. Before he could return to his home upriver, Adriaen's dream to start a new colony in the Catskills had already reached the ear of van Curler, nephew of van Rensselaer and manager of his colony. His report was no doubt enroute to his uncle in Amsterdam.

* * *

At the end of summer, Adriaen was informed by van Curler that his contract as Schout of Rensselaerswyck would not be renewed. His termination came as no surprise, and as van der Donck had already decided to leave Rensselaer's employ, it had little impact.

But the West India Company resolution that had accompanied Rensselaer's termination letter was a blow, denying Adriaen's petition for the patroonship of the Catskills. Discouraged but determined, he started making plans to establish a law practice in New Amsterdam. Central to that practice was his commitment to advocate for self-governance and to implement the tolerance that had been instituted in the homeland, but not yet afforded to the citizens of the New Netherlanders by their corporate overlords.

* * *

When Adriaen arrived in New Amsterdam with all of his worldly possessions, he temporarily moved in with Michiel Janszen who had relocated there from Rensselaerswyck.

He also reconnected with Cornelius Melyn, who had fled to New Amsterdam from his Staten Island colony, along with his family and all of the surviving settlers, after the Hackensacks began to retaliate against the Dutch for the massacre of their women and children in the nearby village of Pavonia.

This was merely one of dozens of assaults and retaliations between the Dutch and the surrounding tribes that became known as the Kieft War. The director ignored his own Council of Twelve, a group comprised of prominent local citizens who strongly advised Kieft against brutally attacking the Wilden. Instead, he listened to the likes of van Tienhoven, who went on to lead the cold-blooded massacre in Pavonia. The Twelve had since been disbanded and replaced with the Council of Eight Men, chosen by the people.

After nearly three years of bloody reprisals by both sides, most of the farmers in the surrounding countryside had been murdered by the Wilden and their settlements destroyed, erasing more than a decade of Dutch progress in America.

Settlers who had lost everything now huddled in New Amsterdam and placed the blame at the feet of Kieft. Word spread throughout the city that new petitions against him were being secretly sent to his superiors. Unknown to Kieft and Tienhoven, Adriaen was behind the scenes, employing his legal skills to raise the petitions initiated by the Eight to a more professional and effective level.

*　*　*

After his move to Manhattan in the fall of 1644, one of the first legal cases Adriaen took was on behalf of Cornelius Melyn, his friend and voyage mate from their Den Eyckenboom crossing three years earlier, now one of the leading members of the Eight.

After a secret meeting of the Eight at the house of Michiel Janszen, Melyn took Adriaen aside and explained his legal quandary. Tienhoven, who despised Melyn, had impounded his small seaworthy shallop for alleged unpaid tariffs.

She was a sleek shallow draft sailing vessel with forty feet of waterline, designed for coastal waters navigation. Tapered at both ends, her rudder, masts, oars, and tackle were reversible, allowing her to easily back out of narrow creeks and rivers.

On Adriaen's advice, Melyn encouraged Tobias Feake, the son of one of his former English trading partners in Connecticut, to make an offer to acquire the boat for half the amount of the unpaid fine. Seeing it as another jab at Melyn, Tienhoven approved the sale.

What he did not know was that Adriaen had arranged a deal with Feake, who would repay Melyn for the fair value of the ship by quietly moving tobacco and other Dutch goods from Manhattan to the New England colonies for himself and his new partner, Michiel Janszen. In addition to Melyn's customers, Tobias brought to the table his contacts up the Fresh River in the Connecticut Colony, and beyond Long Island as far east as the Bay Colony. He promised the return trips to Manhattan would be filled with Scotch whiskey, the best English tea, and the finest fabrics from the East, all goods that Melyn knew were in high demand by wealthy women.

Melyn and Feake were in agreement on one important thing. They would not let Kieft and his henchman steal their cargo under the banner of their exalted positions using trumped-up tariffs that were little more than legal thievery.

* * *

During negotiations for the sale of Melyn's ship, Adriaen became friends with Tobias, who was just a few years younger than he. One night at the home of Janszen over several mugs of beer, Tobias began to reveal more about his time living in the Connecticut Colony and the Bay Colony before that.

"I was in the village of Stamford near Greenwich with my uncle Robert when his trading partner and comrade in arms during the Pequot War, Daniel Kirkpatrick, was accosted by the Dutch privateer Captain Willem Blauvelt, or Bluefield as the English call him."

Adriaen was aware of the scores of privateers who had received their commission from the Dutch States during their war of independence with Spain, but Blauvelt had secured his commission directly from Kieft. Serving as his private navy, the goods and riches Blauvelt captured on the Spanish Main in his frigate *La Garce*, were returned to New Amsterdam in exchange for a hefty cut of the spoils.

Tobias continued, "Making it clear that his orders were from Tienhoven, Blauvelt demanded that Kirkpatrick lead a full-scale attack on the Wilden villages upriver. Considering Blauvelt to be nothing more than a pirate with no authority in Connecticut, an argument broke out when Kirkpatrick became dismissive of his demands."

"I've met Blauvelt. He is a violent and unprincipled man," Adriaen interjected.

Tobias nodded. "That is true, and as the argument became more heated, Blauvelt flew into a fit of rage. He pulled out his pistol and shot Kirkpatrick dead in front of his wife Annekan van Beyeran, and their five children."

"How horrific. What has become of them?"

"Before Uncle Robert returned to England, we moved the family to a new home in the village of Vlissingen on the north shores of Long Island, further from the Indian conflict. There, they are among the many English who have fled New England for religious freedom."

"How are they faring without the father?"

"After losing him, my heart went out to the family. I moved to Vlissingen where I could look after them, and have since become a surrogate father to the youngest ones."

Chapter 17

Peace with the Wilden

Kieft became so distraught about the war with the Wilden that had now gone on for more than three years, he sought council from van der Donck. He knew from the Catskill colony petition that he spoke their languages and had connections among tribal leaders.

Receiving a summons from Kieft, Adriaen marched into the Stadt Huys with a much different attitude. Last time it was he who made a request and was denied. It was now Kieft who was in need, and it was going to cost him.

He briskly walked through Kieft's open office door and came to a stop in front of his desk.

"What do you want?" Adriaen asked, skipping over the usual pleasantries.

"I want to hire you as an interpreter and negotiator, to make peace with the Wilden."

"I am a patriot and will do so without payment," Adriaen said as he watched Kieft lean closer, "but there is still the matter of land."

"Of course, resubmit your petition for the Catskill colony."

"I'm afraid the sun has set on that opportunity."

"So, what do you propose?"

"If I get you the ear of the chiefs in the north, I want another tract of land on the east side of the North River above Spuyten Duyvil creek."

"Agreed, but you will still need to pay a fair price for the land."

"Of course, a fair price based on the work I've done for you. And one more thing," Adriaen said, lowering his voice, "Tienhoven will not be a part of this expedition." Leaning closer he added, "They know who he is."

* * *

The peace delegation, led by Kieft and van der Donck, along with a detachment of Dutch soldiers with their snaphaunce muskets and finest uniforms, arrived at Beaverwyck in late summer. Word had already been sent upriver and the tribal leaders were prepared to meet at a temporary encampment near the falls.

Adriaen's reunion with his friend Agheroense was warm and genuine, and their initial exchange was in both Dutch and Mohawk. Kieft, who had been afraid to leave the safety of Fort Amsterdam or the nearby Stadt Huys throughout the war, was stunned when the two men from very different worlds embraced each other as brothers.

Agheroense, wearing his dress buckskins and war feathers, led the Dutch party up the main trail along the Mohawk River, to a small ceremonial encampment in the forest erected for these negotiations. The chiefs of the Mohawk and Mohican nations stood in front of their lodges, accompanied by a contingent of their honored warriors.

At Adriaen's insistence, the peace treaty was to be negotiated with the two largest tribes first, knowing that each of them had an extensive network of defense alliances with the smaller tribes downriver.

Kieft quickly realized that without the help of van der Donck there would be no talks. Kieft also realized the tribes considered him to be weak, held in low regard by the Wilden because he had tolerated Tienhoven's brutality and sexual assaults on their women and young girls. Kieft agreed to ban Tienhoven from any further dealings with the Wilden, and while Adriaen was not convinced, the chiefs accepted Kieft at his word.

Once details of the Dutch peace proposal met with the satisfaction of the chiefs, they sat quietly around the fire and waited for Kieft to make the next move. The intermittent song of birds in the surrounding trees and the crackling of the ceremonial fire were the only sounds that broke the stillness.

"What are they waiting for?" Kieft whispered to Adriaen.

After a few quiet words with Agheroense to confirm all parties had the same understanding of the terms, Adriaen turned back to Kieft. "They are waiting for you to finalize the proposed treaty."

"And how do I do that?"

"With a gift worthy of the significance of the occasion. You see the poles standing beside the entries to each of their lodges?"

"I do. What of them?"

"That is where you hang the gifts you have brought to them. If they take them and return to their seats, the treaty is approved. If they return them to the post, the negotiations are over. There will be no treaty."

The blood drained from Kieft's face. "What are you saying? There are no gifts. I've brought nothing," he sputtered.

Adriaen did not respond. He simply shifted his gaze away from Kieft and toward the chiefs sitting quietly across from them. Watching them.

The director lowered his voice. "You've tricked me. You know I have nothing to offer them. We'll be lucky if we get out of this alive."

Adriaen's smile was reassuring, but his eyes had hardened. "I have brought gifts I am sure will meet their approval."

"This is not the time to play games, van der Donck," Kieft said in a low growl. "What do you want?"

"The colony we spoke of at the Spuyten Duyvil. Transfer the patent on the land to me and I will help you end this long and bloody war."

* * *

On his return voyage to New Amsterdam, Adriaen was filled with a great sense of achievement. Not only had he helped bring peace to the province, but he now held the patent for the colony he had dreamed of for years. Knowing how slippery Kieft was, Adriaen drew up the legal patent for his patroonship at Spuyten Duyvil. The director signed it before they left the Wilden encampment.

But there was something else on his mind as the boat drifted down the North River. Lying on deck those warm August nights, his thoughts turned to Mary. After their initial encounter in the court room, he had several occasions to visit with her and her family at their new residence in Vlissingen, or Flushing as the English now called it. Her father, Francis Doughty was now the village minister.

Adriaen had also become fond of young Elias, younger brother of Mary who could already speak better Dutch than his sister. He dreamed of one day becoming a wealthy planter, and he pestered Adriaen at every opportunity about matters of law, land ownership, and trade.

The Doughty's were neighbors of Tobias Feake and Annekan van Beyeran. Adriaen, who had become their attorney, now had an additional excuse to call on Mary. They conversed mostly in English, but her Dutch was noticeably improving. In spite of their language difficulties, they seemed to have no end of things to talk about.

Adriaen had fallen in love with Mary and had hopes of marrying her one day. Standing on deck, he pulled the patent out of his coat pocket and read it again. With a plantation waiting for him, their future need no longer be a dream. He started to rehearse the speech he would give her father before he asked for her hand in marriage.

Chapter 18

The Jonk Heer and the Minister's Daughter

Through Tobias, Annekan, and the Doughty family, Adriaen had become well known in the village of Vlissingen among the established households, including Eduard Hart.

Hart was one of the English who had fled from New England's religious tyranny and settled by Vlissingen Creek on the north shores of Long Island. In the several years since his arrival, the village had grown substantially.

Hart shared his dreams of Vlissingen becoming a proper town with Adriaen, but confessed he had no idea how to move forward. Over the course of several meetings at Doughty's church, eighteen of the local landowner's signed the final petition crafted by Adriaen, asking that the proposed charter of their town be recognized by the Dutch authorities.

Maintaining civil relations with Kieft in the aftermath of the peace treaty, Adriaen was able to get him to sign off on the petition. It helped that he knew Kieft was under pressure from the West India Company to get more settlers into the province, including New Englanders if they swore an oath of loyalty to the Dutch States. What Kieft did not yet know was the year prior, Adriaen had secretly assisted Melyn and the Eight in preparing a petition to have him removed from being Director of New Netherlands.

Van der Donck and Hart had made it clear in the Flushing Charter that the people in the town would have the same *Freedom of Conscience* and other rights as afforded to all those living in the Dutch homeland.

* * *

On the cold October evening of the Charter signing, a spontaneous celebration broke out at the home of Eduard Hart. Many had already gathered in his home, including Adriaen and the Doughty clan. Out in the street, the neighbors built a large bonfire, drawing an even larger crowd. The hard cider and warmth of the fire were perfect on the cold autumn night.

When the celebration was at its height, Adriaen shouted from Hart's front stoop, calling for everyone's attention. Word had already gotten out about his new plantation and cheers of "Jonk Heer" could be heard in the crowd, the Dutch phrase for *Young Gentleman*. Usually reserved for a notable young landholder or professional, Adriaen had now become both.

It took a few minutes for the crowd to settle down, but he now had their attention.

"Mary Doughty. Are you out there?"

"I am," she answered haltingly.

"Would you please step up here beside me?"

Blushing from such public attention, she made her way through the crowd and slowly climbed the steps. Adriaen took her by the hand and whispered something in her ear. Then surprisingly, he got down on one knee and looked up into her eyes, now welling with tears. A hush fell over the crowd.

"Mary Doughty, before the witnesses gathered here tonight, will you be my bride?"

Her answer was impossible to hear over the cheers of the crowd. Pulling Adriaen to his feet she kissed him before burying her face into his shoulder to dry her eyes.

* * *

Young Elias, now a young man of thirteen, was thrilled by his sister's acceptance of Adriaen's proposal. To Elias, he was not only a decent man, the kind he thought his sister deserved, but the smartest man he had ever met. Now he was soon to become his brother.

He was of great help to his sister, scribing her formal wedding invitations and delivering them to those residing in Flushing.

Eduard Hart, who had recently been chosen Town Clerk, was so impressed with his written invitation that he offered the young lad the occasional job of making duplicate copies of official documents.

* * *

Word of the union between the two prominent families spread through the upper circles of New Amsterdam society. Only two weeks away, it was shaping up to be the biggest social event of the year. Friends fondly referred to it as *The Wedding of the Jonk Heer and the Ministers' Daughter*.

When it became obvious to Tienhoven that he was not invited to the celebration, he obsessed over what he considered a serious breach of etiquette. After all, he had been the second most powerful man in the province for more than ten years. Perhaps even more powerful than Kieft, he grumbled to himself. It was a shame that no one knew what he did for the province.

Kieft had kept him in the shadows, and he was still furious he had been left out of the talks with the Wilden. More so, he was angry the director had agreed to give van der Donck a patent for the land he'd had his own eyes on, much as he'd had the previous year on the lovely Mary Doughty. Being married with children had never interfered with his lustful and aggressive pursuit of young women. White or native, it did not matter as long as he got what he wanted.

Tienhoven came to realize he should have left van der Donck to his Catskill colony instead of revealing his plan to Rensselaer's agent. His hatred grew by the day. By being the only other lawyer in the city, and in charge of the court, he was certain the perfect opportunity for retribution would eventually come his way.

Chapter 19

Wedding in New Amsterdam

The wedding day took place on the twenty-second day of October in the year 1645. One Mary Doughty of Flushing was to marry Adriaen van der Donck, Esquire, at the Reformed Church of New Amsterdam.

Friends of the bride and groom showed up in great numbers filling the largest church in the province to capacity, including the extra chairs placed in the nave and side aisles. The Reverend Francis Doughty, father of the bride, presided over the union after being given consent by the Dutch minister.

Honored guests included chairman Cornelius Melyn and the Council of Eight, Michiel Janszen, the tobacco planter Adriaen had temporarily lived with in his Manhattan home, the new town clerk of Flushing, Eduard Hart, and Tobias Feake, seafarer extraordinaire and trader of fine things.

Even Director Kieft made an appearance. Although he suspected most of those gathered despised him, his wife had insisted on attending. She had a new gown, and was determined to flaunt her good taste and money. Seeing the couple walk into the church, Tobias looked twice before realizing the fabric of her dress was made of an Indian silk he had recently smuggled in from Rhode Island.

Reverend Doughty performed the ceremony in both his native English and passable Dutch to the diverse group of people in attendance.

Although rooted in Dutch law where tolerance of others was considered good for business, the mixing of cultures in the New Netherlands, as evidenced by those in attendance, was transforming the inhabitants of this new province into something previously unknown to the world. A new kind of people that worked together in spite of their differences. Americans.

* * *

Reports of those attending the wedding soon reached Tienhoven's ears through his spy in Flushing. His report suggested that the whole town avoided paying tariffs by routinely trading goods with the English boatman from Connecticut and beyond Long Island, but of this he offered no real proof. In the depths of his tortured mind, Tienhoven believed that van der Donck was somehow behind the smuggling operation, along with his silent partner, Cornelius Melyn.

Tienhoven regretted allowing Kieft to approve the Flushing Charter. Even though the tolerance the charter implied was attracting more New Englanders willing to pledge loyalty to the Dutch as planned, they were now espousing strange new beliefs, far more radical than the ideas that got Reverend Francis Doughty tossed out of Massachusetts. Although Tienhoven had drifted far from the righteous path, he would be keeping a keen eye on these blasphemous foreigners.

* * *

The morning following the wedding, Adriaen and Mary departed from the East River quay of New Amsterdam aboard the *Pride of Flushing*, as Tobias Feake had named his shallop. With Elias Doughty assisting on the sails, the *Pride* quickly followed the tidal surge upriver beyond the Spuyten Duyvil to the new mooring posts at the freshwater creek near the center of his new estate.

Adriaen had tall wooden pilings driven deep enough into the river bed to withstand the ever-changing currents in the North River. The mooring piles supported a small deck and the outer end of a rope bridge spanning across to terra firma. He stepped out and onto it first to confirm it was strong enough to hold their weight, but cautioned it was damp and slippery. Traversing one at a time, the new bridge sagged to within a few feet of the water's surface at its midpoint.

Once on shore, along with a few small trunks of personal items, they followed Tobias up the wooded path from the river bank to a high meadow overlooking the imposing North River Valley. When Mary laid eyes on their new home for the first time, it was just as Adriaen had described, the first phase of a grand manor. Currently standing was a three-room cabin, but the footprint of the stately home it would someday be part of could already be seen on the ground.

The house was strategically positioned in a clearing on higher ground from which one could view the entire twelve miles of riverfront that formed the western boundary of his vast plantation, a place Adriaen named *Colen Donck*, Dutch for the *Van der Donck Estate*.

Mary took to the land like a duck to water, and by winter's end she and Adriaen had a new sawmill built on what they renamed Saw Mill Creek. With the help of Tobias, the *Pride* was regularly transporting hardware, seed, and general supplies upriver to Colen Donck, and returning to New Amsterdam loaded with freshly sawn timbers from their mill. And like Adriaen, he was elated about his recent marriage to Annekan van Beyeran and the adoption of her children.

Part Five
(Present Day - New York City)

Chapter 20

Brooklyn FBI Field Office

Since his promotion, Sharky enjoyed an office across the bullpen from Martin. Assigned exclusively to her special detail with the governor, he was determined to take down the people responsible for the bombing. Killing political opponents went against everything he believed democracy stood for.

He glanced at the framed picture of Ricardo and him exchanging vows, and was grateful how much simpler his life had become since coming out. He no longer had to live a dual life. Yet he was deeply troubled by the idea that a moment so meaningful to him could cause such a strong reaction in others, even to the point of violence. He was outraged that the governor had been targeted, narrowly escaping the assassination attempt that had killed Senator Torres, by simply trying to eliminate the perverse use of nonprofit religious privilege to manipulate partisan politics.

He was following up on a short list of names culled from the thousands of calls that came through Brooklyn's cell towers around the time of the bombing, when Lucius Fletcher, his liaison with NYPD on the museum bombing, walked through his office door.

"Special Agent Obsharski. Sorry to bother you, but we just received a bulletin from the 84th Precinct regarding a young woman named Sydney Rogers. She was brutally assaulted when she apparently interrupted a burglary in progress at her apartment."

Not yet sure why this was relevant to their investigation, Sharky tilted his head to one side. "What's her condition?"

"She's being treated for blunt force trauma to the head at Brooklyn Methodist. They currently have her in a medically induced coma."

"So why is NYPD bringing this to our team?"

"Because of her connection to the Brooklyn Museum. She's employed there as an intern."

"Okay, now you've got my full attention."

"Right, my feelings exactly, so I immediately scrolled down our list of those in attendance the night of the bombing. She was one of the interns who volunteered to help at the reception that night, so she was in the lobby all evening. I spoke to the other volunteers and one of them remembered her taking pictures at the event."

"We need to see those pictures. Now. Did NYPD find her phone?"

"No, it wasn't on her person or in the apartment."

"Was anything else taken?"

"Nothing that the responding officers were able to verify before the paramedics wheeled her out. She was barely coherent when they arrived at the scene."

"Hmm, a burglary and brutal assault, and just for a phone. Did she have a laptop?"

"I just returned from her apartment and there was no sign of one."

"Have one of your detectives check her workspace at the museum for one," Sharky ordered, "or anything else that might make sense of the burglary."

* * *

Annah sat on a bench in the back yard garden of their Prospect Heights apartment, enjoying the warmth of the midday sun on her back. Living in the city was always invigorating, but she was looking forward to heading back to the Catskills.

With a renewed focus she believed came from his interactions with Mary Lou, and a few weeks of hands-on work at the museum, Will had the historic print shop exhibition moving in high gear. Most of the remaining narrative and design work could be done remotely.

Will had left early that morning for a meeting with Theron at the archeology lab to go over his progress on the translation of the printer's proofs. Annah was taking the opportunity to have an early lunch with Martin.

Having escaped death together more than once, they had become the sisters neither of them had. Over the short time they'd known each other, Annah had shared so many tantalizing tales about her home in Kerala that Martin moved it to the top of her vacation wish list, while Martin's vivid descriptions of the great National Parks of America had moved Annah to read books about each of them. Yellowstone was on the top of her list.

They'd not seen much of each other since the bombing. While anxious to see her, Annah was trying not to let the disturbing dream that woke her that morning upset what was otherwise a beautiful morning.

* * *

Annah was mulling over the menu at one of her favorite Keralan style Indian restaurants when Martin arrived.

"Annah, it's so good to see you."

Annah was immediately comforted by Martin's strong familiar voice, and rose to her feet to greet her in a warm embrace.

"It is good to see you too," Annah replied.

Not wanting to waste their time together on talk of the investigation, Martin asked, "How's Will? And tell me about the farm."

"Well first off, it has been a fascinating experience watching Will and Mary Lou become an item."

"Mary Lou?" Martin replied, leaning closer to Annah to learn more about this mystery woman. "Do I have to shoot somebody?"

"Well, she is pretty seductive for a therapy horse."

Martin laughed out loud.

"I might need a bigger gun."

It was Annah's turn to laugh. "Maybe just an apple. She is a sweetheart."

In a conspiratorial tone, Annah lowered her voice and scanned the dining room from side to side.

"I want to hear more about you and Albert."

"Well, I can tell you that it takes a lot of will power for us not to spend all of our time together. I've never wanted to lose myself over a man, but I am definitely under his spell."

"Intimacy?" Annah ventured.

Martin uncharacteristically let out a giggle. "Well, we do occasionally play *Boris and Natasha*. That's what Albert calls our spy game."

"Just watch out for *Moose and Squirrel*," Annah teased, having become a Rocky and Bullwinkle fan at Will's urging.

Martin's phone buzzed, interrupting their girl talk.

"Excuse me while I take this call," she said turning to her side.

"What have you got for me Sharky?"

"Could be nothing, but one of the museum interns helping at the exhibit opening was mugged and robbed in her apartment last night. She's currently in an induced coma at Brooklyn Methodist to combat brain swelling.

"What was taken?"

"As far as we can tell, the only thing the assailant took was her phone. I have NYPD detectives at her museum workspace looking for her laptop, or any other devices or clues that might shed some light on the break-in."

Hanging up and returning her attention to Annah, Martin asked, "Sydney Rogers, does the name mean anything to you?

"Yes, she's one of our interns at the museum."

Somber and professionally stoic, Martin continued, "I'm sorry to tell you that she was mugged at her apartment last night."

"How horrible! Is she alright?"

"They have her in an induced coma while they try to reduce brain swelling around the point of impact."

"Good Lord," Annah groaned, stunned by the news.

"I know this is a lot to process at the moment, but can you think of any reason she might have been targeted?"

"No. I can't imagine anyone wanting to harm such a gentle soul."

Martin took another mouthful of baingan bharta on a small piece of naan. As she savored her food, she noticed a dip in Annah's spirits. There was a tell in her eyes, as though she was remembering something horrific.

Finally raising her gaze, Annah whispered, "Please be careful."

"Now you've got me spooked. What's going on?"

"I had a vision in a dream this morning. You were shot."

"And what was I doing?"

"Protecting me."

Chapter 21

The Serbian Connection

Using his direct access from the governor's suite into confidential criminal investigative records, Albert discovered some disturbing facts about the mysterious Sofiya Balashov, recently killed in her Staten Island home. According to FBI forensics, she was murdered by a fairly sophisticated assassin. If not for the current, statistically unlikely rash of violent deaths in the Russian community, they might have missed the traces of duct tape adhesive on her wrists and the tiny injection mark behind her ear.

She first moved to America during the fall of the Soviet Union with her now deceased husband under his Priority Worker's Visa. She achieved her own green card for her humanitarian work prior to her husband's passing. Delving deeper into her history, Albert found the referenced humanitarian work claimed in her original visa application to be suspect, but at the time there had been a greater tolerance for Eastern Europeans trying to escape the control of the Soviets.

But her sketchy volunteer work was just the first glimpse into her secret life. With Martin's help, Albert tracked her early years as a single woman. She first went to work for a small temporary placement company that catered to women originally from the old Eastern Block. They were later investigated for human trafficking and shut down, but she was never indicted. A few years after that she was suspected of running a small prostitution ring, but the charges were dropped when the two Ukrainian girls who had agreed to testify against her, suddenly disappeared.

But after that incident, her record with local authorities was clean, not even a traffic ticket. According to tax records, she had been operating a small legitimate temp agency, selling end-of-life insurance and cemetery plots on the side. The hit on her made no sense to him.

* * *

Albert's highly encrypted and rarely used cell made one of several distinct buzzing patterns, that of Drazen Novak, his former MI6 contact in Dubrovnik.

"Albert, my old comrade, our system just flagged an ongoing relationship between Sofiya Balashov and a suspected Serbian arms dealer."

"Is that all?" Albert asked with feigned disappointment. With a chuckle he added, "Does he have a name?"

"We have confirmed that a Serbian named Caslav Nedic has been the love interest and business partner of Sofiya Balashov for a good part of the last decade.

"On the surface he's a well-connected exporter of electronics, and although he is suspected by Interpol of having his hands deep into the illegal weapons trade, they were never able to make the charges stick. All of his closest associates go back to the Serbian security forces that fought in the Kosovo War. Several were later tried and convicted for war crimes."

"How did Nedic take the news of Sofiya's death?" Albert pressed.

"Not good. The news of her murder sent him into a rage."

"He knew it was murder? We haven't made that public yet."

"We believe he learned the murder was made to look like a heart attack from his mole inside the NYPD. Caslav apparently despises *dirty spy shit*. When he kills someone, he leaves his calling card."

"Anything else?"

"Yeah, he's the kind of guy known for settling the score with a vengeance. Word on the street has it that one of his nephews living in Brooklyn has been trying to identify Sofiya's killer."

"One of his nephews?"

"The one he had doing occasional work for Sofiya. We're still looking for the other hypothetical nephews in Brooklyn."

* * *

Martin was returning to her desk at the Brooklyn field office when her cell buzzed. The familiar face on the screen brought a smile to her face.

"Is this my favorite Cornishman, or is that Cornwaller?"

"Albert will do just fine," he replied with a touch of mock annoyance.

"All business this morning, eh?"

"More like the thrill of the hunt. I think I can shed some light on your antique Serbian detonators," he added.

"Tell me more."

"Sofiya Balashov had a close relationship with a Serbian arms dealer, apparently both romantic and business."

"So maybe she was placing more than just temps?"

Albert chuckled, "We have to stop meeting like this."

"You know where to find me."

* * *

Albert was determined to find the threads that led back to the grand master behind the whole murderous enterprise. Linking Caslav to Sofiya made it a near certainty that the explosives used in the museum bombing came through them. Someone did their best to erase some of those threads with the murder of Sofiya, and most likely all of the other dead Russians in Brighton Beach. He was not hopeful of finding any other second tier assassination operatives still alive.

He briefly entertained the thought that Sofiya might be the ringleader

Curt Ench

of the bombing, but quickly dismissed it. Her motives were unclear. If it was done just for the money, the intense heat coming down from law enforcement would have made it a bad gamble.

He had found no trace of political bias or allegiance in her file, or any evidence of fomenting hostility toward the governor. Her social media was boring and untended with no discernable agenda.

But not so with her boyfriend Caslav, who held a deep and abiding hatred of America for its part in driving the Serbs out of Kosovo and leading the NATO bombing that killed his sister. He saw the likely possibility that Sofiya's participation in the plot was simply out of loyalty to him.

Albert hoped that surveillance on Caslav and unearthing his alleged nephews might pick up that thread again.

* * *

After a long day, Albert met Martin for dinner at their favorite American grill. Over seared scallops and grilled asparagus, they avoided talking about the latest in the case until they'd had their fill of gazing into each other's eyes. It seemed the seafood was an aphrodisiac, but truth be told, most cuisines were.

Albert was the first to break the spell.

"Caslav Nedic, lover of Sofiya Balashov and the arms dealer who supplied her with the explosives and detonators used at the museum, is thought to have two nephews living in Brooklyn."

"Nephews. Hmm. Any names or faces?"

"Nothing yet. My source believes they have different last names. Small help I know, but he is fairly certain that one of them did the occasional odd job for Sofiya."

"I'll have my team get on identification of the nephews, and whatever their latest odd jobs entailed. By the way, how did Caslav take the news of her death?"

118

"Not well. He apparently found out it was a staged heart attack, and went ballistic." Albert lowered his voice and added, "Word is he's prone to extreme violence and retaliation."

About to take the last bite of her molten chocolate cake, Martin paused to ask, "But who would he be coming after?"

Chapter 22

Brooklyn Museum – Archeology Lab

Dark clouds gathering in the north were stealing the late afternoon daylight in the lab as Will got ready to lock up for the day. He gathered his copies of Theron's most recent translations of the old printshop records that had been left spread out on the long window counter from his morning meeting.

Some of the history coming to life through these records gave a stunning portrayal of Dutch colonial life in the sixteen hundreds, along with volumes of intimate details on some of the most influential early settlers.

As he leaned forward to reach the last sheet, a blinding bolt of lightning struck the lawn below the windows. The deafening crack rattled the glass. As Will jumped back, the brilliant flash lit up the page in his hand. The large typeface was burned into his memory. *Cornelis van Tienhoven - Suspected of Murder.*

Another blinding lightning strike knocked out the building's power and left him standing in the dark. Unsure whether to wait out the electrical storm and the rain that was soon to follow, he decided to make a run for it.

* * *

The powerful thunderstorm rolled into New York City that afternoon with a vengeance, pelting Annah with wind driven rain drops as she ran up the front stoop of their apartment.

Juggling her keys and several large shopping bags, she pushed through the entry. She'd spent the last couple of hours filling her shopping list of supplies for the Garrison farmhouse.

They planned to leave for the Catskills in the morning. With Will's Dutch colonial printshop exhibit moving ahead nicely, they wanted to spend time in the country. At this point most of their remaining work on the exhibit could be done from the farm.

Annah knew Will would enjoy spending a few more weeks with Mary Lou, and Kari had agreed without hesitation when she'd called him. He had seen the empathy this gentle horse had for Will, and getting to know him better, he had begun to share those feelings.

The rain was beating on the window panes with a deafening roar. She worried that she had not gotten a call from Will who was due to return home with some takeout. She looked out the large front windows through the rain as it sheeted over the gutter. All she could see was a watery grey blur.

Between the pounding rain and thunder, a thud coming from the bedroom hallway caught her attention. It sounded like something fell onto the carpet.

As she entered the bedroom, now darkened by the storm, she could see the curtain billowing from a slightly open window, which had knocked the lamp off of the nightstand. Often leaving it open a crack for fresh air, she must have forgotten to close it.

Crossing the room, she bent down to pick up the lamp. A flash of lightning lit the floor, revealing large wet footprints. Operating on recently challenged survival instincts, she grabbed the lamp and turned around swinging.

Her blind swing caught the intruder on the side of the head and sent him reeling. Taken by surprise, the hooded figure regained his footing and ran toward the front door.

On the stoop and about to collapse his umbrella, Will heard the commotion. As he swung the door open, he saw a hooded man running down the hall straight toward him, Annah close behind wielding a lamp.

Will braced himself. Just as they were about to collide, he grasped the man by the forearm and flipped him over his back into the wall beside the door.

The man righted himself before Will could tackle him. Scrambling to his feet, the intruder darted out the open door into the murky darkness.

Will eventually gave up the chase when he lost sight of him in the rain. Drenched from head to toe, he returned to the apartment where Annah almost knocked him over as she rushed into his arms.

"Are you okay?" she asked, still trembling from the adrenalin rush. Wiping the rain from the side of his face, she kissed his cheek. Then pushing away just enough to get a good look at him, she broke into a big grin. "I couldn't believe my eyes when you showed up and tossed him into the wall."

"You couldn't believe it? I wish I had a picture of you coming after him with a lamp!"

"That would be nice. At least we'd have a picture of his face!"

* * *

After a few hours of restless sleep, they put on the coffee and packed for their road trip up the Hudson Valley. Annah hadn't seen very much of the state so Will suggested a sight-seeing trip on their way to the Garrison farm.

The police had come, but the wet footprints were dry by the time they got there. Annah had thought to snap photos of the prints, but the most that could be deduced was they were made by a man with big feet. The guy wore gloves, so there were no prints. Since nothing was stolen, the police report was rather routine.

Will had called Albert, who promptly advised them to get out of town given the break-in occurred right on the heels of the Sidney Rogers assault. He instructed Will on evasive techniques, like making random turns on his way out of town and making strategic pull-offs to see if he was being followed. He also mentioned, that in the case of a car chase, the importance of taking pictures of the car and license plate. From anyone else Will would have thought this a bit paranoid. Annah had no problem with Albert's advice.

It was Sunday morning and traffic was relatively light in the city as they drove with the top down in Riley's old VW Beetle. The classic car had been offered to Will by her mother, an offer he gladly accepted.

The weather was balmy for early October and Annah was enjoying the air rushing through her hair as they tooled up the FDR toward the Bronx.

"I'm glad we're getting out of the city," she said as they turned north on the 9A. Pausing she added, "Do you think the intruder was connected with Sydney? Or maybe, to Rayne Ashcroft and the Mandate?"

"We've seen crazier things. I'm already a bit spooked after talking to Albert, so I think it's good for us to disappear for a while."

"Disappear?"

"You know, have an adventure. Speaking of adventures, I'm psyched about Theron's latest work on the Dutch printshop records."

"That will be fun to sort through on a road trip," Annah said with a hint of sarcasm, peering at Will over her Ray-Bans.

"I was thumbing through some of the translated documents referring to Adriaen van der Donck's patroonship," Will continued. "Colen Donck, the plantation that he founded, bordered the Hudson River on the west and the Bronx River on the east. It extended twelve miles upriver from the northern tip of Manhattan encompassing all of what became modern day Yonkers, the city that bears his nickname. The southern terminus of Colen Donck was where the Harlem River merged with the Hudson at a place called Spuyten Duyvil, Dutch for 'Spitting Devil'. The strong tidal influx and constant reversal of flow in both rivers has long been known for creating strange whirlpools and tumultuous sprays at their point of convergence, giving the place its name."

"Isn't Yonkers just up ahead?" Annah asked, pretty sure of her geography.

"Yep, about two miles, but we'll be entering Colen Donck as soon as we cross the Harlem River."

As they crossed to the other side of the bridge, Annah started to laugh. She pointed to the first exit sign on their right. *Spuyten Duyvil this exit.* Looking over at Will, she said, "You must be psychic!"

Chapter 23

Mechanic On Duty

While Martin stayed on the Serbian connection, hunting for Caslav's nephews, Albert turned his attention to the matter of the mechanic. He realized any one of these threads could be a path back to the top of the whole conspiracy. Someone was handling Hollis Marsh.

Albert got word back from one of his underworld contacts in the gambling syndicate that Marsh's habit went well beyond on-line sports betting. With the usual *you didn't hear it from me* disclaimer, he confirmed that there was a large overdue mark against Marsh from a rough local backroom poker operation.

After catching a cab to Williamsburg, Albert quietly entered Marsh's first floor apartment, careful not to disturb a thing. The space was relatively upscale for a single mechanic's budget.

Scanning the living room, he recognized a strong female touch in the furnishings and artwork. This was quickly confirmed by several distinctively feminine winter coats in the hall closet.

He crossed to the kitchen area and noted an escape route out the back door. Reassured, he entered the master bath and went straight for the medicine cabinet. Among the assortment of lotions and pain relievers next to a pregnancy test kit, was a prescription for one Darcy Wells.

Proof of Marsh's marital status stood on the large dresser in the master bedroom. A prominently placed silver frame highlighted the smiling bride and groom on their wedding day. As Albert snapped a picture with his phone, he had the impression they were truly in love. He wondered if she'd known about his gambling problem and mounting debts before she'd married him. It might explain why his records still documented him as single, and why she may have wanted a degree of separation in their public lives.

A noise outside alerted Albert. Someone was at the front door. He stealthily slipped into the kitchen and out the back door without notice, just as someone entered through the front.

* * *

Darcy Wells worked on the town hall advance team for the governor's reelection committee, responsible for coordinating local officials and the parts they played in various events. She routinely sent her reports to the governor's security detail to help them define a secure perimeter and run background checks on people who would publicly interact with the governor. In the last election, Tess's opponent had shared the stage with a city manager who was later discovered to be a registered pedophile in another state. Not a winning strategy for her opponent.

Since the assassination of Senator Torres, Darcy had been living a nightmare and the deal she made to save her husband's life haunted her every thought. She'd convinced herself that what they told her was true. *They were only going to eavesdrop on the governor,* so she agreed to have her husband look the other way at the limousine garage. After the bomb went off, she knew she'd been lied to.

She wanted nothing more to do with any of it and began looking for work out of state. Her plan to free herself from their grip ended abruptly when Hollis rolled up on their curb after being dumped from a moving car.

As she was preparing to leave work for the day, a distinguished looking gentleman walked up to her desk and introduced himself.

"Darcy Wells, I am Everett Pendrake," he said in his finest British accent as he politely offered his hand.

"Darcy, whose mind had been a million miles away, stared at him blankly for a moment before replying. "Is there something I can do for you?"

"Perhaps you missed the memo. I'm the governor's official biographer. I was hoping to get a few quotes from various people working for her."

Her well-honed public smile was shaky as she tried to decide if Pendrake was for real.

"I hope this won't take long. Have a seat."

"So, I see in your file that you are not married."

"That's correct. How is this relevant?"

"I'll explain, but first would you explain your role in scheduling the governor's public appearances?"

Albert watched as a grip of uncertainly took hold of her. She sat motionless, organizing her response.

"I meet with local public officials to develop a short list of people for the governor to invite on stage with her."

"I came across your name while looking into the Brooklyn Museum bombing. Were you there that night?"

At the mention of the bombing, he saw her hand start to tremble. "No, fortunately I was at home that night."

"Yes, of course. With your husband."

"Yes, I mean …," searching for a lie when Albert broke in.

"Maybe I can help. Your husband. Hollis Marsh?"

* * *

Albert took a taxi downtown and met with Myles Cassidy, his contact in the gambling underworld of New York City. Myles ran a small dive bar in downtown Manhattan that catered to a peculiar mix of local government officials, law enforcement, Wall Street traders, and people in the entertainment business. Customers came to drink, gamble, and cheat on their spouses.

Myles described the guy who picked up Hollis Marsh's markers as a big muscular white guy. Known for his weird circus tatts, the word *Strongman* was prominently inked on his right forearm.

And it wasn't the first time Strongman had picked up someone's marker. He confessed he had no idea how things worked out for those indebted to him.

Strongman moved from game to game, never staying too long before moving on to another area of town. Myles recently heard he'd found a game to his liking at the White Eagle Bar down in Brighton Beach.

Chapter 24
The Big Fish

The cleanup from the botched bombing attempt on the governor's life was all but complete. In spite of their best efforts to put the whole episode behind them, the director of ORC covert activities was still wary. The Dark Lord, a name given to him by his underlings in yet another Tolkien reference, had a reputation for dispensing brutal and often fatal punishment for failure.

Stories of the particularly bloody military campaigns he had commanded as a young man preceded him, and they all knew he was one person you didn't want to get on the wrong side of. It was rightfully assumed that he had another completely separate covert operation ready to replace the whole lot of them.

His was the final word, and he trusted no one, especially the flunkies on the bombing team. Using extreme caution, he was never seen in public with any members of his clandestine operations, and he used an electronic firewall between himself and his team leaders, Grimes and Daggert. Beyond their common membership in the Originalist Confederation, no other evidence connecting them existed.

Meetings were always held in their private SKIF, a secure meeting room on the second basement level where no recording or transmitting devices of any kind were permitted. The room was swept daily for electronic bugs.

With the elimination of Sofiya Balashov, Grimes considered the museum bombing episode closed, and was anxious to move on to their current planning.

Not so with the Dark Lord, whose steely eyes glared at Grimes. "Why hasn't Bass Drexler been eliminated? He's the last loose end of your failed assassination attempt which can lead law enforcement back to you and Daggert, and ultimately to our organization."

"Killing Bass was never part of the plan," Grimes argued, reaching for his handkerchief. "My God, he's one of us."

He did his best to sound convincing, even though his support for Drexler wasn't entirely out of loyalty. Grimes knew Drexler had serious dirt on him and would use it if push came to shove. But as he spoke, he could feel the Dark Lord's cold, reptilian eyes burning into his chest.

In a low voice void of emotion, the Dark Lord said, "I see. Perhaps he's not the only loose end."

His meaning did not escape Grimes.

* * *

Since learning from his Uncle Caslav that Sofiya was murdered, Rybak had been sleeping with one eye open. His involvement with Sofiya was always done in the shadows, nothing ever on record. What Sofiya didn't know was that Rybak had been ordered by Caslav to keep an eye on her. He was seething with anger, and wrestling with guilt at having failed his uncle.

As far as he knew, he was the only one still alive from Sofiya's operation. He thought of every angle and although there was virtually nothing that linked him to Sofiya, her murder had been done by professionals. There was no way of knowing what she may have told them before she died.

The burner phone he maintained solely to communicate with Caslav began to buzz.

"What have you learned about the bastards who murdered my Sofiya?"

his uncle growled, skipping the usual small talk.

"Not much. She kept the entire operation to herself for security reasons. Everyone downstream of her is dead. Except me."

"Someone was paying her for the operation," Caslav added. "I want to know who."

"I remembered her calling him the *Big Fish,* but I've not been able to trace that to anyone."

"I'll have my contacts look into this fish man." Then with genuine concern for his nephew's safety, Caslav asked, "Do they know about you?"

"I don't think so."

"You need to be certain. And careful. An assassination attempt such as this requires the resources and coordination of some very powerful and committed men. Find them before they find you."

* * *

Rybak decided to risk exposure by making contact with his main rivals in the Brooklyn illegal arms and munitions business. There had been an informal truce for the last few years as there was no shortage of customers to fight over. He and his uncle kept to their European and Middle Eastern clientele while the Paraguayan Cartel serviced the Latin Americans.

The last time there was violence between the two gangs was when the Paraguayans began muscling into the Croatian and Slovenian manufacturing circles in a move to undercut their Serbian suppliers. After the number of funerals became uncomfortable for everyone, they agreed to a truce, knowing it would be more profitable for both sides and attract less attention from the authorities.

Rybak had known Luis Cardoso since they were young men working on the boardwalk at Coney Island. Their brief friendship ended abruptly when the amusement park that employed them was destroyed by Hurricane Sandy. Over the intervening years, Rybak learned that Luis had worked his way up in the ranks of their Paraguayan competitors.

Rybak reached out to Luis through his grandmother who still lived in midtown Manhattan. Remembering young Rybak, she was happy to pass on her grandson's number. Later that day he received a text from Luis suggesting they grab a beer in a neutral location down on the boardwalk.

"Luis. You haven't changed a bit," Rybak said as he stood to greet him.

"Rybak, my friend. What have you been doing all these years?"

"If I told you I'd have to kill you."

"Same for me," Luis laughed. "Can you believe this is the same place we worked at when that storm kicked our butts?"

"It's okay but I liked the old places better."

The waiter arrived with two Modelo Especials, along with limes and frosted mugs.

"This is the only way to drink it," Luis said, taking a swig from the icy rim.

"It is good to see you. I appreciate you making the time to meet me, and I promise this isn't about business."

"Yes, I think it's better not to talk about business."

"Agreed," Rybak answered with a knowing glance.

"So, what is this non-business?"

"I need to find someone."

"A customer perhaps?"

"Perhaps someone who occasionally shops in our markets. But this is personal."

"I'm guessing this might have something to do with all the people showing up dead in Brighton Beach," Luis deduced.

"To avoid getting our paths tangled, all I can say is he's known on the street as the *Big Fish*.

"I've encountered such a man. He's a very dark spirit."

"Do you know where I can find him?"

"I can't help you with that but I have a name. Not sure if it's an alias but I believe his name is Bass."

"That makes sense. A bass can be a big fish."

Luis laughed, "I didn't catch that. I'm not much of a fisherman."

"Last name?"

"Like the old NBA player, Clyde Dres ..." Luis paused, searching his memory.

"Drexler?"

"That's it! Bass Drexler."

"I owe you," Rybak said.

Downing the rest of their mugs, they bid each other peace in the coming year and left by separate exits.

Chapter 25

Down by the River

It was midafternoon and Annah had no idea where they were spending the night. They'd spent most of the morning in a sidewalk café near Van Cortlandt Park, before exploring the exhibits at the Van Cortlandt House Museum.

Annah was pleased to see how excited Will was about his Dutch heritage. The more he dug into Theron's translations of the old Dutch print shop records, the more traces he had found of Adriaen van der Donck's pivotal role in early colonial America.

Will imagined Adriaen hiking through his family farm on his many wanderings through the Catskills on his quest to create a new colony. And although the Catskill colony never materialized, his friendly relations with the chiefs of the neighboring tribes, combined with his ability to speak to them in their own languages, placed him in the perfect position to negotiate a peace treaty between them and the Dutch.

In a bit of historic irony, it was this ability to facilitate peace that opened the pathway for Adriaen to finally realize his own colony, a request he had previously been denied in the Catskills by Director-General Kieft.

Will's growing interest in Adriaen led him to explore the area east of the Cortland Museum where the original van der Donck manor house was thought to have stood. Sitting beside a grove of locust trees along the lake, Will closed his eyes and allowed the sounds of nature to seep into his quiet mediation.

This was the heart of Colen Donck, the powerful dream of this trailblazing Dutchman. The reverberations set in motion by this new American's courage who imagined a path of tolerance and justice for everyone in this vast country, could still be felt.

* * *

Will surprised Annah when he turned off the 9 in downtown Yonkers, and slowly drove down Dock Street toward the Hudson. The recently restored Saw Mill River, unearthed after decades of flowing through concrete tunnels, was now the centerpiece of the town as it meandered its way through the middle of a new urban park.

"Seems like your boy is everywhere," Annah said, laughing as she pointed to a sign that said *Van der Donck Park.*

He turned around at the tracks and made his way back toward Mill Street.

"Shouldn't we be finding a room for the night?" Annah asked.

Will slowed to a crawl and pulled into a reserved parking spot. Having been annoyingly silent, he broke into a smile and said, "Look no further."

"We're staying in Yonkers?"

"Yes, as long as that's okay with you."

"Well, they do have a nice river."

* * *

The front stoop of the apartment was adorned with pumpkins and other seasonal trappings. Will reached under a cluster of brightly colored Indian corn and punched in the lock code to the apartment door.

Holding the door open for her, Annah walked in ahead of him and stood inside the entry, instantly liking the clean contemporary vibe and inviting sleeping loft. But the most impressive feature was the view from the large living room windows onto the Mill Street extension of the Saw

Mill River restoration project.

"This is lovely," Annah said flopping down on the big sofa.

Will went back out to the car for their luggage and returned to find Annah thumbing through the restaurant guide.

"Someone's hungry," he said. "I understand there's an abundance of great ethnic food in the neighborhood."

"I vote for the Cuban restaurant."

The place looked great online and was only a block away. Her plan was an early dinner, followed by some well-deserved snuggling time.

* * *

The raised walkway above the river was a pleasant shortcut to the restaurant. They were early enough to get a table in a nice spot by the window. People-watching was one of their favorite pastimes, often veering off into wild guesses as to their names, relationships, and occupations. After a while, their speculations devolved into people's hobbies, favorite movie quotes, and farm animals. No one was spared their silliness, but Will seemed distracted.

"You've been quiet since we left the park," Annah said, after deciding on the spicey salmon tostones.

"Dreams from the woods have slowly worked their way into my waking state. I'm seeing pathways everywhere I look"

"Tell me more," Annah said leaning closer.

The waiter politely interrupted their conversation as he placed two icy mojitos on the table, for a moment reminding Annah of the professional waiters back in Kerala.

After a long sip, she leaned back in the booth, locking both arms behind her head. Will found her beauty intoxicating, particularly as she was then, relaxed and with her guard down.

"Take a picture. It'll last longer," she teased shyly, noticing his eyes on her.

"Exactly," he said reaching for his phone.

Albert's words of caution were miles away.

* * *

After an amazing meal, they hurried back to the apartment in the grip of a romantic emergency.

Pieces of clothing were strewn on the stairs leading up to the loft as their desire coursed through them like an out-of-control fire. Each touch was magnetic and every nerve in their bodies alive.

Will slowed their pace as they stood at the foot of the large king bed. Pulling Annah toward him, she gasped as he brushed her neck with his lips, then whispered words meant only for her. Suspended in time, they explored each other once again, still wanting more.

Exhausted, they laid in each other's arms for the longest time, whispering, laughing, sharing stories. It was all part of the irresistible attraction they shared.

Annah slept in Will's arms. In the dim moonlight, he studied the contours of her face, the face he loved, until the distant sound of the river and her steady breathing lulled him, too, into a deep sleep.

* * *

Will woke in the dead of night, still musing over the tales of van der Donck and the early Dutch settlers. He quietly rolled out of bed and recovered his clothing, one piece at a time, as he snuck down the stairs. Breathing the fresh night air, he walked by the old storefronts on Main Street drifting toward the Hudson. Other than a few late-night bars, the shops were closed and the streets empty.

Something in the window of the old hardware store caught his eye, and he crossed the street to get a closer look. The display showcased antique hand tools and measuring devices, and from what he could make out in the dim light, appeared to be a museum in a single storefront window. The backdrop was a hand painted mural straight out of colonial America.

Descriptive plaques in front of several items dated as far back as the mid sixteen hundreds, and it was easy for Will to imagine Adriaen using similar tools to build his home.

Lit only by moonlight, Will recognized a transparent reflection of himself in the glass, superimposed over the display of tools. His ghostly image seemed to become part of the historic setting.

He was captivated by his face as it began to transform into someone he didn't recognize. But it wasn't just his face. His clothes looked like they were out of a Rembrandt painting. As he moved closer, his image was erased by the glare of a lantern held high by a man who hurriedly walked by.

Mesmerized, Will's curiosity compelled him to follow. As he approached the river, he could feel his heels digging into the soft clay. Oddly, there were no lights on the water, other than the flickering reflection of campfire light scattered along the opposite bank, and the glow around the man now standing on a small wooden dock as he slowly swung his lantern from side to side.

Part Six
(Year 1647 - Saw Mill River at Colen Donck)

Chapter 26

Saw Mill River

Tobias Feake caught the incoming surge on the North River, making the short trip from the inner bay where he received his delivery from the cargo ship, *de Statyn* before she anchored in the East River. This was standard practice by the boatmen on shore to avoid the special tariffs of Herr van Tienhoven.

Ships like *de Statyn* would remain in the outer harbor for several days, waiting for the high tide to come in the late of night. As planned, Adriaen stood on the small dock with lantern in hand at the confluence of the North and Saw Mill Rivers at high tide, as he had done for the last several nights.

His patience paid off on the fourth night as Tobias Feake sailed up river in the *Pride of Flushing*, the name he had given to his shallop.

"That was first rate navigating," Adriaen called over the distance as the *Pride* drifted toward him. "Throw me the rope."

With a mighty heave, Tobias tossed the bow line to his good friend.

Moments later, Adriaen had the *Pride* close enough for Tobias to jump off with the stern line.

They embraced on the dock as the good friends they had become.

* * *

The sun rose on the valley as they spent the next few hours unloading cargo onto Adriaen's wagon. Once secured by canvas and rope, the sturdy wooden wagon, pulled by two large Zeeland draft horses, meandered up the newly cleared roadway to the manor house on the ridge.

Mary was there to greet them at the doorway of their modest three-room cabin, built of logs in the style of the Finns down on the South River. Adriaen's future plans for the house included a second floor and large conservatory for propagating plant species.

"What have you boys been up to," she asked with a demure smile as she stood in the front doorway with her long gun, looking very much like a typical pioneer woman.

"Riches from the East my dear," Adriaen replied, happy to have made it uphill to the manor without incident.

Setting the gun aside she gave both a warm hug.

"You must tell me of your dear Annekan and her children," she said to Tobias.

"They are all well. You'll be the first to hear of our plan to wed in June."

"That's wonderful! She's a fine woman, and I know you'll be happy."

"Already happy, ma'am."

The two men made short work of the ropes and were soon carrying several large crates into the house containing furniture made by Dutch craftsmen back in the homeland.

From the front porch, they saw a rider appear at the edge of the clearing, and quietly picked up their guns. Since Kieft's War with the Wilden, it had become habitual among the settlers to take a defensive posture when someone approached.

They lowered their guns when they recognized Elias Doughty slowing to a trot on his grey stallion.

"Elias, you look troubled," Mary said to her brother as he dismounted.

"I have news. There has been a major development in New Amsterdam that you need to be aware of."

"Come inside and have something to eat while we talk," Mary said after embracing him.

Young Elias, now in his fifteenth year, had ferried over from Flushing and raced up the Bronx River trail. He dismounted and handed the reins to Tobias, who led his horse to the corral.

Catching his breath, he spoke again as he entered the house, "Kieft has been ordered back to the Netherlands to account for his deeds."

"That is great news. How did you come by it?"

"The order was delivered in person by his replacement, Director-General Pieter Stuyvesant. He's already causing quite a stir at the Stadt Huys."

* * *

The petition to have Kieft removed was finally successful, but the relief they'd hoped for was soon replaced by the dictates of a stern disciplinarian and devoted Calvinist. And to add to the growing concerns of the local inhabitants, Kieft's replacement kept van Tienhoven on as his head administrator and provincial schout.

Stuyvesant was something of a legend in the Caribbean, where he had a leg shot off in a battle with the Spanish. He was known for swift punishment of those who crossed him.

Upon arrival, he handed Kieft orders to return to the Netherlands to account for his actions, and although Stuyvesant found Kieft cowardly and despicable, he had equal distain for those who had challenged his authority.

After Cornelius Melyn and Joachim Kuyter demanded further investigation into Kieft's misconduct, Stuyvesant disbanded Kieft's council of Eight. As punishment for what he considered rebellious behavior, he ordered them to return to the Netherlands to stand trial for libel and treason.

Melyn and Kuyter set sail for Amsterdam aboard the *Princess Amelia*, as did former director Kieft. In a strange twist of irony, the *Princess Amelia* was shipwrecked on the rocks in the Bristol Channel. Melyn and Kuyter managed to swim ashore, but Kieft went to the bottom wrapped in his fancy robe.

* * *

In an effort to make a clean start, Stuyvesant had the citizens elect eighteen men, from which he chose a new council known as the *Nine Men*. This was done to appease the populace, as he had no intention to seek honest advice.

Offered passage on the *Pride*, Adriaen and Mary arrived in New Amsterdam the following morning to meet with the newly ordained Director-General of the New Netherlands. As he had with Kieft, and Rensselaer before him, Adriaen straightaway offered his services, while strategically remaining silent regarding local politics. He needed time to size up the new Director-General.

Stuyvesant and his wife, Judith Bayard, invited them to their home that evening for dinner. Judith and her children were taken by Mary's kind disposition and, for an English woman, her reasonably good Dutch.

Yet however gracious van der Donck was in his dealings with him, he soon realized Stuyvesant was an autocrat who believed his word was law. He also saw himself as a defender of the faith, which in his case was a stern version of Dutch Reformed Calvinism. He showed no tolerance for others' beliefs, although he tactfully avoided mentioning the strange religious notions of Mary's father, the Reverend Francis Doughty, who was currently with a congregation in Flushing.

Stuyvesant soon made it clear that he and his superiors at the West India Company felt Kieft was not only incompetent, but far too lenient on his unruly subjects. Their view of the citizenry was in direct opposition to

Adriaen's own belief that the law should arise from the basic goodness and common sense of the populace.

* * *

Not long after it was formed, the Director-General disbanded the first assembly of the Nine Men, claiming they were ineffective in stemming the influx of complaints by their fellow citizens. But the underlying motive for dissolving the council was more nefarious, done at the urging of Tienhoven, his head administrator and provincial schout who was concerned the men were spreading rumors about him cheating at cards. While no legal action was ever taken against Tienhoven, it had become much harder for him to find a seat at a game with anyone who knew him.

Adriaen remained close to Stuyvesant during that first year as he had with Kieft, but continued his advocacy for the people behind the scene, opposing authoritarian rule and collecting notes of complaints by the citizens. Many of the complaints that carried over from Kieft to the new director were related to the corrupt tariffs and confiscation practices occurring all along the waterfront. This system of graft and extortion was particularly dear to Tienhoven, as it provided the financial backing for his insatiable lust for gambling and young women.

Chapter 27

Remonstrance of the New Netherlands

By the fall of 1649, Stuyvesant had made his mark on the province, pushing several public works projects ahead in New Amsterdam and negotiating borders with the neighboring English colonies. His vision of properly ordered society started by restricting the religious practice of everyone to a single state sanctioned faith, that being his Dutch Reformed Church.

And although the policy of tolerance toward other religions had been steadily growing among the Dutch, the other unsanctioned congregations were prevented from any form of public worship, even in the homeland, forcing them to meet privately. In his familiar dictatorial manner, Stuyvesant took this a step further, and forbade others from any kind of gathering, including in their homes. This further amplified public unease about his harsh proclamations.

In response to the spreading unrest in New Amsterdam about his corrupt and capricious governance, Stuyvesant held a special election to form a second council of Nine Men, this one with Adriaen van der Donck as its president. Predictably, this did not go well with Tienhoven in his dark quarters.

* * *

In private meetings beyond the spying eyes and ears of Tienhoven and his lackeys, members of the Nine pushed for stronger resistance against

Stuyvesant and his crooked administrators. Finally, their petition to remove Kieft had been successful with the help of van der Donck's legal skills, so it was natural they turned to him regarding their ongoing grievances.

With Adriaen's added insight, the Nine recognized the urgent need to establish good and fair governance, agreeing that the first logical step was to secretly assemble all of the complaints and issues with Kieft and Stuyvesant into one comprehensive petition. Included would be a thorough report on the state of the province. The document was to be named *The Remonstrance of the New Netherlands*.

But secrecy was the fertile hunting ground of Tienhoven. Discovering the secrets of others gave him leverage and corrupt influence, so he kept his spies well paid in liquor.

It was common knowledge that van der Donck stayed in the house of Michiel Janszen whenever spending the night in town, and that typically occurred around the time of formal council meetings with Stuyvesant. But what his spies also discovered was that on many of those nights, other members of the Nine stayed on at Janszen's house into the late hours. He could only imagine they were conspiring against lawful authority.

The morning following one such late night meeting, and Tienhoven was certain van der Donck was still in town, he persuaded Stuyvesant to call an emergency meeting of the Nine Men. Once van der Donck and his accomplices were all assembled at the Stadt Huys, he broke into the house of Michiel Janszen and riffled through all of the letters and documents in his office.

Posting guards at Janszen's door so no one could enter, Tienhoven hurried back to the Stadt Huys where he barged into the assembly. Ignoring Stuyvesant's annoyance, he walked up to the table and spread out a handful of written complaints from the draft remonstrance that were specifically directed at Stuyvesant.

After skimming the first few pages, the Director-General flew into a fit of rage. Identifying van der Donck as the ringleader, he demanded an explanation for his insolence. Adriaen calmly reminded the director that he had instructed the Nine Men to identify grievances and complaints from the citizenry before they blew up in the director's face. Stuyvesant glared at him silently.

Adriaen continued. The Nine were working on a proposal to hold a convention open to all inhabitants of the New Netherlands. From this, they planned to prepare a remonstrance to be sent to the authorities in Holland. A petition that compiled a list of grievances and proposed solutions that addressed the needs of the colony.

Considering Adriaen's explanation brazen, Stuyvesant marched down the street to the Janszen house to discover the full extent of their rebellious plot.

Within hours, Adriaen was arrested for treason and jailed.

* * *

Not fully aware of the Jonk Heer's popularity among the common people, Stuyvesant was shaken by the outpouring of support for Adriaen from the far corners of the Dutch colony. Having become a folk hero for ending Kieft's War with the Wilden, he was known to everyone in Manhattan and the surrounding villages for his brilliant legal advocacy in court, on behalf of both rich and poor alike.

Under growing pressure to release van der Donck from jail, Stuyvesant had a stroke of genius, or at least he thought as much. He would send van der Donck and Tienhoven back to the Hague to argue before the high court of the States-General.

With van der Donck's growing political prominence and the mounting accusations being made against Tienhoven for his corrupts ways, he saw this as a chance to eliminate two of his biggest irritants in one move.

* * *

Mary was overseeing the final installation of the blades on their new sawmill, wrought of Swedish iron and driven by a finely crafted Dutch gear assembly. The mill would soon be up and running.

Learning her husband was going to stand trial at the Hague, she vowed to join him in the Netherlands as soon as she settled their current business affairs.

Adriaen was an advocate for the innate goodness in people, something he believed would ultimately allow them to govern themselves. His outlook was elegantly simple. When everyone is a potential ally, people generally get along, respect each other's differences, and prosper. However, when people are treated as adversaries, their fear drives them to hoard, even between themselves, creating artificial shortages that cause others to go without. She respected him for raising these fundamental questions about humanity and would be honored to stand by his side.

* * *

On release until his ship sailed, Adriaen and his wife traveled to Flushing aboard Tobias' shallop. Their visit was two-fold. Elias needed to be told about Adriaen's order to return to the Netherlands to appear before the high court. They also needed to enlist his help so Mary could join her husband as soon as the mill was in production.

Her brother lived in the small house built on the Doughty farm just beyond the edge of the village. Despite his young age, Elias had ably managed the farm from the age of 17, when their father had left for Virginia the previous year.

The Doughty farm had been deeded to Mary as a wedding gift by her father. Seeing that her brother was more than capable of caring for it, she had made plans to hand the deed over to him, and now she would be asking him to add the responsibility of Colen Donck to his burden.

Tobias tied the *Pride* on the largest of three new piers in the bay near Flushing Creek. Anxious to talk to her brother, Mary thanked Tobias and started down the main road through the village, leaving Adriaen to catch up.

After a short walk on the trail that wrapped around a heavily wooded section of marshland, the two of them came to the Doughty house. Mary spotted Elias around back, working the ground in his vegetable garden.

"Sister! What a surprise!" Elias shouted from across the yard. Dropping his shovel, he ran over to warmly embrace her, then turned to face Adriaen.

"Brother. It is always an honor and a pleasure."

Adriaen once again was struck by the self-assured manner of Elias, even at his young age. Some men never achieved what he already had. Aside from being a gentleman farmer, he still scribed important legal documents and proclamations for Eduard Hart.

Adriaen's tone was serious when he spoke. "Elias, we have important news for you. I will be traveling back to the Netherlands by order of Stuyvesant, where Mary hopes to soon join me. I am going to defend what is good for the people of New Netherlands, and point out what needs to be improved. Unfortunately, while our remonstrance spells out these facts in fine legal detail, the creation of the document itself has been deemed an act of rebellion by the director, and I have been directed to stand trial at the Hague."

Mary added, "Adriaen may need to be there a year or more, and I would like to join him in the spring, but we would need your help. If we lose the case, we could face expulsion from the province."

"Of course, sister. What can I do to help?"

"When I leave, we would need you to manage Colen Donck," Mary said.

When Elias did not respond, Adriaen broke the silence.

"You will have all the backing you need here in Flushing from Tobias Feake. We have already spoken to him. We've also spoken to Michiel Janszen about being your assistant at Colen Donck. He is currently expanding his own plantation on Staten Island, just a few miles downstream from our land, so he will be able to oversee the operation when you are in Flushing."

Elias surprised both of them with his excitement. "I have always wanted to run a plantation. And, I have already studied your plans and schedules for the current operation. I expect the sale of lumber alone will make you both wealthy."

"Don't cut them all down," Mary replied with a hint of concern.

"Of course I won't. I will cull the trees according to Adriaen's master plan. You won't even notice they're gone."

Chapter 28

Year 1651 - Amsterdam

Adriaen arrived at the waterfront as the sun rose, having received word that the *de Statyn* had docked in the port of Amsterdam in the middle of the night, bringing his beloved Mary to join him. It had been a long and lonely winter without her, spent with kinfolk down in Breda. He would soon take up residence with Mary in a cozy home along one of the newly built canals.

All of Adriaen's time between court appearances was dedicated to promoting immigration and investment in their new colony. He had spent a good deal of time that first winter commissioning a colored map of the New Netherlands by Nicolaes Jansz Visscher, which contained an attractive image of the booming village of New Amsterdam. Engraved by Johannes Blaue, it had been inserted in the lower right corner. The map was an incredibly effective marketing tool for attracting prospective emigrees to the new frontier. Abundant land with plenty of fresh water was an enticing reward for the bold and adventurous.

Adriaen's mother, Agatha van Bergen, was independently wealthy and according to Dutch law able to divorce her philandering husband. Following her son's advice, Agatha pulled up stakes in Breda and ventured to Manhattan, along with several other close relatives.

* * *

The Treaty of Munster in the previous year had changed the focus of many of the more influential members of the States-General. There was a political movement toward a more restrictive version of Dutch culture.

Many on the high council in the Hague agreed with the West India Company's position that the provinces should be viewed strictly as a business enterprise in which individual rights were often an obstruction and not guaranteed. This creed was repeated over and over again by Tienhoven, who had been sent by Stuyvesant to repudiate all of van der Donck's naïve and traitorous evidence.

Yet after each round of fallacious testimony by Tienhoven, Adriaen provided a detailed rebuttal filled with facts and notarized personal accounts from prominent New Amsterdam residents. He proved over and over again that autocratic rule was not good for business, but rather interfered with the settler's prosperity, and thereby injured their sponsors back in the Netherlands.

His positive manner was in direct contrast to Tienhoven, gradually winning over most of those sitting on the high court.

Tienhoven began to falter during his presentations, often forgetting his arguments or slurring his words. There were no settlers or Wilden to blame for his lack of concentration, only the well-founded tales of his drinking and womanizing. Adriaen provided eyewitness reports describing Tienhoven's proclivity to dress like a "Wilden" and sexually assault young native girls.

As his instigation of the Kieft War and deadly participation in the Pavonia Massacre were brought to light, he became universally despised by the Dutch. In his deranged mind, he began to consider having his legal rival killed, but soon realized Adriaen had too many powerful friends in the Netherlands. He would keep his dark thoughts to himself, at least for now.

Tienhoven's position went from bad to worse when it was discovered he had seduced a young woman named Liesbeth Croon in the Hague, this while his wife Rachel Vigne, twenty-two years his junior and only sixteen years old when they married, faithfully awaited his return in New Amsterdam with their three children.

After Tienhoven was summoned to court to answer for his adultery, he fled on a ship departing for New Amsterdam, along with Liesbeth who he lured aboard with the promise of marriage. Unfortunately for Liesbeth, there would be no happy marriage in America, only the scorn of Tienhoven's wife Rachel and her children who were waiting on the dock.

* * *

The sudden disappearance of Tienhoven left Stuyvesant and the West India Company without a legal advocate versed in the issues of the colony. With his main antagonist officially barred from any further proceedings in the high court, Adriaen quickly moved for resolution.

He had been in the Netherlands for three years pursuing the rights of colonial citizens. The States-General finally decreed that the city of New Amsterdam and its residents would have the same rights as a proper Dutch city, governed by elected representatives.

Although this was a tremendous victory, Adriaen was not able to secure the same right of home rule for the rest of the colony, which would continue to be governed as a trading outpost of the West India Company. That fight would have to be fought another day.

Adriaen's cohorts, Jacob Van Couwenhoven and Jan Evertsen Bout, two members of the original remonstrance contingency, were the first to return to New Amsterdam with the declaration that a city charter was to be formed on the model of Amsterdam, its namesake, and its authority recognized by Stuyvesant. Begrudgingly, the director allowed the charter to be written and elections held, becoming the precedent for all future freedoms demanded by Americans.

Chapter 29

Year 1653 – New Netherlands

Although Adriaen had successfully earned the chartered city rights for New Amsterdam, the court deemed him to be potentially disruptive in the face of their changing political landscape. The Dutch states had recently earned their independence from Spain, but suffered several internal power struggles. It had only been a few years since the Prince of Orange tried to overthrow the republic in a failed coup attempt, making anyone politically active suspect.

Finally permitted to leave the Netherlands, he set sail for his adopted new home. Mary had returned a few months earlier that year and was staying with brother Elias in Flushing, and Adriaen was longing for their reunion.

After Tienhoven had fled from his accusers in the Netherlands, Adriaen and Mary agreed it would be wise for her to go home to look after their interests, and spread the truth of what had happened at the Hague.

She was stunned to find that Director Stuyvesant accepted Tienhoven back into his fold. His duties, however, were reduced to little more than a tariff collector and keeper of the peace on the waterfront.

There were rumors he was gambling with the Wecquaesgeek camped up on the Bronx River where his reputation as a cheat had not yet reached everyone's ears. Of late, he had been seen with large caches of high-quality wampum, and there were whispers of him using firearms and gunpowder as table stakes in those games.

Stuyvesant dismissed the rumors, confiding in friends that even if true, it was not the same as selling guns to the Wilden, which would be a serious crime. As this information made its way into the wider community, it led others to suspect Stuyvesant was the one selling the guns to Tienhoven.

* * *

The hatred Tienhoven had for van der Donck had grown during the course of their battles at the high court in the Hague did not dissipate after his return to Manhattan. While losing his former power and status, van der Donck had become a folk hero, beloved by the people.

When Mary arrived in port without Adriaen the previous spring, he immediately began watching her. Hiding in the shadows of the heavy forest, he remembered the lust he had felt for her that morning in court long ago, over a libelous song.

Mary did her best to avoid the overblown pig of a man. And even though she was not a spiteful woman, she felt no pity for him when she heard his wife consigned him to permanently sleeping in the barn after she learned about Liesbeth Croon, his hopeful, but spare wife.

* * *

In the few years Mary had been away, her younger brother had grown into his own man, held in high regard within the community. It gave her great pleasure to watch the bond between Adriaen and Elias grow even stronger since Adriaen's return.

Elias had always looked up to Adriaen, perhaps more so than his own father who had moved to Virginia. He was impressed with Adriaen's work as a statesman and lawyer, and admired the bold adventurer who made friends with the Wilden and learned to speak both Mohawk and Mohican.

They shared countless stories the first few days after Adriaen's return. Elias brought his brother-in-law up to date on all the improvements that had been made at Colen Donck, happy to report that the sawmill was paying dividends, as well as providing the fine hardwood used to construct the new conservatory at the manor house.

Elias mentioned that while riding his gray stallion through Colen Donck on his routine inspections of the works in progress, he twice spotted Tienhoven on the Bronx River trail heading upriver toward the Wilden encampment at the White Plains. Oddly, he appeared to be wearing buckskins and a head scarf as if to hide his appearance, but his horse and Dutch saddle had given him away.

* * *

The evening of the long-awaited house warming party for Adriaen and Mary had finally arrived. The conservatory was completed and a blazing fireplace kept the October chill at bay. They had made provisions for guests who chose to stay over, and Tobias had his shallop ready to ferry those from Manhattan back home after midnight.

The light mist on the grounds glowed in the orange crescent moonlight, adding an eerie contrast to the warmth and music spilling from the new windows in Colen Donck manor. Eduard Hart and Mary played several duets on the harpsichord as Michiel Janszen added haunting violin melodies.

The scent of pumpkins and spice filled the air as Annekan and her oldest daughter brought out fresh baked bread from the kitchen. Tobias followed behind with a new batch of rum punch. A snappy fiddle tune from Michiel brought everyone to their feet and the party was in full swing.

Elias felt like a proud parent, having overseen most of the recent improvements to the house and gardens while Mary and Adriaen were away. The lantern lit pathway to the gazebo added a touch of charm to the landscape, and gave a place for young lovers to escape from the crowd. Elias was hoping that the lovely Sarah O'Neal might join him there before the night was through.

* * *

Several children who were out playing on the lawn, ran into the house looking as though they'd seen a ghost.

"We saw a face in the woods," the oldest boy said. Catching his breath he added, "We heard branches breaking as he ran off."

This was the time of year when imaginations ran wild, with talk of Heinrich Hudson and his men haunting these woods. In the dim moonlight with a forest full of creatures, it could have been anything, but Elias ran out to check. As he approached the edge of the clearing, he caught a strange odor. A foul human smell lingered in the woods. Not the earthy smell of the forest dwellers, but one of rotted meat and alcohol.

"All's clear, probably just a raccoon," he announced returning to the house. He had his suspicions of who had been lurking in the woods, but chose to speak to Adriaen after guests had left to not further frighten the children.

"Make sure your mugs are full," Elias added as he ushered everyone back into the conservatory for a toast that Adriaen and Mary planned to make to commemorate the occasion.

From Adriaen's experience in legal proceedings, and recently before the high court in the Netherlands, it had become second nature for him to stand before crowds and make his thoughts known. But Mary, not used to speaking in front of a crowd, found herself taking a deep breath as she tried to calm her nerves.

Searching for words, she scanned the room and found it filled with people she loved.

"We are blessed to be surrounded by friends and family who support us with such care and warmth. And with your help and encouragement, we promise to make Colen Donck an example of tolerance, good will, and the self-governance we have tirelessly fought to established for the entire colonial province of the New Netherlands. We have won those rights for the city of New Amsterdam but at a great cost to Adriaen, who is now barred from participating in provincial politics. I, however, am not and will speak out against tyranny and injustice whenever the opportunity presents itself. Like now. To justice and freedom," she said raising her glass.

"Hear, hear!" Elias called, taking a generous swig of punch.

"But none of this would be possible without my amazing husband," she said, taking hold of Adriaen's hand and raising their arms.

A cheer erupted in the room, "Jonk Heer, Jonk Heer, Jonk Heer…"

Moved by the support of their friends, Adriaen was about to step forward when there was a loud rapping on the garden door.

The crowd quieted as Elias walked across the room to open it. Several men instinctively stepped in front of their wives and children.

As the door swung open, a large Wilden dressed in the finest suit of buckskins and ceremonial beadwork stepped inside. The only sound in the room was a collective gasp.

As the room quieted, he asked in perfect English, "Is there room for one more friend of the Jonk Heer, Adriaen van der Donck?"

His voice was unmistakable to Adriaen. "Aghar, my dear friend. What a welcome surprise."

Mary had heard many stories but this was her first meeting with the legendary Mohawk. Majestic, his half shaven head crowned with ceremonial feathers, he wore a white buckskin suit with a beaded breastplate suitable for a chief. Everyone stared in silence as Adriaen crossed the room and embraced his friend. He turned and nodded to Janszen, who picked up his fiddle and began to play.

Mary took Aghar by the arm and followed Adriaen over to the fireplace. "I am very pleased to meet you. Adriaen has spoken of you so often, I feel as if I know you already," she said taking a good look at his face. "And your attire is quite impressive."

"I wore it to celebrate your husband's return," he answered, nodding to Adriaen, "and to honor him in front of his neighbors and trusted friends.

And as I'm certain that most of your guests have never met a Wilden other than the few poor beggars camped by their villages, I thought it was a good time for them to meet a Mohawk warrior in formal attire."

She laughed when she realized how proper his English was. "You are clearly accomplished in languages. And you taught the Iroquois tongue of the Mohawk to Adriaen?"

"And the Algonquin tongue of the Mohican. Language is the gift given to me by the *Great Spirit*. This was confirmed to me at an early age by my grandfather, who is among the wisest of my people."

Aghar then turned and addressed those gathered, "To all of you who have shown respect and tolerance to the Wilden, like our friend the Jonk Heer, you have become known to my people as *Jonkees*. It is meant to set you apart from the vile and murderous allies of Tienhoven."

Then taking Adriaen aside, Aghar lowered his voice. "I would like a private word with you when you have a moment."

"Of course. Mary, would you excuse us?"

The night sky was clear and the air crisp as they walked toward the garden, the low sound of the river now softening the music coming from the conservatory. "Perhaps this would be a good time to speak," Adriaen said quietly.

"My people have a legal matter with West India Company and the Mohican would be grateful for your help. More importantly, Grandfather asked me to bring you a message from the Elders, given to him in a dream, as a gift to you. In the vision, they spoke of a possible future of peace and prosperity in this land for all of the people."

Although weary of the politics in the New Netherlands, Adriaen received the gift as good news and smiled.

"Grandfather did not say how long this will take."

Pausing to stress the importance of his next words, Aghar added, "The vision also contains a warning."

Part Seven

(Present Day - New York)

Chapter 30

Return of the ORCs

"This crap the governor calls tax reform has to be stopped!" the covert director of the ORCs shouted, more enraged than Bragg had ever seen him. "The goddam floor vote could come any day now, and she won't waste any time signing it into law."

The Honorable Byron Bragg was not a religious zealot like many of his ORC associates. He did his best to appear neutral in his public statements, but ever since being elevated to the New York Court of Appeals with the help of the Originalist Confederation, Bragg privately endorsed extreme policies related to their planned religious makeover of America.

His face still red with anger, the director collected his thoughts. "If the Israelis can have a *Jewish democracy*, why the fuck can't we have a *Christian democracy*? The United States was never meant to be a secular democracy. Our country was originally based on religion being the harness and reins on people's behavior, rather than the laws of a representative government. The revolution was against the British parliament, not the king."

"Your Originalists are dug in far too deep to be easily swept away by this soon to be ex-governor," Bragg insisted. "She'll be just another unhinged liberal thrown onto the scrapheap of history."

"Maybe, but she's poised to sign the act into law at a ceremony held in a historic location, somewhere in the Hudson Valley. I have men scouting the proposed stops on her current townhall tour as we speak."

"If it's ever brought to the high court, you know you can count on my support."

"What about the other judges?"

"They're hard to read. Religion is a particularly thorny issue with them. They'll likely lean toward traditional values, but where the line finally gets drawn is still anybody's guess."

"It's better if it never gets signed."

* * *

Grimes was still unnerved by the suggestion that he too, was a loose end. The Dark Lord was not known for bluffing, and Grimes worried that he may have learned of his past association with the Russians. It was something that could still get him killed.

He saw his status with the Confederation and perhaps even his own life riding on the successful outcome of the second assassination attempt. His man Drexler had done everything right the first time. How was he to know of the governor's sudden change in plans? But his higher up and the powers that be in the Confederation didn't want to hear it. They were looking for someone to punish.

As he emptied the last of a large bottle of scotch into his heavy glass tumbler, the burner phone used only with Drexler began making its familiar buzz.

"What can you tell me?" Grimes pressed.

"I'm in Tarrytown sitting in an outdoor cafe. Our intel says it's one of the stops on the governor's Hudson Valley tour to promote the new tax legislation. We've confirmed that her presentation will be in the old music hall, just a block up the street from where I'm currently sitting."

"We need to be one hundred percent certain of success before making the call."

"I'm doing the detailed reconnaissance we need to determine if this is the best location for my snipers. We're not leaving anything to chance."

"And a plan for cleaning up loose ends after it's done?"

Ruffled by the casual way he referred to the really ugly treachery that Grimes himself could never do, Drexler answered, "You'll be the first to find out."

Drexler's words hung in the air over Grimes like a dark cloud.

Chapter 31
Turning the Tables

"Darcy, what do you have for me?" the voice asked.

The burner phone that Everett Pendrake had delivered to her was still set on speaker so that he could listen to the conversation on his remote device.

After their initial encounter, Darcy remained convinced that cooperating with Albert was far better than a certain prison sentence. He couldn't guarantee a completely clean slate for her and Hollis, and they would surely have to get new jobs. But for now, she needed to follow his directions precisely.

She agreed to install his remote listening equipment in her home while she waited for the next call from the dreaded voice. The system allowed her to listen to Albert through an earpiece while on the call. They had tested the system and Darcy was comfortable activating it.

She sat upright when Albert's sound piece went live in her ear.

"Just give him the general info on the town hall locations, just as we discussed," he whispered. *"You've got this."*

Darcy cleared her throat. "She'll be in Tarrytown on Friday, then, Peekskill, Newburgh, Poughkeepsie, and Kingston next week."

"We already know about Tarrytown," he grumbled. "I need specifics on her other stops; dates, times, facilities."

Trying to hold back her tears, she muttered something inaudible.

Albert heard her voice falter. *"Try to keep him on the line a little bit longer. Tell him you should expect an update tomorrow morning,"* he whispered.

Now following Albert's direction almost robotically, she added, "I expect an update on the town hall schedule tomorrow."

"You better be right if you want to see Hollis again." he said before hanging up abruptly.

"Well done," Albert said in a calm tone. *"I've got his location."*

"I need to see Hollis. It sounded like they've abducted him."

"Don't worry. As long as they need you, he'll be alright. I now have a way to track them down."

Albert knew that if she was right about Hollis' abduction, she would be under immense pressure, often the cause of fatal decisions.

"Darcy, remember to activate the link if you find yourself in immediate danger."

* * *

Albert was sitting in the corner booth at the White Eagle in Brighton Beach, a bar Strongman was known to frequent. His patience had paid off. He spotted Strongman's tattooed forearms at a table several booths closer to the backroom entry.

He was waiting to capture a good facial image with his phone when the call alert came in from Darcy. As he listened to the conversation, Albert's cell phone locator tracked the dark voice on the other end of the line to the bar. Virtually the same room he was in.

His deduction that the extortionist was connected to her husband through gambling was about to pay off. Albert watched as the tattooed man and Darcy ended their phone calls at the exact same moment. This coincidence, combined with the cell locator, gave him double confirmation that Strongman was the voice who was threatening her and her husband over the phone.

He was now deep into a second phone call, and Albert casually walked over to the bar counter. While ordering a beer and fiddling with his phone, he caught a clear image of his face in the backbar mirror, including the *Strongman* tattoo on his arm.

Throwing a few bills on the table, the tattooed man bolted out of the bar. A few steps behind, Albert followed him out onto the sidewalk. Halfway down the next block, Strongman jumped into a late model muscle car and headed northbound on Ocean Parkway.

* * *

Rybak had Drexler in his sights, and his directive was simple. Uncle Caslav wanted retribution. As he began to squeeze the trigger, a large muscular man walked into his line of fire.

Events had been unfolding quickly since Rybak had first caught a lead on the *Big Fish*. It didn't take long for Caslav and his New York assets to identify the Fish as Bass Drexler, a man with a long resume as a security consultant for some very high-end Manhattanites.

The name of one client stood out in particular, that of Garson Grimes, known by his friends as the *Banker to the Frackers*. Their association went back several decades to when Grimes hired Drexler fresh off his last tour in Afghanistan, to help put down a union movement in his natural gas fields. Accusations of violence and murder followed Drexler but criminal charges were never filed.

Over the following years, Grimes paid to have his record sanitized, then referred him to a handful of associates. Drexler had a special skill set that was in high demand among his confederates.

The only other information unearthed was an old address of Drexler's in Queens from years before. That was enough for Caslav, who immediately sent his name, the address, and a photograph to Rybak by encoded fax, over the land line in an old Dubrovnik coffee shop. He wanted to be sure there was no record of their communication. Rybak knew his orders. He didn't need them spelled out.

After surveilling the Big Fish for several days, Rybak began to recognize a pattern. There were two locations he visited daily, one a sleazy bar with a backroom card game, and the other a swanky address in lower Manhattan, a place Caslav learned was also a frequent haunt of Gaston Grimes.

Caslav was sure that Grimes was the one giving the orders. But for now, he wanted Rybak to focus on Drexler.

* * *

As he had done before, Grimes tried to convince the ORC leader to allow Drexler to be point man for the second attempt on the governor, over the strong objections of Clay Daggert. The Dark Lord finally conceded, allowing Drexler to continue, but only under the close scrutiny of Daggert's foot soldier, Burle Strong.

As soon as the meeting ended, Daggert called Strong who had just finished his latest tattoo session, and now sporting the image of his own head in a lion's mouth.

"Stay close to him. He botched the first assassination attempt, and we can't allow that to happen again. Who's to say the feds aren't already on to him. If you see even the slightest hint of compromise or incompetence, take him out."

Daggert's orders were clear, and within hours, Strong caught up with Drexler in Tarrytown where he was evaluating the site for the next attempt on Governor Hendriksen. As expected, Drexler was methodically taking pictures with his phone of the streets around the old theater. It all seemed to be normal surveillance work.

He had nothing personal against Drexler, and considered him his equal in the dark ORC underground. But if it came down to it, he'd take Drexler out without a second thought. He wasn't about to cross Daggert.

Strong watched patiently from a distance. After investigating the inside of an old vacant storefront building a block down from the theater, Drexler turned down a side street and crossed over to a small sidewalk café. The waiter seated him at an outdoor table with the sun on his face and a brick wall to his back.

* * *

Rybak casually walked down the sidewalk toward an alleyway across the street and a few shops down from the café where Drexler was sitting. Seeing no onlookers, he ducked into the alley.

Peering around the corner in the shadow of an old brick building, he now had Drexler in his line of sight. For a marksman like Rybak, it was an easy shot. This time there would be no reprieve.

Chapter 32

The Old Dutch Churchyard - Sleepy Hollow

The first thin rays of dawn pierced through the slit in the heavy curtains, moving across Annah's face as she rolled over onto her side. She squinted at the illuminated clock on the nightstand with sleepy eyes. *6:45...*It was simply too early to be awake.

Something rustling in the living room caught her attention. She sat up and rubbed her eyes to get a better look through the glass panels below the loft guard rail. In the dim light she could see Will slouched in the large upholstered chair. Oddly, he was fully dressed, but his pant legs were rolled up.

She slipped out of bed and descended the loft stairs. Will was barefoot and his socks and shoes were lying on the floor beside him.

"Will," she whispered, as she moved closer. "Are you awake?"

He stirred but didn't answer. She reached down to pick up his socks and shoes to find they were both wet and muddy.

Trying to imagine a scenario that made sense, she quietly placed them on the entry mat, then put on a kettle of water in the smartly appointed kitchen. Waiting for Will to wake up was going to require a strong cup of tea.

* * *

While Will slept, Annah thumbed through several tourist brochures that had been neatly arranged on the end table for guests. The one about Washington Irving caught her interest. She was pleased to learn that the scene for much of his writing, the Old Dutch Church of Sleepy Hollow, was just a few miles upriver.

The aroma of Annah's green chai seeped into Will's dreams. Annah was sitting on the sofa across from him when he woke.

"Smells good. Any more chai?"

"Could be, if you have a good explanation for the wet pant cuffs and muddy shoes."

"I'll think better with tea."

Annah conceded and headed for the kitchen.

"I'm not sure what happened," he shouted to her from the living room. "I woke up sometime after midnight and couldn't get back to sleep, so I went for a walk down Main Street."

After handing him a cup of chai, Annah returned to the couch.

"That sounds reasonable," she said. "But the muddy shoes?"

"That happened on the path by the river. This is where it gets strange."

"I'm all ears."

"There was a man with a lantern on a dock down where the Saw Mill River enters the Hudson."

"A man on a dock with a lantern? What time was that?"

"Right. It makes no sense."

* * *

They agreed to put the strange events of the past night on hold until they'd showered and had breakfast. Annah was still excited about Sleepy Hollow and Will agreed that it would be the logical next stop on their road trip.

After breakfast in a small café in Irvington, Will got back on Broadway heading north.

Annah took a long look at the vehicle behind them in the passenger side mirror.

"I thought I saw the same orange land rover following us back in Yonkers. Are you heeding Albert's cautions?"

"Not really, but I'll turn on the next block and go through the neighborhood to make sure.

"Good idea. So, tell me about the man with the lantern."

"He was dressed in seventeenth century clothing, and I saw him signal to a boat that tied up on the dock. They unloaded several crates and moved them onto a cart. I followed them up the creek."

"Were you time traveling, or do I need to check your head for bumps?"

"Already did that."

"Okay, when did lantern man first appear?"

"Down on Main Street, at the old hardware store. I was looking at a display in the storefront window."

As they neared Tarrytown, Will slowed the beetle to a crawl, coming to a stop behind a line of cars. Traffic was backed up for blocks as police redirected traffic down side streets. Nearing the center of town, they saw police gathered in front of a building cordoned off by crime scene tape.

Will rolled down his window and called out to a pedestrian walking down the sidewalk. "What happened?"

"There's been a fatal shooting."

* * *

Clouds had been building all morning and the weather report predicted a slight chance of rain. The leaves on the trees were well into their autumn change and glowed with color wherever the sun broke through.

As they entered Sleepy Hollow, the first few sprinkles of rain fell on the windshield, and Will pulled over on a side street to raise the convertible top. The last few rays of sunlight that were scattered over the rooftops were disappearing, as the misty gray bank of rain grew nearer.

"How much farther to the Old Dutch Church?" Annah asked, trying to trace their route on the sketchy tourist map in the brochure.

"Should be just up…oh, there it is!"

A strong architectural statement in simplicity, the church and surrounding churchyard were right out of the sixteen hundreds.

"Let's check out the graveyard before it starts pouring," Annah said as she folded the tourist map and put it in the glove box.

They parked in a small lot south of the church and followed the main sidewalk uphill to the church entry. The walls were skillfully laid up in rustic stone masonry, and crowned by a classic Belgian Gambrel roof.

Just beyond the formal entry to the building, Annah impatiently pulled Will through the churchyard gates.

"We need to get a move on," Annah said. "It's getting darker."

"Dark and rainy. Perfect weather to stroll through an old cemetery."

"Do you think the lantern man was a ghost," Annah asked, snuggling closer to Will's side.

"After all the mysterious encounters we've had, I can't be certain where ghosts leave off and visions through the veil of time begin. He paid no attention to me, yet I strongly felt he sensed my presence."

"Will, if there's more to it, I'm certain it will become clear to you."

They continued up the slope and wandered through some of the oldest grave markers.

"Will! Come look, it's a Gerritsen. I wonder how he died."

"Are you thinking of the Hessian rider?"

"Who?" she teased.

"The headless horseman."

"Oh sure, he was here."

A loud crack of thunder ended their excursion through the tombstones. Big drops pummeled them as they raced back to the recess at the church entry just as a ragged bolt of lightning tore across the sky.

Illuminated by the bright flash, Annah caught a glimpse of something bright orange on the ridge above the cemetery.

* * *

Clovis Helms was a police force dropout when Dell Thatcher first crossed his path, picking him up from the criminal justice scrapheap in his early thirties. Always on the lookout for candidates to do his special projects, he preferred someone with a law enforcement background who had been compromised, and Helms was already in deep with some crooked cops before being let go for domestic violence.

After working for one of his side security businesses for several years, Thatcher managed to get him a position on the governor's security detail using the sanitized background he had created for him.

As someone reporting directly to Thatcher, no one had reason to question his work, which consisted mainly of doing his boss's dirty work. He had nothing he could pin on Thatcher, as their interactions were always done in person to avoid an electronic trail. Helms either followed orders or faced exile.

The Sydney Rogers incident wasn't his first fuckup. His instructions had been simple. *Get her phone and laptop.* Putting the young museum worker in the ICU had been a really bad move.

Thatcher realized Helms knew too much about his business. His first choice was to figure a way to get more out of him. Then quietly eliminate him. His second choice was to eliminate him now. So far, he'd been operating under the first choice, but that could change in a heartbeat.

* * *

Once again, his orders were simple. *Get Devar's laptop.* Helms knew if he screwed this up, it would be the last time. He'd managed to put a tracking device on their car back in Yonkers the previous night, and after a miserable night sleeping in his car, he woke up stiff, cold, and hungry.

He patiently followed Devar and Garrison, waiting for an opportunity where he could be certain of success. Turning around to get a better view of the church, Helms killed his headlights and eased onto the shoulder of the road as it started to rain.

* * *

During his extensive review of the closed-circuit security footage from the night of the bombing, Thatcher was becoming obsessed with what may have been captured by camera or video on Sydney Roger's cell phone. He made a mental list of the calls he had made in the minutes leading up to the explosion.

The first call had come from Drexler with the news that the governor's schedule and mode of transportation had changed. He had then made two calls to Sofiya trying to get her to call off the detonation, both of which went unanswered. He was making one last attempt to reach her when the bomb went off.

Sofiya took the fall for it, and now Thatcher's long held belief that he was too important for Grimes and the other ORCs to take out was becoming less certain.

His latest security update from his FBI liaison, Johanna Martin, indicated they were rapidly culling through the cell calls that night, comparing them to the available security footage, looking for anyone speaking on their phones. He was satisfied that he wasn't captured on any of the museum cameras.

He was not so certain of Sydney Rogers, who could actually be seen on the security footage taking random photos of the guests. In his growing paranoia, he began to worry that she had also made videos.

Helms did manage to get Rogers' phone, but nearly killed her in the process. They found a text from Annah Devar asking her to take some candid images of the opening for the web page but no pictures were ever transferred, likely because the photo files were too big for texting.

Assuming that Rogers had sent the picture and videos over the internet, he had ordered Helms to get Devar's laptop without being seen.

* * *

Helms watched in amusement from the top of the hill as Garrison drove around in random loops before leaving town, just as he had in Tarrytown.

Chapter 33

Follow the Tattoos

Martin got a call from Patrick O'Malley, the Tarrytown chief of police.

"We have a murder up here that I think you'll be interested in."

"Who's the victim?"

"A guy by the name of Bass Drexler. But he's not why I'm calling."

"Okay," Martin said, not certain about where this was going.

"We ran through all of the street cam footage immediately before and after the shooting. We spotted the same guy near the crime scene several times. He disappeared from view in an alley diagonally across from the victim's location just before shots were fired."

"Did you catch a good facial image?"

"He was careful to keep the bill of his cap pulled down and never looked up, like a professional. But we lucked out and caught his reflection in an old glass storefront. Apparently, the FBI's facial recognition service can read backwards."

"We call it FACE, cute right? So, did it identify the shooter?"

"We believe he's a man you've been looking for. The official name in his naturalization records is Rybak Sadouski."

"Serbian?"

"Half. The other half is Belarus."

"Anything else?"

"He's was suspected for all sorts of crimes when younger, but nothing stuck. His current age is thirty-eight. Closest relative, a Serbian uncle named Caslav Nedic, brother of his deceased mother."

"That's our man. Send us everything you've got."

"One more thing. There's a witness, another man at the café table when Drexler was shot. His driver's license confirmed his name as Burle Strong. We've insisted he remain available to our investigators."

"So, you let him go?"

"Yes, but we placed a locator on his car."

"Good work. Compliment your team for me. I'll keep you apprised as things develop."

* * *

It had been a while since Albert made a surprise visit to Martin's special operations center in the Brooklyn FBI field office.

"So, is it Harwood or Pendrake I have the pleasure of seeing this afternoon?"

"I'm flexible on that."

"Not too rigid, eh?"

"We'll have to discuss rigid later. But I've got some developments that I'm sure you'll find provocative."

"Go on."

"I've turned one of the assassin's pawns, a young woman named Darcy Wells. She's part of the governor's advance planning group. She's working for me now."

"Impressive."

"Basic spycraft," he said with false modesty. "She gets her directions from a guy we call Strongman."

"Tattooed on his arm?"

"How did you know that?"

"Basic police work." She enjoyed turning the tables on him. He was usually ahead of her.

"I showed you mine. What have you got?"

"We identified Caslav's nephew, Rybak Sadouski. We believe he assassinated a man named Bass Drexler in Tarrytown, one shot in the head and a second through the heart."

"Ouch."

"Get this. Drexler was having breakfast at an outdoor café with …"

"Strongman?"

"His real name is Burle Strong. He was released after questioning, but we're surveilling the address he gave to the local police."

Albert's jaw dropped. He was impressed.

"And so, our paths intersect once again," he said.

"I love it when you talk dirty."

* * *

Martin's task force was working in high gear following the trail of Rybak Sadouski, while Albert followed up on Strongman and continued monitoring Darcy Wells. She was focused on getting to the bottom of Rybak's connection to Drexler.

She now knew that Rybak had a relationship with Sofiya Balashov through his Uncle Caslav, all clearly involved with the execution phase of the bombing. With Albert's details, she also knew that Drexler's breakfast friend, Strong, was operating Darcy Wells and her mechanic husband.

She now thought it likely Drexler was the one running Sofiya, and that Rybak was now in charge of carrying out Uncle Caslav's revenge for killing her.

Background data on Drexler was bubbling up all around her command center.

"Martin, I've got his sealed military records from the Pentagon," Sharky shouted.

"What did you have to give them?"

"Not a thing. After we explained he might be involved with the assassination of Senator Torres, they handed it right over."

* * *

It appeared likely that Strong and Drexler were both directly connected to the financial and planning levels at the top of this sprawling assassination pyramid. As he was walking out of Martin's office, Albert stopped at the door and turned around to face her.

"I have a strong feeling there is something in Drexler's connection to Strong that holds the key to finding the higher ups in this unholy alliance."

Martin agreed. She ordered her team to comb through every bit of evidence in the case again, starting with the dead Russians in Brighton Beach and working their way up to Drexler and Strong.

That afternoon, her team was scouring Brighton Beach, starting at the White Eagle Bar where Albert identified Strong.

After Martin leaned hard on Grigoriy, the owner of the White Eagle, he confirmed that Drexler and Strong were both regulars at the house game. Grigoriy also recognized Hollis Marsh, although he claimed he had not seen him around lately. As suspected, the bar was clearly the place where Hollis was recruited.

As Martin gathered updates from the team, Sharky presented his financial analysis of Drexler. Bank records showed his most recent paychecks came from a sketchy bank in Cyprus. It would take days, if ever, to trace corporate ownership back to the individuals responsible for the deposits. But finding out was a priority.

He did, however, discover something very revealing in the process. Burle Strong was receiving his paychecks from the same bank account. This proved he and Drexler were coworkers.

* * *

It was cold and rainy the following morning when Albert returned to the governor's offices in Manhattan. He needed to update Tess on the new developments in their investigation, and access the secure server through her direct link.

"I could use a cup of hot chocolate," he announced as he entered, carefully hanging up his rain-soaked coat by the door.

The governor stepped out of her office to greet him.

"Good to see you, Everett. Please come in and tell me about your progress on our project."

Closing the door behind her, she pointed to the comfortable chairs around the coffee table by the floor to ceiling window that offered an unobstructed view of Lexington Avenue.

Taking a seat, Albert began.

"We have a growing cast of suspects related to the case, all still alive until yesterday morning."

"Go on."

A man named Drexler was shot dead at a sidewalk café. We believe the shooter was a man name Rybak Sadouski, who we believe killed Drexler in revenge for the murder of Sofiya Balashov, his Uncle Caslav Nedic's partner and love interest. Our investigation points to Sofiya and Nedic as the source of the museum bomb."

"I'd say that's progress."

"Yes, but we believe Drexler is mid-level, between Sofiya's group at the bottom and his bosses, who are yet to be identified, at the top."

"So much for the lone wolf theory."

"But here's where the story opens another line of investigation. Drexler was having breakfast with a man named Burle Strong when the shooting occurred."

"Some name."

"It turns out someone in your employ had been compromised by Strong. Apparently, Darcy Wells, a member of your Town Hall advance planning team, has been passing specific details about your itinerary to Strong."

"Have you made an arrest?"

"Wait, there's more. Although her employment records show her as single, she is actually married to one of your personal limousine mechanics, Hollis Marsh."

"My God. Where does this conspiracy end?"

"That is what I am going to find out. Right now, Darcy Wells is cooperating and I have her on a very short electronic leash. That's how I was able to track down Strong."

"How did you find her?"

"That's a long story, but the security link on your computer helped point me in the right direction."

"So, what's she doing now?"

"She's coming to work as usual per Strong's directions, and reporting any new schedule details to him, that is if she doesn't want to see her gambling addicted husband cut into pieces. Strong made it clear that Hollis was grabbed for added leverage to keep her in line. I've checked with the limo garage and Marsh didn't report for work today.

"We have enough to hold Strong right now, but that could jeopardize what very well could be our only thread back to the top of this conspiracy. For now, we'll settle for the wiretap warrant just granted to us under seal by Judge Bayberry."

"She's a good one. Have you spoken to Agent Martin?" Tess asked.

"Yes, we've coordinated our investigations. She's following up on Rybak and Drexler while I try to run down Strong. We've made progress but so far, haven't found the people at the top. I'm afraid we can't guarantee they won't try a second attempt on your life. Maybe you should postpone your upcoming town hall tour."

"That's the one thing I won't do. I plan to sign the new tax bill into law at one of my town halls. The House Speaker thinks he'll have the final vote by Wednesday, in time for me to sign it at a ceremony in Kingston."

* * *

Sharky walked into his office to find Thatcher staring at the open folder on his desk containing the most current analysis of the burner calls made five minutes before and after the bombing. Sharky had been in the middle of preparing his daily update for Martin and had been gone from his desk only long enough to warm up his coffee in the microwave across the hall. He found it odd that Thatcher would be behind his desk at that moment.

Of the thousands of calls made in Brooklyn close to the time of the bombing, the taskforce had been able to distill them down to a few dozen of interest, particularly several that had been repeated.

"What can I do for you, Thatcher?" Sharky asked abruptly.

Startled, he replied, "I was in the neighborhood so I thought I'd drop by."

"Sure, have a seat," Sharky said neutrally, still feeling something was off about his sudden appearance. He casually gathered the papers spread out on his desk and closed the folder.

"Any new developments? I want to make sure I understand the risk assessment before continuing on the governor's town hall tour."

Thatcher managed to sound all business, but he could feel himself unraveling. He only had thirty seconds to scan the list of phone numbers listed before Special Agent Sharky walked in, but it was long enough to recognize the number of one of his burners on the short list.

Chapter 34

Up to Esopus

Annah's dreams were filled with ancient mysteries and mythical characters, much like her time in Cornwall by the lake and bees. They found a charming hotel room in Sleepy Hollow and woke up hungry.

"I thought India had a corner on spirits and demons, but this place is freaky."

"Bad dreams?"

"More like weird dreams. It feels like I've walked these grounds before."

"Karma?"

"Isn't it always? I think it strange that many Americans think of karma only as punishment."

"It must be our collective guilty conscience," Will chuckled.

Annah snuggled against Will. "Just before I woke up, I sensed somebody stalking us, a dark shadowy figure."

"It wouldn't be Sleepy Hollow if you didn't."

* * *

Will and Annah had a late breakfast in the village of Sleepy Hollow before heading north toward Peekskill. The rain had passed and the air was fresh and clean.

Will pulled in to a small independent grocery along the roadside. He had woken in the middle of the night thinking it would be a treat for Annah to have an authentic American picnic across the Hudson in Bear Mountain Park. As he was checking out, he noticed a headline in the local paper, *Governor's Townhall - Paramount Theater Today.*

With everything for a picnic packed neatly under the hood, with the exception of a basket, Will lowered the convertible top and continued their tour. They soon entered downtown Peekskill where traffic had slowed to a crawl. Security barriers were up on Main Street, diverting traffic around the historic theater where Tess would soon preside over the townhall. Annah was sickened by the sight of protesters in death masks, picketing along the police perimeter tape. After the shooting in Irvington in broad daylight, the police were taking no chances.

Once out of traffic they drove over the Bear Mountain Bridge and entered the park.

Annah was thrilled to be out in the fresh air, surrounded by nature. The natural beauty of the hills and river vistas were moving. She imagined generations of painters standing where she stood, trying to capture its glory.

She particularly liked the Trailside Museum and Zoo, finally getting to see authentic Black Bears. When Will had mentioned them in reference to his grandfather's gun, she thought he was kidding. But that was part of an episode she'd sooner forget.

The geology and vistas stirred the scientist within her. This terrain, much like that in her beloved Kerala, was timeless and ancient. Standing on the edge of a scenic overlook, she spotted two bald eagles down the ridge, their majestic white heads catching the midday sun. One followed the other as they plummeted toward the river in search of the day's catch.

Will laid down two large beach towels on the soft grass and spread out their culinary treats. Opening the Petite Verdot, they leisurely ate brie on herbal fig crackers, along with dried apricots and cashews. Jalapeno chocolate and the last of the Petite Verdot was the perfect end to their picnic.

"This is heavenly," Annah cooed.

Will leaned over and gently kissed her.

"It is with you here."

* * *

When they returned to the beetle, Will noticed that the glove box was open. Someone had been searching through their stuff.

"Anything missing?" Annah asked with alarm.

"Where's your wallet and phone?"

"In my front pocket. I think I got the habit from you."

"Maybe we scared them off," Will said without conviction.

Annah turned and pointed down the park entry road. "Something just caught my eye."

"Was it orange?"

* * *

"Should we call Albert and Martin?"

"Not yet. I'm going to lose them and then backtrack over to the east side of the Hudson.

"Sounds like a good plan. I'll keep lookout with my mirror."

Will was about to ask for details when Annah pulled an enormous mirror out of her purse.

"Women never know when they're going to need one," she giggled.

Convinced no one was following, Will raced back over the bridge and sped north on the 9D.

A few miles further up river, Annah saw a large sign that said *The Town of Garrison*. "Really? Did you drive this way to show me the family town you forgot to tell me about? Kinda like the Garrison Farm?"

"Okay, I confess."

"And is your *town* our destination for today?"

"No. I thought we could have a nice dinner in Cold Springs, not far from here. It's also great for window shopping."

"I can do that," she said cheerfully.

"Then we'll head up to Beacon. I'll book us into a sweet little hotel I know on historic Main Street. They have a spa."

"Say no more," Annah sighed, scooting deeper into her seat and putting on her shades. She didn't ask if he'd been there before with another woman. Anyway, it wouldn't matter to her. Their relationship was solid.

* * *

Will called ahead and made reservations for a window table at a cozy bistro on Main Street. The candlelight and white tablecloth added a touch of class, and they ordered a sparkling wine that added to the feeling of celebration.

Both of them were pescatarians and the menu offered a nice variety of fish entrees. Predictably, Annah ordered halibut while Will ordered the swordfish.

They were good at inventing reasons to celebrate, and getting out of the city was a good enough excuse that evening. But Annah still hadn't shaken off the creepy feeling of being followed.

"I hate to break the mood, but something's been bothering me," she finally said.

"Go on. I trust your instincts."

"If someone is following us, how did they pick up our trail in the first place?"

"Good question," Will answered. "They'd have to have been on standby in their car, waiting for us to leave, and have pretty good tailing skills to follow us out of the city."

"Or maybe they used one of those things Albert sticks on people's cars?"

"You know I stuck one of those on Reddick's car back in DC, under the rear fender on the passenger side. According to Albert, that's where trained agents place them."

* * *

They were still reeling from the discovery of a tracking device as they drove north toward the historic village of Beacon. Will found it just where Albert would have placed it, and tossed it into the middle of a pond near the roadside.

It was dark when they arrived at the inn. At check-in, Annah wasted no time scheduling appointments for the spa the next day. She hoped a massage would relieve the feeling of dread that had formed in her gut when they found the tracking device. Although it was some relief getting rid of it, the fact that it was there at all freaked her out.

* * *

Helms watched from a distance as Will pulled the Beetle onto the shoulder and threw something in the lake. Instantly, his tracking program lost its signal.

"Damn it. Those things aren't cheap," he mumbled, seeing no way to recover it.

But the VW was highly recognizable, so he'd have to track them the old way, by keeping them in sight. The dim light of dusk was fading and he was able to drive closer. His orange vehicle didn't stand out as much at night as it did in the daylight.

Helms stayed back a block as they entered Beacon. The Beetle slowed and pulled into a parking spot just off of Main Street. Already imagining scenarios for getting Devar's devices, he watched Garrison carry their luggage into an old hotel.

Not looking forward to another night in the car, he convinced himself it would be better to get a room and keep an eye on them from the hotel. From across the street, he watched through the large hotel windows until Devar and Garrison got their room key and left the lobby.

As he crossed the street hoping they still had a room available for the night, his cell rang. It was Thatcher.

"I've learned that Sydney Rogers' brain swelling has significantly improved. They're planning to bring her out of the medically induced coma tomorrow. I need to know what's on the pictures she took at the Museum, and you and I both know it's likely Devar has them." Thatcher hung up before he could respond.

"Can I help you?" a pleasant voice from behind the reception desk asked.

"Yeah, I'm looking for a room for the night."

* * *

After a good night's sleep and a hot shower, Will and Annah were ready to go down the block to a little café for breakfast. As they descended the central staircase from the second floor, they didn't notice the man watching them from the landing above.

Helms raced back to his room and climbed out the window onto an old iron fire escape and down the steps to the second floor, where he quickly headed toward the window to Devar's room. Based on the ashes and cigarette burns on the railings, it was obviously the place smokers used in the quaint, non-smoking hotel.

With the chiseled end of a tire iron grabbed from the trunk of his car the night before, he pried up on the lower sash. Concerned the glass would shatter at any moment, he was relieved when the old double hung latch between the two sashes broke loose. He was able to raise the window with little effort and quietly slip in.

* * *

He had one of their laptops in his hand and the other on the foot of the bed when the door swung open, items Will had forgotten to lock in the room safe.

Helms turned toward the window as Will dove across the room. The force of Will's weight drove him onto the bed, knocking the laptop out of his hands.

Wriggling out of his grasp, Helms ran to the window with Will two steps behind him. Half way out the window, Will grabbed him around the mid-section just as they tumbled onto the fire escape. He hit him with such force that Helms went over the rail, managing to grasp a crossbar, where he dangled for a moment before losing his grip. Will reached out to grab him a moment too late, and watched as he fell from the second story, landing awkwardly onto a recycling bin before bouncing onto the pavement. Before he could lower the fire escape ladder, the intruder had staggered off. Will ran down the alley but the man had disappeared. Fortunately, Will had gotten a good look at him before he did.

"Are you alright? What in the world are you doing down there?" Will looked up to see Annah standing on the fire escape.

"Chasing your headless horseman," he yelled up to her, trying to muster a bit of humor.

As he traced his steps back to the fire escape, he saw something glint in the sun. Annah must have seen it at the same time.

"Is that a cell phone?" Annah shouted.

"Looks like he left us a present."

* * *

The fire escape was too much for Will, so he walked around the hotel and entered the lobby on the Main Street side. He rang the bell on the reception desk.

Devasy, the night manager who was still on duty, promptly came out of the small office behind the desk.

"How may I help you?"

"I'm in Room 210. I want to report a break- in."

"Is anyone hurt?" he asked.

Will found it reassuring that his first thoughts were for their safety and well-being.

"Nothing serious. Just a few bruises."

Straightaway, he latched the entry doors and put a *Return in Ten Minutes* sign on the glass.

"Please, show me your room."

They climbed to the second floor. Before Will could pull his key card from his wallet, Annah opened the door.

"I'm Devasy, the manager. Are you okay Ms. Devar?" he asked with a soft but noticeable accent.

"Yes, thank you. It was all over before I got back to the room."

She paused, "Your accent sounds very familiar. Kerala?"

"Yes, I am Nasrani from Kochi."

"As am I," Annah smiled.

"I know the name Devar. It is highly respected. Please, tell me what happened and I will have the police come and make a report."

* * *

Since no one was hurt and nothing missing, the police noted a forced window latch and attempted burglary in their report and left the scene.

Will and Annah didn't mention the tracking device found on their car, or the cell phone dropped by the burglar, correctly assuming that Albert and Martin would want to hear it first. Nor did they mention the break-in at their Brooklyn apartment, or their suspicions about being followed.

192

Will called Martin and gave her the phone number of the burner and the calls made on it. He assured her he had carefully picked it up and wrapped it in a tissue, hoping her team could pick up fingerprints or DNA on it, as well as Annah's laptop. She told them to stay put until her investigators arrived.

* * *

Martin was unexpectedly sitting in the hotel lobby when Will and Annah came down from their room to meet the FBI team. She had arrived at their hotel at the same time as the CSI team.

"It's really good to see you," Annah cried, as she raced to embrace Martin.

"Thanks for coming all the way up from the city to check on us."

"I would have come up from the city, but I was already in Kingston with the planners of what the governor's now calling The Great Town Hall, to be held in two days. She's expected to sign her new tax bill into law in the old Senate House in Kingston, which in her words, is a place of great historic significance."

"We won't be far away. We're heading up to the Garrison Farm later today," Annah said. "You should drop by when you're in the area."

"Albert has fond memories of the farm. I'll see if he can join us."

"By the way, we already have solid leads from the numbers you gave us from the burner. Albert has confirmed with Sharky that two of those numbers are on his shortlist of suspicious calls. The timestamp on those calls indicate they were made within a minute or two both before and after the bombing.

"And Sydney Rogers is conscious. They brought her out of the coma this morning. We're hoping the doctors will allow me to interview her soon. She may be able to shed some light on the assailant."

"Do you think he's the same guy who's been following us?" Annah asked.

"There was no DNA evidence at her apartment, so the only way to prove it is to find a witness."

"I got a good look at the intruder this time," Will said. "I made a sketch of him before I forgot details."

Taking the drawing from Will's hand, she studied it for a moment. "Very impressive."

Will shrugged. "Required art classes."

* * *

Devasy was off shift, but returned to the hotel at Martin's request.

"Do you recognize this man?"

"Yes, I believe him to be the man that checked in last evening."

"Was that before or after Will and Annah checked in?"

"I remember clearly that it was shortly after. He checked in to Room 307 as Kenneth Hess."

"I'm guessing that's not his real name."

"He had an ID. It looked legitimate."

"When did he check out?"

"He didn't. The maids knocked on his door and found his room empty."

* * *

They said their goodbyes to Martin and began their drive up to the farm. They drove up through Poughkeepsie in silence, trying to process the recent events swirling around them.

Will took the westbound exit and crossed the river on the Mid-Hudson Bridge. Annah broke the silence as she gazed out over the river.

"Everything's been happening so quickly since the night of the bombing. First the assault on Sydney Rogers, then two more on us. Is it the same man? What are they looking for?"

"Let's break this down," Will said. "If the attack on Sydney was by the same people and for the same reason as those on us, then it must have something to do with the museum. That's really the only connection."

"You're right, and perhaps more specifically, about the opening of our exhibit."

"And therefore, most likely about the bombing. What else could make them so desperate?" Will speculated.

As he merged into the northbound exit lane for Kingston, Annah twisted around and squeezed between the front seats to reach her laptop. While facing back, she glanced out the rear window at the road behind them.

"I'm seeing orange cars."

"You've got me seeing them too," Will added.

"Could he be brazen enough to come after us again?"

"Or desperate. There must be something on your laptop he's looking for."

"Sydney Rogers. She's the clue. She must have sent me something."

She booted up and opened her email.

"I don't remember seeing anything from her."

"Junk mail?"

"I'll look again."

She scrolled back to the night of the opening but there was nothing from Sydney.

"Have you checked *your* junk mail?" she asked pointedly.

Five minutes later, Annah had Will's laptop up and running. She opened the email manager and scrolled through his *Inbox*. Buried with dozens of older emails marked as *Read*, she found one from *srogers* with attachments.

"Sweetie, I found an email from Sydney Rogers buried in your *Inbox* that came in a few days after the bombing. You must have skipped right over it."

"She emailed me? Shit! I was inundated with messages right after the bombing, and haven't been very focused since then. I wasn't expecting anything from her."

"Her message says that she tried to send it to me, but it bounced back. I'm guessing she left the last letter off of *Annah*. The attachments are photos and a short video."

Annah scanned through the still images, recognizing many of the special guests at the museum reception. Tears filled her eyes as she was reminded of how beautifully the evening had begun.

"These images are wonderful. There's one with both of us talking to the governor that's priceless." Her heart sank when she realized it was taken just before the blast.

"What's on the video?"

"Keep your eyes on the road while I take a look."

Annah started the video and began to laugh. "Sydney caught Albert and Martin as they entered the lobby and signed the guest book. They look like royalty."

She continued watching. "The video follows them over to where we were standing."

She stopped the video, realizing she had been entirely focused on Albert and Martin.

"I'm going to play it again in slow motion, and focus on the other guests in the lobby."

Half way through the short video, she paused it. "There's a familiar looking man in the background talking intently on his phone."

"Let me see him," Will said reaching for the laptop.

"Wait. Keep driving while I enlarge the image."

Once she had a tight blow up of the man, she held the laptop near the dashboard where Will could glance at it.

"I've met him. Isn't he part of the governor's security entourage?"

Part Eight

(Year 1654 - New Amsterdam)

Chapter 35

A Legal Matter Upriver

Symon Claesz, captain of the *Geldersche Bloom*, the *Flower of Gelder* to the English, navigated his vessel up the North River on the final leg of one of her many voyages across the Atlantic Ocean from Amsterdam to Beaverwyck in the Patroonship of Rensselaer. They were delivering a dozen more immigrant families, and much-needed supplies to Jan Baptist van Rensselaer, second son of Killian van Rensselaer.

Adriaen bought passage on the *Flower* for both him and his adventure thirsty brother-in-law, Elias Doughty. When Elias, now a man in his own right at the age of twenty-two, first learned of Adriaen's legal mission up north, he was determined to make the journey with him.

Elias wanted to see the legendary settings for so many of the adventures told to him by Adriaen van der Donck. He adored his brother-in-law and trusted him with his life. His fiancée, Sarah O'Neal, while supportive of his trek into the primordial forest, quietly told Adriaen to make sure he came back in one piece. Their marriage was planned for the following spring, something she greatly looked forward to.

* * *

They boarded the *Flower* in Manhattan with their horses, but were only sailing half way to Beaverwyck. Their destination was the village of Esopus some seventy miles upriver. They could have ridden up the river trails, however Adriaen wanted Elias to see the country as he first did.

Elias' curiosity was insatiable and he remembered nuanced details of Adriaen's views on the law and good governance, based on people's innate goodness, that allowed them to govern themselves. He also knew that Adriaen was instrumental in imbedding the right to freedom of conscience in the original village charter of Flushing.

Elias had vivid memories of his father being harassed for his religious views before being banished from New England. The religious hypocrisy he had witnessed left him with little inclination to become part of a flock, and as the son of a preacher, he felt no need for further religious instruction.

"Elias, I concur with your sentiments about religion. I myself have become tolerant of a wide range of beliefs. I was inspired by the spirituality of the native people, particularly the Mohawk and their concern for future generations. Just remember to use reason as your right hand, but be advised that in these times, legal petitions need to be couched in the precepts of recognized religious principles."

Elias was quiet as he tried to absorb the full import of what Adriaen had said. "Something new is blossoming in Flushing, at the heart of the New World."

"I agree. But the way it all unfolds could depend on the smallest changes made here in our time."

Adriaen's words sent a shiver down Elias' spine. "So how do you know when to act in the face of daily injustice?"

"That is the heart of wisdom," Adriaen answered. "I am still working on that."

* * *

The *Flower of Gelder* sailed close to the western bank and found anchorage just beyond the point at the mouth of the Rondout Creek in the land of the Esopus, a branch of the Lenape tribes. Adriaen, Elias, and their horses were lowered onto the shore barge and ferried to a short wooden dock on the north bank of Rondout Creek.

After guiding their mounts across the gangplank and down the dock to terra firma, they repacked their gear and supplies for the ride up the river trail to the sacred highlands of the Catskills.

There had been a long-standing agreement between the Mohawk, Esopus, and Munsee that their tribal boundaries were drawn along lines that radiated out from Onteora, the tallest peak in the high mountain wilderness. Each tribe wanted to settle on land that maintained their access to the great rivers.

Aghar proposed that there be permanent landmarks established so these key locations could be entered into the court records of the New Netherlands to prevent unnecessary future disputes between the tribes. The records would also make it official in the Dutch manner what land was still retained by the tribes. The current dispute arose when the Mohawks thought an Esopus sachem was selling Mohawk land to an Englishman.

Once on shore, they followed the old road that ran through the small Dutch settlement up to the Esopus Creek trail. As planned, they met Aghar at his temporary camp on the banks of the Esopus, in the old forest just beyond the last Dutch homestead.

* * *

It was already midday by the time they passed the first Esopus village on the trail that led up to Onteora. Elias had spent a good deal of time in the thick woods around Colen Donck, but had not seen the majesty of these primordial forests. The maples and other hardwood trees were as wide as he was tall, and the pines and firs towered toward the sky. He was hoping to see his first black bear, while Adriaen and Aghar were hoping he wasn't eaten by his first black bear.

Evening was approaching and the shadows grew long, having already been mid-day when they finally departed Aghar's camp by Esopus Creek.

"These forests were alive before there was time," Aghar said to his new friend.

"You mean they are older than the people," Elias asked.

"I mean that the ancient forests have no concept of time."

"The trees have concepts?" Elias countered, a bit perplexed.

"Do you doubt there is a living consciousness in those trees?" Aghar asked.

"Meaning they have ideas and dreams?"

"Can you prove they don't?"

Elias conceded with a laugh, finding it absurd to play games of logic in the ancient forest.

"How much farther to the meeting place?"

"Only another day's ride," Aghar reassured.

"Oh! I expected we'd be there today."

"Our journey will give you the opportunity to sleep in these ancient woods. You may want to pay attention to your dreams," Aghar said with a smile before riding ahead to join Adriaen.

* * *

They stopped in a clearing below a waterfall that cascaded down a narrow gorge in the densely forested hillside. The majestic sound of the tumbling water overpowered the random thoughts running through Elias' mind.

"Adriaen, does the sound of the falls make you as sleepy as it does me?"

"I've heard stories, Brother, of people under the spell of the forest sprites who have slept for days."

"Forest sprites. Is Adriaen trying to trick me, Aghar?" Elias asked over his shoulder.

"I think we should eat before we all fall under their spell," Aghar replied. "Are you good with rabbit stew tonight?"

"It's my favorite."

"Just like your brother."

* * *

Sparks from the blazing campfire spiraled upward through the pines as night fell over the mountains.

The moon shone like daylight where it broke through the trees, lighting the pathway beside the gorge. After eating his fill of rabbit, carrots and squash, Elias decided to wander up the path to where the mist from the waterfall cast rainbows in the moonlight. The place reminded him of the mythical scenes in stories read to him by his father as a small child.

The soft dappled moonlight on the forest floor and the rhythmic sound of falling water eased him into deep contemplation. He laughed off the tales of wood sprites that mischievously cast sleep spells on their victims, imagining they were stories the Wilden told to keep their children from wandering off too far.

He sat on the rocks at the top of the falls, imagining what tomorrow's gathering might look like. His eyes felt heavy and were beginning to close when he heard footsteps coming up the river path.

Elias assumed it was Adriaen as he turned his focus toward the sound. No one was there. Confused, he peered through the darkness once again.

On the path midway up the gorge, backlit by the moon, he saw the silhouette of a maiden. She approached slowly, unaware of his presence. As she entered the mist, the dancing rainbow colors seemed to move through her.

Stopping beside a patch of ground brightly lit by moonlight, she reached down to touch a man peacefully lying in a patch of fine grass. Rising to his feet, the two quietly walked up the path deeper into the woods.

Speechless, Elias was compelled to follow. As he walked faster to catch up, the wind began whistling in his ears. He didn't notice his feet weren't touching the ground until he was eye to eye with an owl sitting on a large limb high above the forest floor.

Astounded, he abandoned his pursuit, choosing instead to fly higher, up where he could see the silvery light reflecting on the surface of a great wide river. He continued his flight to the south where the river met the sea. The sky around him was teaming with night birds.

He recognized the outline of Manhattan and Long Island, surrounded by unchanged channels and bays, but the land was different. The buildings and carriages were illuminated by a thousand lanterns, like swarms of fire flies in June.

And then he spotted Flushing Bay, his home on Long Island. The village had grown beyond recognition, filled with people celebrating in streets that were lit from above. People from a hundred different countries who spoke a hundred different languages, held as many different spiritual beliefs. Tolerance was the fundamental nature of their law.

Walking down the wide avenue through throngs of people, he was joined by Adriaen on his right and Agheroense on his left. Then he was flying once again, this time with two men at his wings.

As they passed the Spuyten Duyvil and over Colen Donck, Adriaen spoke these words before vanishing.

"You will know what to do when the time comes."

* * *

Aghar found Elias sitting by the waterfall. As he guided his young friend back to the campfire, he said, "You were gone so long I decided to come and make sure the bears didn't get you. Where did you go?"

"I had a dream or maybe, a vision. I flew down to the sea and over my home in Flushing. Everything was different. There were all kinds of people in great number living peacefully together. You and Adriaen showed up and guided me back home."

"Did we fly as well?"

"Yes, but Adriaen disappeared over Colen Donck."

Adriaen's role in the dream confirmed something Grandfather had told Aghar, something he could not repeat, something Elias was not ready to hear.

The following week, Elias was caught between his waking and dream states. He had been gifted with the vision of a wonderful possible future. But he was also filled with emotion about the enormous changes that were to come, and the realization that none of them would be there to see it.

On their return journey to Flushing, Elias had a new understanding of the cultural and physical patterns being established in this new land, and how the examples they were setting would have a profound effect on future generations, sometimes for the better, too often for the worse.

He was anxious to return home and share these new revelations with his sweet Sarah, soon to be his bride.

Chapter 36

Religious Based Authoritarian Rule

Religious refugees from Europe and New England continued to pour into the New Netherlands with a variety of new beliefs and doctrines. Mary and Elias Doughty were accustomed to alternative religious views, growing up with a father who was a minister, driven out of New England because of his unorthodox views that they considered heresy.

But after emigrating to the New Netherlands, Reverend Doughty never quite squared with the colony directors, Stuyvesant and Kieft before him. He eventually left for the Virginia colony, but not before granting his farm in Flushing to his daughter, Mary.

In the years after their return from the Netherlands, Adriaen and Mary maintained close ties to Flushing. Her brother, Elias Doughty, and good friend Tobias Feake had become distinguished citizens of the thriving village. And village clerk, Edward Hart, remained a trustworthy ally.

News of Stuyvesant's crackdown on Lutherans, at the behest of his Dutch Reformed Church ministers, did not sit well with the people in Flushing. Already a tolerant mix of Dutch and English, they came from diverse religious backgrounds, including Calvinists like Stuyvesant's own Dutch Reformed Church, Presbyterians, Lutherans, Baptists, Jews, the emerging Quaker movement, and even the traditional worship of a freed African slave.

Although forbidden from engaging in political affairs in the New

Netherlands as part of the terms that allowed him to return home from Amsterdam, Adriaen secretly aided the Lutherans and others in need of legal petitions against what he considered the unlawful acts of Director Stuyvesant. To avoid the personal wrath of a growing number of colonists of faiths other than his, Stuyvesant thought himself clever to pass the Lutheran petition on to his corporate higher ups in Amsterdam.

The West India Company sided with the Lutherans. They dressed Stuyvesant down for bringing the matter to them publicly. The eyes of devout Calvinists were always on them, so they wanted to keep religious matters in house. The crackdown was bad for business, theirs being trade and colonization. He was ordered to deal with these issues locally in the future.

From that day on, his animosity toward other religions grew even stronger. He believed he had been given clear authority by the Company to deal with these matters however he liked. He shared his suspicion that the Lutherans had received legal help with their petition from van der Donck with van Tienhoven, who quickly volunteered to have his spies keep tabs on him. In truth, it was something he had been doing for quite some time.

* * *

In light of being reprimanded by the West India Company, Stuyvesant made a series of unpopular decrees, the latest a stern warning regarding religious assemblies. It was now illegal to assemble without the oversight of a minister approved by himself.

Tobias Feake had growing concern for Hannah Feake, his first cousin and sister for all practical purposes. Both having been raised in the same household, she had been exploring other paths since her father abandoned their family.

Hannah, along with Mary Doughty and Adriaen van der Donck, joined Tobias on one of his trading expeditions to the Providence Plantations. Adriaen was keen on meeting their newly elected president,

Roger Williams, who had originally founded the colony on the Providence River a decade earlier.

Adriaen was in accord with his views on the complete separation of church and state. And now with the growing diversity of spiritual beliefs in the New Netherlands, he was also highly motivated to explore Roger's ideas about religious tolerance and noninterference by the state. This was technically the same legal position in his Dutch homeland, a right Adriaen clearly restated in the Village of Flushing's founding charter. He now saw this civic tolerance being perverted by the dictates of Director Stuyvesant.

Roger and Adriaen were also like minded about fair dealings with the Wilden. Roger had heard the tales of Adriaen van der Donck negotiating peace with the Lenape and Mohawk peoples. He himself had managed to dissuade the Narragansett tribe from joining the Pequots in their war against the Bay Colony.

Upon their arrival in Providence, the group was well received by the new president, as informal ambassadors of the Dutch colony. Rogers, born in England, was also fluent in Dutch, and several of the native tongues, another thing he and Adriaen had in common. His philosophical discussions with Adriaen became quite detailed and lengthy, switching back and forth between English and Dutch.

Young Hannah was spellbound by the strength and clarity of Roger William's words. They were in striking contrast to the mad ramblings of her own father, who she watched as a young child descend into insanity before completely abandoning them.

She was also taken by the esteem in which women were held in the new colony, women who were allotted ownership of strips of land just like the men. Hannah remembered the scorn her mother had faced from the more rigid members of their religious community for the simple fact that she owned property after being abandoned.

Later being accused of adultery after remarrying, her mother faced threats of execution. It was only her blood relation to Governor John Winthrop of the Bay Colony that spared her from execution by hanging. Her current marriage was not recognized until she moved to the Dutch colony, and Hannah inherited her mother's contempt for the pious and unforgiving ways of the Puritans and Pilgrims. Losing faith in the male dominated New England Puritan society, she began her search for another spiritual path.

Hannah learned the history of a local woman named Jane Verin, who attended church services at the home of Roger Williams against the wishes of her husband who chose himself not to attend.

Her husband, Joshua, wanted the governing council to punish his wife for disobeying him for what he claimed to be biblical law. In an act of enlightened fairness, the council found in favor of Jane, forbidding future punishment of anyone for not worshipping according to the demands of others.

Sadly, the council declined to punish her husband for severely beating her, and Jane Verin was forced to move to the Puritan dominated Massachusetts Bay Colony with her husband, beyond the protection of Providence.

* * *

Hannah was happy to be back in Flushing. She dreamed of a day when she and other women would hold themselves to be equal to a man in all matters of spiritual and intellectual pursuits.

As the *Pride of Flushing* approached the dock on Flushing Creek, they were greeted by John Bowne, an emigree from England by way of the Bay Colony. Being a gentleman, he helped Mary and Hannah down from the Pride and onto the solid wood decking of the pier after tying up the shallop.

He had first met Hannah some five years earlier when she was a brash fourteen years old. Impressed at the time with her intelligence and thirst for knowledge, he now found himself smitten by the beautiful young woman standing in front of him. She was like a bud that had burst into full bloom and he was captivated by her.

Their courtship ignited that day on the pier, and although not *required*, they were soon given the blessings of Tobias Feake, Hannah's sibling cousin and protector.

Chapter 37

Year 1655 – The Peach War

Tienhoven was left in charge of the colony's affairs in the Stadt Huys while Stuyvesant, along with most of the garrison from Fort Amsterdam, were on a military campaign against the upstart colony of New Sweden on the South River, called the Delaware by the English.

Due to a serious lack of understanding of the alliances along the South and North Rivers between various native tribes and other Europeans settlers, Stuyvesant started a row of dominos falling in New Sweden that didn't stop until it reached the palisaded walls of New Amsterdam.

Unknown to Director Stuyvesant, the Susquehannock had a mutual defense alliance with New Sweden. His attack on the Swedes was the first domino, and the counter attack by the Susquehannock was the second. The next domino in play was the mutual defense alliance between the Susquehannock and the Munsee, both being closely related Lenape tribes. This too, fell when five hundred Munsee warriors in sixty canoes swept into Manhattan and overwhelmed the city, burning and pillaging houses as they went. Incredibly, no one was killed.

The sachem met with the governing council at Fort Amsterdam and agreed to have their warriors leave in peace at sunset. As the Munsee prepared to leave the island that evening, the Dutch colonist Hendrick van Dyck was wounded by an arrow.

The arrow was clearly in retaliation for the death of a Munsee woman, shot dead by van Dyck shortly before the uprising, and certainly an underlying cause for the initial attack on New Amsterdam. His explanation for the murder was a claim that she was stealing peaches from his orchard.

In a predictable reaction by the bloodthirsty Tienhoven, he ordered a hastily raised citizen militia to open fire on the Munsee. While few were killed on either side, the Munsee crossed the North River and launched attacks on the settlers in Pavonia and on Staten Island. All told, forty colonists were killed and one hundred women and children were taken hostage.

Other raids and attacks spread across the southern half of the colony, carried out by the Munsee, Raritan, Hackensack, Tappan, and other close allies.

* * *

Upon his return to the escalating terror in New Amsterdam and the surrounding villages, Stuyvesant discovered that Tienhoven had once again ignited an unnecessary war with the same bloody results. Enraged, he sent a formal request to his West India Company superiors for Tienhoven's immediate dismissal.

One of Tienhoven's many spies who worked closely with Stuyvesant advised him of the letter. He was in debt, and without his regular pay would be indentured. Between his hand in the death of thousands in the Wilden wars and his relentless corruption issuing arbitrary tariffs on the docks, he was unrivalled as the most hated man in the New Netherlands.

Tienhoven's hatred of van der Donck had grown so great that in his twisted, diseased mind, he imagined van der Donck was behind the letter, using it as an attempt to replace him as the chief schout and administrator of the province. He had spies watching van der Donck at Colen Donck and in Flushing with his mongrel friends and associates, and entertained the idea of arresting him for secretly being involved with politics, in violation of his word given to the States General in the Hague.

But it was van der Donck's success in his personal and social life that Tienhoven truly despised him for. Aware that that kind of success was unreachable at this point in his own life, he reasoned that with enough money he could live a comfortable life of leisure. All he had to do was quietly book passage to Curacao, leaving his home and family behind.

But his syphilitic brain fed his rage and delusion. Convinced van der Donck would execute his diabolical plan and put him in irons, he had no time to waste.

Tienhoven's survival instincts kicked in and his first order of business was money. Under the cover of darkness, he stole into the clerk's office and made several false entries in the book of accounts before sneaking out of the Stadt Huys with four thousand guilders. Intentionally leaving clues that pointed to others who had access to the vault, he figured by the time they traced the theft to him, he would be long gone and living comfortably in the Caribbean.

Chapter 38

Colen Donck

Mary and Adriaen finally felt settled into their new life at Colen Donck. Adriaen could not have endured being in the Netherlands for over three years if Mary had not crossed the ocean to join him, as he advocated tirelessly for the rights of colonials to be equal to those of people living in the homeland.

But now the fields and orchards of Colen Donck were planted and beginning to bear fruit. In the verdant paradise filled with new life, their minds turned toward children, something they very much wanted to share.

They spent the morning on horseback, making their rounds to the far corners of Colen Donck to witness progress on several important projects. The second mill bed and saw blade added by Elias while they were in Europe nearly doubled production and was now paying for the improvements to the manor house in progress.

Mary was particularly keen about the new grist mill, much needed by the farms up the North River from Manhattan. The small percentage of flour they would take in milling fees would be enough to feed the two dozen Dutch and English families already living on the estate, several Siwanoy families that tended their livestock, and the immigrant farmers expected to arrive over the next few years.

Adriaen was elated as they rode across the estate, and his wife and partner Mary, was proud of the courage and determination he had maintained over the years to see his dream come to fruition. He had become a folk hero, and neighbors were already calling the estate Yonkers after his nickname.

* * *

Adriaen sat in front of the fireplace in the late afternoon waiting for Mary to join him.

"A sizeable sum of money has been transferred to our account from revenues generated by your book back in the Netherlands," Mary said as she brought tea and placed it by the fire. "Your work has inspired hundreds of land-starved Dutch farmers to risk everything and come to America. This is all because of you, Adriaen."

"Kind words for someone confessed to love me. The money will help build a second grist mill and my patroonship will continue to prosper long after I'm gone. Yet, in my gut I know that this large estate landlord-tenant farmer model of colonial development will soon outlive its intended purpose. It is my fervent hope for the people who come to these lands, to be governed by fellow citizens who are honest, civil, and fairly elected."

"This current conflict with the natives…"

"Aggravated once again by Tienhoven," Adriaen interjected.

"Yes, Tienhoven. Allow me to read what you wrote about the Wilden in your book, *Description of New Netherland.*"

"*We are beholden to the Natives in the highest, who not only yielded this rich and fertile country, and for a trifle in compensation ceded it to us. It is now our great shame, and fortunate would we be, had we duly acknowledged this good deed, and in return for what the Natives have shared with us, had endeavored to share with them the eternal good, for as much as it is in us. It is to be feared that on the last day they will rise up against us for this injustice.*"

"I fear for these good people, people like Aghar."

"As do I, my darling husband. Your empathy and thoughtfulness are examples for others to follow. I also want to thank you again for your kindness and generosity toward Elias."

"It is an honor to be his brother," Adriaen murmured, pulling her closer.

"And it is an honor to be your wife," she said, walking into his arms as the fire blazed on.

* * *

Tienhoven paid his weekly visit to the makeshift camp of drunks and gamblers north of Colen Donck. Two among them were Wilden from an eastern tribe who had yet to catch on to his sleight of hand and thus were indebted to him for gambling losses.

It occurred to him that the current chaos in the colony would be the perfect cover to dispense some very personal retribution, and agreed to waive their gambling debts in exchange for a favor. One they were certainly capable of delivering.

* * *

Tienhoven's two native accomplices, disguised to look like Munsee warriors, rode down river to Colen Donck and quietly tied their horses in the thick woods near the manor house.

Under cover of a black, moonless sky, they crept closer to the manor, following the glow of the firelight that spilled out from the new glass windows.

Part Nine
(Present Day - New York)

Chapter 39

Lower Manhattan

In late afternoon, the fire alarm sounded, sending everyone toward the marble staircases leading to the exit in the main lobby. Men in expensive suits, some still chewing their gourmet lunch from the exclusive club restaurant, poured onto the sidewalks of lower Manhattan.

As if on cue, rain began to fall, casting a gray pall over the streets. The emergency response team from the NYFD was there within minutes. As firefighters streamed into the building and began meticulously clearing each floor, several Confederation members huddled under the entry canopy of the neighboring bistro, unsuccessfully trying to stay dry.

Without warning, one of them stopped talking mid-sentence before collapsing on the sidewalk.

Blood seeped from a small hole on the side of his temple. Simultaneously, they heard someone in the crowd shout *ACTIVE SHOOTER!*

Panic rippled through the crowded street. People scrambled for cover, trampling each other as they sought safety behind cars and recessed entry ways. Taking advantage of the chaos, a lone man pulled up the hood of his raincoat, merged with the crowd and ran toward the man lying face up in the rain. As if confirming he was dead, the runner bent over the body for a moment before he turned and disappeared down the crowded street.

* * *

Sharky's telltale ring tone began buzzing on Martin's cell.

"What've you got for me?" she asked from the desk in her hotel room in Kingston, where she was preparing for tomorrow's historic bill signing event.

"Got a call from Lucius Fletcher, my NYPD liaison."

"I've met him. Good man."

"He received a report of a shooting from the First Precinct. A man named Gaston Grimes was murdered in front of a private club in lower Manhattan a few hours ago."

"And we need to know this because?"

"The last inter-agency bulletin we issued requested all departments to be on the lookout for any phone number on our shortlist of suspect calls."

"And?"

"The phone number of the burner found on the body of Grimes is on that list."

"Compliment Lucius for me. We need to find out everything there is about Grimes. This should help connect some of the dots in our investigation back to those in charge."

"There's more. One of the most recent numbers called on the phone is also on the list."

"OK. Have your guys make it a priority to track the movements of the two phones with those numbers."

"Hold on. I'm not finished. A delivery runner left a package addressed to Grimes with the receptionist in the main entry lobby of ORC headquarters shortly before the fire alarms went off. We presume it was sent by the killer."

"That's brazen."

"The package contained a handful of incriminating photos of Grimes engaged in lewd sexual acts with minors, apparently going back years."

"Could this get any creepier?"

"One last thing," Sharky added. "I just received the green light from Sydney Rogers' neurosurgeon, so I'm heading down to Brooklyn Methodist to interview her. I've got the sketch Garrison did in case we're dealing with the same guy."

"Has the facial recognition team made any progress on Will's sketch?"

"They said they'll have a few possible matches to me before I reach the hospital."

"Excellent work."

* * *

In support of Martin's taskforce, Albert asked a friend and former associate in British Intelligence to research the Cyprus bank account that had been paying for the services of Drexler and Strong. Reporting back as Albert approached Kingston, he identified the bank as one suspected of laundering billions of dollars for a consortium of wealthy families in the gas fracking business. The funds had been managed by the recently deceased American banker, Gaston Grimes.

As soon as a direct connection between Grimes and Drexler was established, Martin ordered her taskforce to make a deep dive into Grimes' past, starting with his relationship with Drexler and his apparent penchant for pedophilia. She also wanted to know more about the private club he had been in just before he was murdered.

Regarding the shooter, Martin's initial gut feeling pointed to Rybak. The street cams on the block where the shooting occurred were inconclusive, although a hooded man of Rybak's height passed close to the body lying on the sidewalk before vanishing out of sight. At the moment, she was looking upstream for bigger fish. Rybak would have to be NYPD's problem for the time being.

* * *

The relationship between Gaston Grimes and Byron Bragg went back years, becoming friends during an exotic Caribbean junket sponsored by some of their highly secretive international banking clients. Bragg was shaken by the news that photos of Grimes sexual proclivities were delivered to the Originalist Confederation reception desk, most likely by the killer himself. He'd heard rumors over the years of an old KGB blackmail racket, now run by the SFB, and prayed it wouldn't find its way to him.

He scowled as he assessed his exposure to Grimes and the assassination plot. Other than his membership in the Confederation, the weakest link was his association with Dell Thatcher and indirectly, his idiot subordinate. He needed to bring Thatcher in for a grave discussion about his future.

Bragg had no shortage of people on a string when he needed muscle. But this would have to wait until Thatcher returned from his assignment upstate at the governor's town hall meeting.

Chapter 40

Garrison Farm – Esopus Creek

Kari was there to greet Will and Annah when they drove down the long gravel driveway at the old Garrison farmhouse. He was not alone. Will broke into a childlike, ear-to-ear grin when he saw Mary Lou standing beside him.

The road trip up the Hudson had been enjoyable, other than being tailed by the mysterious orange vehicle, the hotel break-in at Beacon, and having someone rifle through the Beetle, but they were happy to be at the farm, which had become their emotional refuge. Annah was already fascinated with the Dutch colonial history in her homeland on the Malabar Coast of India, and now her interest extended to the old Dutch colony of the New Netherlands, now the State of New York.

Impressed with the fundamental contributions they had made to the freedoms Americans still held sacred, she was also grateful to Will's Dutch ancestors. Without them, her friend, lover, and partner would not be by her side.

"Welcome home," Kari said as he opened the passenger door of the Beetle.

Annah untangled herself from her laptop and purse and stepped out of the low-slung car. Her first order of business was to give him a big hug, like she used to hug Thomma. He had a solidness and conviction that reminded her of her brother, who had been lost at the hands of the

Taliban. She'd seen how religious zealotry and bigotry had torn people apart who had once lived peacefully side by side in Asia. She was sickened by reports of this same kind of intolerance and extremism being condoned and promoted by a growing number of American political figures.

"Kari, you're a sight for sore eyes," she said, surprised by the emotion that stirred in her.

"As long as I'm not making your eyes sore?"

Annah chuckled. "Never, my friend."

She turned to find Will already standing next to Mary Lou.

"How's my girl," Will asked, stroking her ears.

The gentle horse reciprocated by nibbling at his hair. Already emotional, their tender greeting brought tears to Annah's eyes.

* * *

Will took Mary Lou for a short ride through the woods while Kari helped Annah bring their luggage and groceries into the old house. She had planned to make curry, and invited Kari to stay for dinner. He sat at the kitchen table as she started to cook and filled her in on the new developments around the farm.

"We have a new family of bobcats living down by the river. They will help keep the rabbits and racoons in check."

"Won't they kill them all?" Annah asked with concern.

"They will eat a few, but mostly they keep them on the move, which helps stabilize the population."

"Well, that makes it sound better," she teased. "Where by the river? I'd like to keep a lookout for them."

"Near the old burial site."

* * *

Down the river trail, Will let Mary Lou mosey and enjoy an occasional mouthful of new grass.

"That'll make your breath nice and fresh, beautiful girl," he said as he stroked her neck.

His heart was lighter when riding Mary Lou. Being partners with such a magnificent being revived his sense of wonder, and he saw the natural world surrounding them differently. He felt his body relax, and soon his mind followed as they approached the banks of the Esopus.

He dismounted near the river and sat on a large rock watching red and orange leaves the size of his hands slowly float over the reflection of the sky. Looking above him, the tree canopy was in its full Autumn display of colors.

Relaxed and in harmony with the sound of the river and woods, he began to drift off as he leaned against the river bank. Moments after he closed his eyes, he was shaken from the lure of sleep by Mary Lou, who reared up and stomped her front hooves on the ground, raising a small cloud of dust. She stepped closer and gave Will a firm nudge with her muzzle.

Looking around he realized they were just downstream from the grassy hollow he and Annah had fallen asleep in. He sat up and looked around for anything that might have spooked her.

He followed Mary Lou's gaze into the deep shadows of the woods. Filtered afternoon light barely made its way to the leaf covered ground, and the only movement he could discern was two hummingbirds darting through the dense branches.

About to turn away, something in the undergrowth caught his eye. There was a slight movement, and then a pair of eyes appeared in the shadows only for an instant, and then they were gone. Will reasoned it was some kind of harmless woodland animal, but nonetheless, he was ready to move on.

"Well girl, shall we get going?"

Mary Lou looked at him with dark eyes and struck the ground with her right hoof.

"What have you got, girl?"

She nodded and took a few steps forward.

Her behavior was puzzling, but he was inclined to let her express herself.

Will mimicked her, taking a few steps beyond her in the same direction. He turned and looked at Mary Lou. "This way?"

She walked up next to Will and snorted as she lowered her head. They were standing at the edge of a clearing, facing an ancient witch-hazel tree. Usually a large shrub, it was nearly as big as a dogwood. Mary Lou relaxed her neck and looked toward the ground. Will followed suit. If not for its distinctive violet blue color, he would not have noticed the object jutting out of a recently eroded rivulet passing between his feet and the trunk of the old tree.

"What do we have here?" he asked, squatting down to get a closer look. Mary Lou snorted.

His scientific training kicked in. Taking his phone out of his jacket, he began documenting Mary Lou's discovery by taking a series of detailed photos.

Using a small twig broken off the witch-hazel tree, he began carefully removing the soil that had encased what appeared to be a small box. As he came closer to freeing the artifact from the ground, a small piece of the blue stained earthen crust broke away from the box, revealing a finely etched brass surface.

* * *

Annah and Kari were about to sit down for a plate of curry when Will entered through the kitchen door, holding something gently in his cupped hands.

"I thought I was going to have to send out a search party for you.

What have you got there?" Annah asked.

"A box," he said with childlike simplicity, delicately setting it down on the kitchen towel lying on the corner of the table.

She smiled and patiently waited until he was ready to continue.

"Looks like a very old brass tinderbox or keepsake box," Will answered.

"Did you open it?" she asked.

"Trick question? Of course not, I'm waiting for a certified archeological preservationist. You know any?"

"And the site?"

"Fully documented with photographs."

Annah couldn't wait. Taking a few quick bites of her curry before it got cold, she put her spoon down and left to get her tool kit.

Will took additional pictures with his macro lens as she painstakingly began removing the violet blue crust, periodically spraying a small amount of distilled water to help lift the corrosion.

Kari looked on in fascination while managing to finish his plate of Annah's curry and rice.

"Now that's Indian food," he said emphatically, making Annah giggle at the clever irony of his statement. Will, too engrossed in the object, seemed miles away.

Nearly an hour passed as Annah worked her magic. Will and Kari filled the time speculating about the age and purpose of the box, logging onto museum and antique sites. They were confronted by a barrage of old brass boxes.

With a section of the etched image now visible, it struck Will as Dutch in style.

"Are those breasts?" Annah asked, handing the magnifying glass to Will.

"Are those nipples?" he replied, handing it back to her.

"What is this, early American porn?" Kari asked. This time, Will chuckled.

With a bit more cleaning it became clear they were looking at the half naked female figurehead of a sailing ship. The image was a finely engraved vignette of a ship's bow sailing toward you in perspective. The name of the ship, *de Statyn*, was etched on the gunwale behind her.

"I know this ship from Theron's translations."

Will's excitement turned into impatience several minutes later. "Are we ready to open it?"

"A few tiny drops of non-staining preservation grade oil and we'll give it a try."

Annah took out her thin edged hardwood palette knife and gently pried at the latch and joint between the box and lid.

"Don't want to break these old hinges," she whispered to herself, feeling her way like a safe cracker.

The latch was finally loose and with a gentle twist of her blade, the lid opened.

* * *

Night was falling and the fire-light danced up the trunks of the tall maple and oak trees around a small clearing in the forest not far from Kari's corral.

"As soon as I saw the contents of the brass box, I knew we must come to my Kanonhsa, and take council from the elders."

"Kanonhsa?" Will was not familiar with the word.

"Yes, that is what my grandfather called his sweat lodge," he answered as he placed more rocks around the blazing campfire situated directly east of the lodge entry. "I built this lodge exactly as he taught me."

"And what about your father?" Annah ventured.

"I'm afraid he died in the first Gulf War when I was a young boy, before he had a chance to reconnect with the old ways.

"I'm sorry to hear that."

"It no longer saddens me. I have come to see that it was his destiny. I still honor the medals awarded to him for bravery and keep them in a special box. I was reminded of him by the contents of the brass box. I'm guessing they also belonged to a brave warrior."

While the rocks surrounding the blazing fire were super heating, Kari took a sage stick and large feather from his shoulder pouch.

"This box contains powerful medicine. We must prepare ourselves in order to access it respectfully, and to protect ourselves from any dark forces."

He lit the sage and began smudging Annah and Will, bathing each in turn from head to toe with the ethereal white smoke, while brushing them with the feather.

Breathing the sage instantly put Will into a calm and meditative state, as it typically did. Burning sage had become part of his and Annah's morning coffee ritual on the front porch. He had come to believe the smoke of the sage had an awakening property, one that broadcast your empathy and highest intentions to the benefit of others.

"Drink this," Kari said, offering them each a small tin cup of tea. "It will keep you hydrated and help you release any mental blocks you might have."

Annah exchanged a quick look with Will before drinking it down.

Once Kari was satisfied that the rocks were sufficiently hot, he gave Will a forked wooden stick and showed him how to pick them up and pass them through the entry of the sweat lodge. From there, Kari would take them with his own stick and carefully place them in a round depression at the center of the space.

Once everything was properly arranged inside the sweat lodge, Kari called to Will and Annah. They were to crawl in and close the flap tight behind them before taking their places.

With the light from a very small candle, Kari took a braid of sweetgrass that had been soaking in a small pitcher of water, and laid it over the hot rocks. The effect was immediate, transforming the lodge into an unearthly place with its vision-evoking aroma. It vaguely reminded Will of the smell of root beer or sassafras, but sweeter and much more delicate.

Kari placed the brass box, thoroughly cleaned before being brought inside, on the earthen floor in front of his crossed legs.

"Before we ask the spirits to give us more information about this box and its contents, we must cleanse each of the four essential facets of our being and bring them into balance," Kari said in a low voice, "those being our physical, spiritual, emotional and mental bodies."

"Not unlike the chakras we know of in India," Annah reflected.

"Similar, as both are manifestations of traditional knowledge developed in the far distant past. We also know of poorly conceived New Age imitations of this ancient practice that have gone tragically wrong. The sage and feather cleanse your physical body. The sweat lodge will cleanse the spiritual and emotional."

"And the mental?"

"Yes Will, the mental body is almost always our greatest challenge."

"Dirty minds?" Will jested, quickly wishing he hadn't said it.

Kari sensed his regret and responded. "Humor is good. It helps loosen a constipated mind filled with all kinds of conventional wisdom that is anything but wise."

"Meditation always helps put my overly active mental body into a more cooperative state," Annah added.

"That is true. Meditation can be very cleansing. Now, we will sit in silence until our minds are at rest." Kari laid another braid of sweetgrass on the rocks.

* * *

Time seemed to stand still, and Kari waited patiently until everyone's breathing was deep and slow.

"Did we find the balance?" he asked.

Now covered in sweat, Will and Annah nodded in agreement.

To the rhythm of a small rattle, Kari began to softly sing a mesmerizing melody in his native tongue.

Annah immediately felt the healing effect of the atmosphere on her emotional body. Her anxiety and worries seemed to melt away. What she wasn't sure of was her spiritual body. She and Will had been running at a fast clip since the day they left Kerala for Afghanistan, now nearly two years ago. She hadn't taken the time to look deeply at her own spirituality, although she could feel it was stronger than ever.

Will was experiencing waves of emotion. An image of Mary Lou appeared and his eyes filled with tears, not of fear, but of joy. As that image faded, Annah's face came into focus. He felt the full depth of their connection, and their unshakable trust in each other. She knew him as well as he knew himself.

Kari's deep voice cut through the warm heavy atmosphere. "Are we ready to open the box for the elders to examine?"

Annah nodded her agreement, and Will, who felt he was as balanced as he was going to get, did as well.

The finely crafted brass box, tarnished and discolored from years in the ground, opened smoothly for Kari due to Annah's fine work. One by one, he laid its contents on a patterned white bandana.

The first item was a flint knife blade, still sharper than the edge of a broken piece of glass, followed by a kaswentha, a double strand wampum belt made of the finest purple quahog shell Kari had ever seen. The remaining items included several gold coins and a small pocket compass of exquisite design, each described in detail as he laid them in a circle.

Kari's voice faded into the background as Will slowly opened his eyes in the dim light. Curiously, Annah's face had become that of a deer, however he recognized her dark, empathetic eyes and long lashes.

About to comment, Will stopped with a word half formed in his mouth. Like Annah, Kari's face had also changed, but his was more formidable and bear-like.

Reality was becoming more fluid. Will fought the urge to leave the sweat lodge, managing to calm his mind and suspend judgement until the visions passed. The moment he decided to let them become whatever they needed to be, regardless of logic or conventional wisdom, the surrounding environment transformed into a winter's day.

The irony of feeling cold in a sweat lodge did not escape him. As he laughed out loud, he saw two men approaching, both taking long strides over a frozen river. One was dressed in high boots, a green cloak, and a wide brim hat common to early Dutch settlers. The other was dressed in the style of a Mohawk chief, wearing a fur-lined buckskin coat with a lightly feathered fur cap crowning his aged and wizened face.

They greeted Will in English, one with a Dutch accent, the other sounding curiously like Kari, but older.

"Didn't I see you at the dock on Mill Creek?" the Dutch gentleman asked.

"Was that you?"

"Visions are tricky business," added the Mohawk chief.

"Are you one of the elders Kari spoke of?" Will asked.

"Perhaps. I advocate for nature. The oceans and the skies of our planet, the mother of all life, are turning against people. Many plants and animals are suffering because of this, at no fault of their own. This is a mounting debt that humanity must pay."

"I agree."

"People are consumed by their differences, mostly religious in nature, while the efforts of their higher spiritual selves are desperately needed by the planet, and all of our children."

"Yes! People need the freedom to believe or not believe according to their conscience, and a governing system of the people that respects those differences."

"Well spoken, as are the words of your governor," the old man said. "She is standing at a pivotal point between two possible futures, one based on greed, fear, retribution, and religious strife; the other governed by generosity, empathy, tolerance, and an unequivocal freedom of conscience for all people."

The elder looked deeply into Will eyes. With genuine concern, he said, "We have come to warn you that she is in imminent danger. No more than that can we say."

Chapter 41

Hello Mary Lou, Goodbye H…

The moon brightly lit the treetops and barn roof as Will and Annah emerged from the woods into the old barnyard. They were still shrouded in the blankets Kari had wrapped them in after their sweat.

On their walk back from the lodge, the chilled night air helped return them to the present. Neither had yet attempted to describe their experiences.

"Annah, why don't you go on inside and warm up some dinner, while I bed down Mary Lou for the night."

"Are you sure you don't want help?"

"No, I won't be long. Some food and fresh water, a few strolls around the barnyard, and she'll be good. Oh yeh, and a few shovels full of horse droppings."

"Makes the best compost," she chuckled, turning toward the back door to the kitchen.

* * *

Her familiar whinny was that of an old friend. He brought May Lou out of her stall and led her on a loose leader around the barnyard. Her eyes sparkled in the moonlight with an ancient awareness often seen in horses.

On their third lap around the yard, she suddenly stopped and looked into the woods.

"What is it, girl?" He followed her gaze. Seeing nothing unusual, Will assumed it was a racoon or some other forest creature foraging in the shadows.

Mary Lou hesitated for a moment before cautiously following him into the barn. She stood beside the stall gate as she normally did, while Will cleaned and refreshed her sawdust bedding, and filled her feed buckets.

But it was clear to Will that something had disturbed her.

"You're starting to spook me now, old girl," he said, gently stroking her muzzle. "I'll just get some fresh water and you'll be all set."

Will picked up her bucket and headed to the water trough. Dipping it in the water dappled in moonlight, he was caught unaware as an arm wrapped tightly around his neck.

Instinctively, he twisted his body and fell backward over the trough, drenching his assailant beneath him. Slipping away from the dark form now struggling to get out of the trough, he ran toward the barn, intent on grabbing the first sharp tool he could find.

Reaching for an old shovel leaning against the stall, he was slammed into the barn wall as the perpetrator went for his neck a second time.

With the grip on his neck tightening, Will grabbed the man's arms for leverage and lifted both feet off the ground. Swinging them up, he pushed off the barn wall, sending both men to the ground.

Will scrambled to his feet. His assailant rolled over, and in the faint light, he could see the reflection of the man's gun barrel as he pulled it out of his belt. Will saw Annah's face flash in front of him, and he felt the weight of not being able to say goodbye.

As the assailant raised his gun, there was a sudden movement to his right. Will saw the blur of a tail, then as quick as lightning, Mary Lou kicked.

In slow motion, Will watched the man's body fly across the barn and land on an old rusted plowshare, severing his head from his body.

* * *

The disembodied head looked up at him with dead eyes. It was the face he had sketched for Martin at the hotel in Beacon. The authorities later found his orange Land Rover pulled off on a nearby dirt road.

Chapter 42

Kingston, New York

As the crime scene investigators wrapped up, the police suggested Will and Annah find another place to sleep for the night. True to form, Will handled the trauma with humor, glad they had not arrested Mary Lou, even though the deceased clearly had a perfect match of her hoof prints on his side.

At Martin's urging, Will and Annah drove into Kingston and checked into a hotel in the historic stockade district. They were a few blocks away from the small cottage hotel where Martin was staying. Both hotels were only a short walk from the Old Senate House, where Governor Tess Hendriksen was expected to sign her tax reform bill into law later that day.

Their hotel was an adaptive restoration of a landmark bank building, and the room was spacious. Annah wasted no time throwing herself onto the king- sized bed.

"I need to get to sleep before the sun comes up, especially if we are going to make an appearance with the governor this afternoon."

"No problem. I'll just block the homicidal maniac who tried to kill me out of my thoughts," he said, leaning over to kiss her goodnight.

* * *

Kingston was an important city in colonial American history, originally known as Esopus by the native American tribe living there, and later Wiltwyck by the early Dutch settlers of New Netherlands. It was strategically located halfway between Manhattan and Fort Orange, with abundant fresh water and natural defenses.

It was during those years that the Dutch colonial director had a large wooden stockade built in Wiltwyck to fend off a potential British invasion. It's footprint, with centuries of changes, still gave shape to today's historic district.

The Old Senate House was part of a museum enclave of historic buildings surrounding a grassy, neatly mowed commons. The room where the governor would be holding her signing event already held a special place in New York history. The first constitution of the former colony, now the rebellious State of New York, was signed in that very same room in the face of the massive British military occupation of New York City in 1777.

Security had been heightened at all of the governor's events since the bombing, even more so in Kingston after it was made public that the signing would be televised.

* * *

Thatcher was on his way out of the final security deployment and perimeter strategy meeting when Burle Strong walked up beside him.

"I have something you need to see," Strong said, guiding him toward the sidewalk at the edge of the grassy commons.

"We shouldn't be seen together, especially here of all places."

A large Lincoln Navigator pulled up and made an abrupt stop at the curb directly in front of them.

"You should get in. No one can see us with the tinted windows."

Afraid of being spotted, Thatcher climbed into the back of the SUV without question.

"When was the last time you spoke to your man, Helms?" Strong snarled.

"Have you lost your head? What the fuck is going on?"

"Strange choice of words," Strong said, handing a photograph to him.

"What is this?" Thatcher barked, as his eyes tried to make sense of what he was looking at.

It took several moments for his brain to register the image, but as recognition set in, he looked up in horror.

"That's right," Strong said, "It's Clovis Helms, or more specifically, his head."

* * *

Strong was expecting a call from Daggert giving them the final green light, which came as the 9:00 am bells on the Old Dutch Church started to ring.

Although their conversations were always veiled, Strong was never unclear as to his meaning.

"Yo," Strong answered, always avoiding names.

"This needs to be clean," Daggert said. "Not like the last one,"

"One professional, one patsy."

"Right, the lone psycho. He needs to leave fingerprints on the web."

"I've already planted enough on him and his girlfriend over at the AG's office to establish his instability and growing paranoia," Strong reassured.

"With Grimes getting hit on our front steps, things are getting too close to home. Your patsy, is it that guy from security we were looking at?"

"Afraid not. He lost his head in some barn not far from here."

"So, who then?"

"Better you don't know, but I'm certain they'll draw suspicion away from the Confederation."

* * *

Security was tight around the Senate House. As the governor's media team did their last sound and camera check in preparation for her anticipated arrival, Albert got a ping from Strongman's burner phone. He was in the Kingston area, too much of a coincidence to ignore.

Albert headed for the main entry, where Martin was going through the final checklist with her FBI SWAT team. He alerted her to Strong's presence in Kingston and warned that their radios might have been compromised.

"Don't mention anything about Strong over the earpiece. I'll be back as soon as I can," Albert said as he left the Senate House to continue tracking the location of the suspect's phone.

As she watched Albert walk away, Martin's phone buzzed. It was Sharky.

"We've identified the head. His name was Clovis Helms."

"Isn't he connected to Thatcher?" Martin asked.

"Yep, his direct supervisor. Apparently, Helms was one of the operatives he used for special missions. This guy already had a pretty sketchy past when Thatcher brought him over from the State Police."

"I need to see Thatcher. Find him." Martin hung up and called Albert.

After updating him about the head and his connection to Dell Thatcher, she did a quick search of the Senate House and the museum commons but he was nowhere to be found. As the person in charge of the Governor's security team, it was unthinkable on such a security intensive day.

She thought back and realized she hadn't seen him since the morning security meeting. The twisting in her gut told her something was very wrong.

* * *

The press had been gathering all day and media trucks were lined up on Clinton Avenue on the north side of the museum commons. Only members of the press with special passes were allowed inside the old Senate

House meeting room.

As they entered with the press, Will and Annah couldn't believe their good fortune to have seats in the limited guest area during such an auspicious occasion. Annah felt Will's grip on her hand tighten in anticipation.

They were greeted by the governor who sat stoically behind the same long maple table where the New York State Constitution had been signed two and a half centuries before. Just as the founders of the state were on a quest for liberty, willing to risk everything to free themselves from beliefs imposed on them by others, she felt much the same about her tax reform bill, certain it would lessen the growing tyranny of certain religious based groups over matters of individual conscience for the majority of citizens.

The lighting and camera crew from the governor's advance team signaled they were ready. A hush passed over the room as Governor Hendriksen flipped on the microphone in front of her.

"Freedom of Conscience is an inherent right for all of us," she said, breaking the silence. Every camera was trained on her.

"The signing of this new law marks the day when no one person or group will, because of their religious beliefs, receive better treatment under the tax code than anyone else, regardless of what they believe, or if they believe.

"This law restores a right established nearly four hundred years ago when this land was part of the New Netherlands, passed down through English and American law by virtue of the Flushing Remonstrance, and the Treaty of Capitulation between British Admiral Nicolls and the Dutch Provincial Director Stuyvesant, on September 29, 1664.

"The new tax code places equal responsibility on every citizen and organization to support *We the People* in the performance of our sacred duty."

She raised the first of seven pens and began signing her name as required by the state constitution.

The sound of cameras clicking broke the silence in the room as the press core documented the historic moment. Out of the corner of his eye, Will saw a bright flash of light outside the window to his right. Turning his head, he saw the sun reflecting off a rifle scope.

"Gunman!" Will shouted into the crowded room as he pulled Annah to the floor. The warning he had received in the sweat lodge screamed in his head.

In an instant, the solemn room turned into chaos. A bullet shattered the upper pane of the large double hung window as people ran for cover. The governor's bodyguard dove across the temporary stage, knocking her off the chair, narrowly missing the bullet that pierced her arm. In a split second. Martin was crouched beside her with her gun drawn.

"Are you okay?" Martin asked, noticing the blood starting to pool on the floor.

"My arm. It's just my arm. Is anyone else hurt?"

"Not that I know of. My team is combing the commons and other buildings, looking for any trace of the gunman. It looks like the bullet came from a rooftop or a second story window. Stay put and a paramedic will be here soon."

* * *

Due to the twenty second tape delay on the live broadcast, the public did not see Tess sign the first copy of the bill before the feed was cut directly after the shooting.

Watching the signing live on cable news from his Manhattan office, Daggert was eager to celebrate their success, but not until he got a confirmation call from Burle Strong. As he waited impatiently, several sketchy reports came out of Kingston about the shooting and the ongoing search for the gunman. Still, no word from Strong.

Frustrated, he hit redial on his phone. It went directly to voice mail.

"Goddamn it!"

* * *

The man's body was found on the rooftop of a neighboring building. Albert took in the scene as he walked toward the body, carefully stepping around a gun case containing parts of a partially broken-down sniper's rifle. It was startling to see the sniper clutching his chest in a fetal position as if he'd suffered a heart attack, but even more so when Albert saw his face. It was the governor's chief of security, Dell Thatcher.

"The perfect patsy," Albert said under his breath. There was only one problem. Someone hadn't considered the astronomical odds against both he and his flunky, Helms, dying on the same day.

* * *

It was hours before the site was cleared by the FBI. No one else had been shot, and the nasty flesh wound on Tess's left arm had been bandaged.

"Set up the mics and cameras. We're going to finish what we started,"

Her assistant's suggestion to find a jacket to put over her blood-stained shirt was roundly rejected as she strode back to the long maple table.

As the cameras began to roll, the country watched the original footage of the first signing hours after it had taken place, due to tape delay. This was immediately followed by the Governor, now covered in blood, signing the remaining six documents into law.

Phones started ringing on editorial desks across the nation.

Part Ten
(Year 1656 - New Amsterdam)

Chapter 43

Consorting with "The Devil"

Tienhoven entered the darkest phase of his life. He had been a drunk and compulsive gambler for a long time, and now he was also a murderer and a thief.

Stuyvesant returned from his battle with the Swedish colony on the South River, now known as the Delaware by the English, only to discover a gross shortage of revenue in the treasury. Large sums of silver had been embezzled and the books altered to conceal the theft.

Clues pointing to others in his administration seemed contrived and Stuyvesant had little doubt who it was. Tienhoven was summoned to appear before him but could not be found. Even the men known to be his spies admitted they had not seen him for several days, perhaps a week or more. Rumor had it that he had gone north on official schout business, but none of them were certain of his actual destination.

Stuyvesant was livid and sent three soldiers to bring him in for questioning. They checked with the northbound traders on the lower stretch of the North River, and in several small settlements along the river roads to Fort Orange, but no one could confirm seeing him.

The Wilden hated Tienhoven but were reluctant to share information with the Dutch soldiers. The only information given was that he had been seen up near the white plains at the marshy headwaters of the Bronx River earlier that year, gambling and defiling the native women.

* * *

Elias Doughty made an oath to his sister, Mary. He would find Adriaen's murderer and make sure justice was done, the same oath given by close friend Tobias Feake who was now the chief law enforcement officer of Flushing.

The initial report by the Dutch soldiers who first arrived at the manor pointed to a marauding band of Munsee warriors from across the North River. Their proof was a Munsee war club, but according to Mary's recollection of the moments before she was knocked unconscious, the war paint on their faces and weapons looked familiar, more the colors used by the neighboring Siwanoys to the east.

Feake wasn't satisfied with their report either. The evidence sounded as though it had been staged by the killers to send the investigation in the wrong direction. He decided that the attack on Colen Donck was his crime to investigate, seeing that Adriaen and Mary were also residents living in his Flushing jurisdiction.

Elias did not believe the Munsee theory either, and suspected it was the work of Tienhoven. While caring for Colen Donck in Adriaen and Mary's absence, he had observed Tienhoven making weekly pilgrimages upriver in the direction of the Wilden camps. He followed his hunch and went up to the main village in the white plains to find out what those secret excursions were all about. Tobias insisted on going with him.

* * *

They ferried across the East River with their horses and debarked at the Bronx River trail. Both men were armed with pistol, sword and musket as they rode past several new working plantations and orchards where the harvest was being brought in.

After a thorough search of Colen Donck manor, they carefully wrapped and labeled the eagle feathers lying on the floor, and the strips of white cloth used to take samples of the warpaint found on the door.

They continued upriver beyond the Colen Donck fork, toward the higher ground at the white plains. The trail narrowed as it wove its way around massive trees in the primordial forest. Deep in Siwanoy country, they were now beyond the last Dutch farmstead.

Approaching the source of the river, the trail meandered through a labyrinth of small ponds and marshland, all blanketed with a fine white mist floating several feet above the ground. At times the trail disappeared altogether into the misty swamp, but their horses instinctively recognized the path travelled by other men on horses over the decades. They found their way to solid ground without incident.

Elias was the first to smell the campfires of a small Siwanoy village. They rode for another quarter mile before the swamp trail opened on to a large grassy clearing filled with children playing as their mothers industriously prepared food and made clothing. A few men remained in camp helping with the work while the others were out hunting.

The two riders dismounted and were approached by Katonuk, the village sagamore, a man with considerable status based on the feathers adorning his long braided gray hair. He greeted them in well spoken English, likely learned from time spent in the area near Greenwich where the English had a strong foothold.

Katonuk had a stern yet kind demeanor, and Elias took an immediate liking to him. They sat in his wigwam for hours exchanging news and stories about their people. When Tobias finally brought up the name Tienhoven, Katonuk recoiled with disgust.

"That devil is not welcome in our village."

"We understand, and suspect he may have been behind the murder of Adriaen van der Donck," Tobias said.

"I have known Adriaen for many years. It saddens my heart that he is gone," Katonuk lamented. "Do you have proof?"

"We believe that his murder was committed by two Wilden, made to look like they were Munsee from the west."

"And who do you believe they were?"

"Mary Doughty, who is quite a good artist, believes their warpaint was the colors of the Siwanoy, not Munsee."

"Dear Mary. She is also a friend of my people."

"So, we are on the lookout for a couple of Siwanoy who may have gambled and drank with Tienhoven, possibly in his debt. Perhaps Adriaen's murder was in repayment for wampum they were likely cheated out of."

"There is a place back in the swamps where several Siwanoy men are camped, men who have been banned from the village for drinking and gambling. I know they have consorted with that same devil.

* * *

They traveled deeper into the swamp on foot, scrambling to keep up with Katonuk. The trail came to a stream which they crossed using a large fallen maple tree as a bridge.

Katonuk signaled to walk silently just as the faint smell of cooking meat drifted by. Elias noticed a broken rum barrel floating in the swamp water, nearly invisible in the mist.

"Let me approach first," Katonuk whispered as they heard the muffled sound of a voice ahead.

In shadows of the tall thin trees, the old chief guided them forward. As they approached, they heard a woman sobbing as she prayed aloud.

The old chief walked slowly into the clearing of a shabby makeshift wigwam, where an older woman sat on the ground between two lifeless bodies. Katonuk recognized both of the Siwanoy men.

"Are these your sons?" he asked with compassion.

She nodded, and spoke to him in her native tongue.

"These are her sons. Both were shot in the back at close range. Their bodies smell like they were drunk when it happened."

"Does she know who did this?"

Katonuk spoke again to her quietly. The only word they heard her say was *Manetuwak*.

The old chief turned to them and translated.

"She said it was the devil."

* * *

Elias Doughty and Tobias Feake left the white plains and rode to Manhattan Island by way of the road to the Spuyten Duyvil ferry. It was on the ferry that they encountered a platoon of Stuyvesant's soldiers on their way back from Wiltwyck, bound for New Amsterdam.

Overhearing two of them, they learned that the treasury was forty thousand guilders short and that Tienhoven was wanted for questioning. The walls were closing in on Cornelis van Tienhoven.

But he was a sly manipulator to the end. His younger brother, Adriaen van Tienhoven, also employed by the West India Company, had agreed to find his brother passage on a Caribbean bound trader as soon as possible. With rumors flying about his brother's ill deeds, he too vanished that fateful night.

Tienhoven had been hiding in the shrubs near a prearranged point on the banks of the North River. In the depths of the night, he watched as his brother approached on a small shore boat under a brilliant moon. Overly anxious to reach the ship that would sail him to his new life, he had forgotten that the daily influx tide always came with the full moon.

He shouldered his silver laden bag and made his way down to the water's edge, ready to hop onboard. Down river, a large tidal surge rose in the inner bay, spawning a wave that gained strength as it sped past New Amsterdam at the southern tip of Manhattan Island, heading north.

As Tienhoven's brother neared the shore, the wave, now at the height of five feet, lifted the dinghy like a toy boat. It swept Tienhoven into the current, knocking his hat and cane from his grip before taking him and his sack of silver to the bottom.

Chapter 44

Flushing, Long Island 1656

Hannah Feake, first cousin of Tobias Feake, announced her engagement to John Bowne. She had been corresponding with several Quakers in Providence and back in England, and planned to announce her new affiliation to her friends and neighbors in Flushing at the wedding.

The open display of tolerance by the populace of Flushing, gave the village a reputation that attracted people from diverse spiritual backgrounds. Stuyvesant kept a close watch on the spread of these heretical ideas, tracking it mostly through agents he inherited from Tienhoven's old spy network. He was on the lookout for anyone violating his edict that forbade any religious group from meeting without a minister, appointed by himself, being present.

Stuyvesant's pride and stature had been injured several years earlier when the Dutch West India Company ordered him to be lenient with Lutherans, as three of the company's directors were members. But he took their urging to handle matters locally as freedom to deal with other heretics as he saw fit, as long as it didn't raise issues with the directors.

Soon his theory was tested. A large influx of Jews from Brazil arrived in New Amsterdam by ship after the Dutch surrendered their claim to the Portuguese. Stuyvesant refused to let the Jewish immigrants stay in the New Netherlands, arguing that if the blasphemous Jews were allowed to stay, soon the likes of Roman Catholics and other minority religions would emigrate to the province. Unaware that several board members were Jews, he was slapped down a second time.

He was now facing a new crisis. There were reports of Quakers landing on Long Island and openly espousing their corrupt beliefs in public. To make matters worse, most of this was being done without objection from the most prominent citizens.

Stuyvesant considered their belief in a "priesthood of believers" to be total anarchy, and posted a new edict forbidding anyone in the province from entertaining a Quaker, or allowing a gathering of Quakers in their homes.

* * *

The wedding of Hannah Feake and John Bowne was the perfect opportunity for Stuyvesant's spies to find out more about the fringe religions cropping up in Flushing. Each of them reported a good deal of talk about freedom of conscience and their admiration of the new liberties women were being given in the Providence Plantations of Rhode Island.

Stuyvesant believed the new idea of women's rights was a dangerous and direct affront to his church's conservative beliefs, but these were prominent landowners and taxpayers. He could not assault them directly.

But as the rumors persisted, Stuyvesant devised a plan to make an example of the next Quaker from New England who dared to openly preach their aberrant religion in his godly jurisdiction. He would see to it that they were publicly flogged.

Hannah and John's wedding day arrived and not surprisingly, Stuyvesant was not invited. Nor were his spies. Everyone in Flushing knew who they were, the drunks and gamblers left over from Tienhoven's tyranny.

The ceremony was held at the house of Eduard Hart, a beautiful two-story house overlooking Flushing Bay. The crowd gathered on the lawn where the seating had been arranged to highlight the view of the shoreline. The vows would be exchanged in a new gazebo by the water's edge, festooned with flowers and colorful cloth ribbons.

Eduard officiated the ceremonies in which both the bride and groom spoke of the *inner light* when speaking their vows. This phrase revealed their growing alignment with Quakers, as did their pledge to be part of the priesthood of *Spirit* by setting an example of pure love and affection in their own lives.

At the extreme edge of hearing, burrowed into the tall shore grass, was a half drunken spy of Director General Stuyvesant. Predictably, his report was garbled and nonsensical. Talk of light and love was nothing he could use to prosecute them.

* * *

Stuyvesant's jaundiced eyes were filled with frustration as he pondered his next move. And then, as if brought to him by providence, an honest and decent young man named Robert Hodgson who had recently arrived from London, was seen preaching Quakerism in the villages of Long Island.

Hodgson fit Stuyvesant's plan perfectly. Unencumbered by a wife and children, it reduced the risk of excessive public sympathy. Stuyvesant ordered his troops to detain Hodgson and bring him before the court in New Amsterdam.

In the year 1657, Stuyvesant's men arrested Hodgson on Long Island mid-speech. Treating him like an enemy spy, they dragged him behind a cart to the Brooklyn Ferry. He was close to death when they lashed him to a stake in front of the Stadt Haus in New Amsterdam and savagely flogged him.

Citizens across the province were appalled, none more than those of Flushing, where *Liberty of Conscience* was inscribed in the very heart of the village charter.

* * *

The brutal treatment of Hodgson was soon followed by the banishment of Henry Townsend, a Quaker and fellow resident of Flushing, for the crime of holding a meeting in his home.

It was in this period of severe religious persecution by Director General Stuyvesant that Hannah Feake formally announced her conversion to Quakerism, as did her husband, John Bowne, soon after. Given Stuyvesant's obsession with preventing spiritual gatherings outside of his official state religion, and his willingness to use violence to enforce his dictates, Tobias Feake had grave concerns for his sibling cousin Hannah.

Tobias called an emergency meeting with Elias Doughty, Eduard Hart, and other town leaders, to discuss the deportation of their neighbor, Henry Townsend, and the threat to other Quakers like Hannah Feake. With insight that Adriaen van der Donck would have been proud of, Elias Doughty asked a pointed question. If the Director was allowed to do this to Quakers, what would stop him from doing the same to other groups?

Although not a lawyer, Elias had learned the essence of the law from his brother-in-law Adriaen, and retained all of the case files and civil documents from his legal practice. In collaboration with Tobias Feake, the local schout, and Eduard Hart, the town clerk, they drafted a protest against the infringement of their religious freedom by the State.

As Adriaen would have done, Elias and Tobias saw to it that the character of the petition was humbly and politely couched in commonly accepted religious precepts and civil law, and firmly rooted in tangible legal precedent, the first being the religious liberty already established and enjoyed by everyone in the Dutch homeland; the second, the clear and unequivocal establishment of the same principal in the basic fabric of their village charter, as approved by Director General Kieft a decade earlier.

The relevant clause from Kieft's official affirmation of the town's request for a patent, read as follows:

"We do give and grant unto the said patentees…to have and enjoy the liberty of conscience, according to the customs and manner of Holland, without molestaçõn or disturbance, from any magistrate or magistrates, or any other ecclesiastical minister, that may extend jurisdicçõn over them…"

Thirty of the area's prominent citizens, none of whom were Quakers at the time, risked the wrath of Stuyvesant and signed the final document penned by Eduard Hart, arguing for the liberty of Quakers to practice their beliefs unimpeded by the State, and by extension everyone else.

Eduard Hart, following correct legal procedures, had Tobias Feake, the town's schout, submit the petition to Nicasius de Sille, the new provincial schout in New Amsterdam, which was then submitted to the Director General. This document came to be known to the world as the *Flushing Remonstrance*.

* * *

Stuyvesant went on a rampage, arresting Eduard Hart and Tobias Feake, as well as the town magistrates, William Noble and Edward Farrington. He claimed the charges were not for their belief in *liberty of conscience*, but for misconduct of their duties, having appeared to give official sanction to what he called a "detestable letter of defiance."

The two magistrates were released soon after being stripped of their official titles and making pledges "to offend no more", implying they had been seduced by the ideas of Feake.

Feake and Hart were treated harshly, living on bread and water in isolation for a month. Eventually, the elder Hart was released due to failing health. Feake finally recanted. He paid a fine amounting to a year's wages, and agreed to never hold public office again in the New Netherlands.

Stuyvesant continued to insist that his actions were not against their freedom of conscience but against their right to worship in public, outside their own home. But the deed had been done and the Remonstrance existed, quietly waiting for its chance to be argued in a higher court by a brave soul.

Stuyvesant's growing intolerance made that final clash inevitable.

Chapter 45

One Brave Soul

Over the next few years, non-sanctioned worship services from an increasingly diverse number of faiths were cropping up across the colony. Many people like Hannah Feake and husband John Bowne, were now fully engaged in the Quaker movement.

Stuyvesant was frustrated and looked away for the most part, but Quakers still drew his ire. He had always suspected the uppity and outspoken Hannah Feake of being behind the rebellious action of her sibling cousin Tobias, and the whole Flushing affair. And now the recent report from his spy stated that she and her husband were openly holding Quaker services in their own home. It was time for him to settle an old score.

* * *

Flushing Bay was filled with flaxen sails, and the docks were kept busy day and night with the influx of new settlers. Many among the new arrivals were Quakers from Britain. Hearing of the horrific treatment of their brethren in New England and the New Netherlands, they came to support their friends and to help spread their message in this new land.

After arranging chairs for the morning services in the grassy lawn behind her home that gently sloped toward the bay, Hannah sat and watched the shorebirds hunt for their morning meals down on the beach. She thought it would be a sin to sit inside on such a beautiful warm September morning, so she decided they would meet on the lawn in the shade of a large weeping willow.

"Need more chairs?" John hollered from the cooking porch.

"I think this will be plenty. I almost decided on blankets instead of chairs, but I'm sure some will be wearing their best clothes and might object to sitting on the ground."

"I've made sassafras tea for everyone," John said, carrying a large stoneware jug down to the willow.

"I can feel the divine *Spirit* in all of the nature surrounding us," she said, sweeping her hand across the scene in front of her. "It speaks to the *Spirit* that dwells within me, as if we were one."

"As I feel we are one," he said, gently taking her hand and kissing it.

She was deeply in love with this man, strong enough to treat her as an equal in all things. This was a blessed union.

"I believe Tobias would have joined our movement if he hadn't taken the brunt of Stuyvesant's rage. For standing up to the tyrant for all of us, I will forever be in his debt," she said.

"I feel the same about Elias, but instead of a tyrant he had a preacher for a father."

Hannah caught herself before she laughed. Instead, she said, "It doesn't help us achieve harmony with the one true *Spirit* if we laugh at the pain of others."

"Maybe not, but I think laughing at absurdity and irony is forgiven."

* * *

One by one, the neighboring Quakers, and a few guests that had expressed interest in observing their meeting, found a chair on the lawn to their liking and sat quietly.

John brought out a tray of cups and everyone sampled his sassafras.

They had no leader, so when everyone was settled, an older gentleman from Gravesend, new to the group, spoke first.

"I fear we are being watched by the Director's agents."

"That is always a possibility," Hannah said, "but we can't let fear guide us. That is not the path forward."

"I agree," said another member, and then another, until everyone had spoken.

Hannah looked up after pouring a cup of tea. "There is someone else coming," she said, pointing at the silhouette of a tall man emerging from the woods on the east side of the lawn.

With the morning sun at his back, the man walked directly toward the gathering.

"Have you come to join us?" John asked, walking over to greet him.

"Is this your home?" he asked in return.

"It is. Can I help you?"

"And you are John Bowne?"

"I am. What is this about?"

Hannah walked over and stood beside her husband.

Turning to her, the unknown man asked, "Is this a Quaker meeting?"

She asked in response, "Is there a spark of the divine inside of you?"

* * *

There was an early morning chill on the water as Tobias guided the *Pride* out of Flushing Bay. The gulls followed them a short way before returning to boats that were actively catching fish.

Hannah leaned on the rail, thinking of her husband. She had been heartsick since John was taken into custody. He would have appeared if officially summoned. There was no need to take him away on a Sunday morning, other than to satisfy Stuyvesant's growing obsession with Quakers.

Tobias caught the west bound current in the East River bound for New Amsterdam, taking Hannah to John who was being held inside a dungeon at the old Dutch fort. Sick with worry, she needed to know he was not being mistreated. She was relieved to see that he was in good condition even though he had received only bread and water since being arrested, and was being held in a dark and poorly ventilated cell.

"I refused to pay his fine," John said. "He is threatening to deport me."

"I wish you would pay the fine so you could come home with me right now, but I know that if we don't stand up to this injustice, it will never end."

* * *

On New Year's Eve, four months after being arrested, John Bowne was marched from the stockade to the waterfront, where he was to be deported to Ireland on a ship called *D'Vos*.

Hannah was there, struggling to hold back her tears. They were allowed only a few moments on the pier before the guards pulled John away from her and walked him up the gangplank. The captain of the awaiting *D'Vos* was given orders to drop him off in Dublin, their first port of call.

John had plenty of time on the Atlantic crossing to contemplate his next move once arriving in Ireland. He had made an oath to Hannah and himself to fight this travesty of justice all the way to the highest court. Regrettably, that court was in the Hague, still a long way from Ireland.

He arrived in Dublin in late winter and was given shelter by fellow Quakers. They arranged passage for him to Wales aboard the *Grace,* where he began his journey across England on horseback.

News of his mission quickly spread, and he was greeted by Quakers along the full length of his journey as a hero for his refusal to submit to Stuyvesant's unrighteous demands. Fortified along the way by good food and encouragement, he was guided to the port of Gravesend, arriving in good spirits as he boarded the *Helena* bound for Rotterdam.

It was midspring when he finally stepped onto Dutch soil. The roads between Rotterdam and Amsterdam passed through some of the best tended fields John had ever seen, and were bursting with new flowers. The windmills were the same style as those cropping up around his home on Long Island. At the sight of them, he felt the pain of longing, and his mind filled with thoughts of home and his dear Hannah.

* * *

Amsterdam was even more grand than he could have imagined. The waterways and canals were alive with commerce, and it seemed as though there was a boat for every soul living in the city.

And there was an astonishing mixture of people from across the world living in relative harmony, all speaking some variation of Dutch. It didn't take long to find an enclave of Quakers who took him in as if he were a close relative.

Good fortune struck again when he received word that the West India Company directors had granted him an audience. Not only were they willing to consider an appeal of his conviction, they were willing to review Director-General Stuyvesant's edicts against Quakers and the beliefs of others.

The corporate directors already had doubts about Stuyvesant's fitness to govern in the aftermath of the Tienhoven affair. One thing they agreed on was that his extreme policies were not helping business, finding that many prospective settlers were going to Pennsylvania to avoid his zealotry.

The following week, John was standing before the corporate elites in their grand headquarters near the harbor. He carried his satchel on his shoulder and was dressed in the sturdy suit of clothes he typically wore on horseback while managing his plantation. He was a sterling example of what Adriaen van der Donck would have called an American.

His only defense for the crimes he had been accused of were two documents secured in his satchel, the *Flushing Remonstrance* and the *Remonstrance of the New Netherlands*.

* * *

On New Year's Eve in the winter of sixteen hundred and sixty-three, even before John Bowne had completed his journey home, a high-ranking military courier arrived at the port of New Amsterdam aboard the ship *de Statyn* with sealed orders for Director General Stuyvesant.

Word of the courier's arrival, along with sketchy bits of news from Amsterdam, spread through the city like wildfire from the disembarking passengers before Stuyvesant caught wind of it.

Oblivious to the outside world, the director general was comfortably enjoying breakfast beside a warm fire when he was interrupted by a sharp rap on his front door. A cold gust filled the foyer as he stood face to face with a tall Dutch officer in full military dress. He had the look of a serious and uncompromising young man, and had already achieved a rank above what he himself had at the same age.

"Director Stuyvesant?"

"Yes."

"I am Ensign Klaus DeTurk, with specific orders for you from the High and Mighty Lords of the West India Company."

The Director General stood rigidly in the doorway and stared at the young man with contempt.

"You are hereby ordered to read the enclosed document aloud in the public square, and immediately enact its directives."

He clenched his teeth, and in a cold voice asked, "Is that all?"

"I am afraid not. I have been ordered to stay at your side until I witness you breaking the seal and reading the contents of this parcel."

Grabbing the parcel out of the officer's hand, he broke the seal and unfolded the cover. There was one sheet of fine linen parchment with the official header and seal of the West India Company printed across the top.

Regarding worship by Quakers and by all others, you are hereby ordered to allow everyone to have their own beliefs, and to end religious persecution in the colony; to be enacted immediately.

For all of his obstruction and needless infringement on the freedom of conscience of others, Stuyvesant enacted the directive, effectively making the religious tolerance prescribed in the *Flushing Remonstrance* that he had so vehemently opposed, the law of the land.

* * *

On a cool March morning as the fog lifted, Hannah rushed down to the docks to see what new vessels might have arrived in Flushing. It had been a year and a half since John left, and she missed him dearly. His last letter gave her hope that he would be home soon.

As she strained to read the name on a newly arrived cargo vessel anchored in Flushing Bay, shafts of light finally began to break through an overcast sky. The bright rays sparkled on the water like diamonds, momentarily capturing her attention.

The enchanting moment was interrupted by a shore boat from the *Tryall of New London,* with six oarsmen speeding it toward the dock. As it grew closer a man stood up on the bow. It was John, and the smile on his face said everything.

Chapter 46

August 1664 - New Amsterdam

Panic spread through the streets of New Amsterdam as people woke up to the terrifying sight of a blockade of four large English frigates stretched across the inner bay, each warship with its cannons trained on the southern shores of Manhattan.

Each ship fired a blank shot in a rapid sequence to announce their arrival and wake anyone who was still unaware of their presence. The menacing thunder rattled every window in the city.

Stuyvesant had survived his orders for religious tolerance from the directors only eight months earlier, but this time he faced dire consequences, far worse than just losing his position.

As he waited for an envoy from the British fleet to deliver their terms of engagement, three hundred of the admiral's marines moved ashore on Long Island and rallied several hundred of the English settlers to join them. They marched their brigade to the East River shores of Brooklyn where they were reunited with their longboats, and awaited orders to invade New Amsterdam on the opposite shore.

Stuyvesant assembled all of the Dutch troops on the flanks of the Dutch cannon battery on the southern tip of Manhattan Island. He sent runners door to door ordering the men of the city to arm themselves and report to Fort Amsterdam with their families, bringing what provisions they could carry.

As expected, an emissary of Admiral Nicholls came ashore at Fort Amsterdam and delivered a letter to Stuyvesant. His lordship, the Duke of York, offered unusually favorable terms as he wanted the colony fully functioning and intact, rather than a ransacked and smoldering shell of what it had been. In a rage, Stuyvesant tore up the letter, destroying evidence of the offered terms from his people. He was ready to fight.

But word of the admiral's terms was revealed to the public through pamphlets passed out by the marine soldiers. Within days, a large crowd of townspeople, including nearly a hundred local burgers and magistrates, descended on Stuyvesant's headquarters, demanding he negotiate for peace. Tobias Feake, Elias Doughty, John Bowne, and others from Flushing were among them.

* * *

Impatient for a response, the admiral moved his warships closer to the fort and readied their cannons as the people were nearing the point of revolt. Stuyvesant finally succumbed to their demands and agreed to negotiate terms for a peaceful surrender.

A meeting was held at the Stuyvesant farmhouse, between Nicholl's second in command and a group of prominent merchants and landowners. Their final version of the negotiation was entitled *The Articles of Capitulation* and was signed onboard the admiral's ship by Stuyvesant's lawyer and chief negotiator on September 6, 1664.

Two days later, the entire company of Dutch troops marched to the docks and boarded the *Gideon* bound for the Netherlands, and Nicholls pronounced himself governor of the colony.

"Freedom of Conscience" was one of the many rights guaranteed in the *Articles of Capitulation* to the citizens of the New Netherlands.

Part Eleven

(Present Day - Esopus Creek)

Chapter 47

Blueberry Pancakes

Tess woke up in the down bed in the Garrison's second floor guest bedroom, disoriented for a few moments until the events of the previous day came rolling back to her.

The sudden knock on her door sent a bolt of fear down her spine, until she heard the familiar voice of Martin.

"Are you coming down for breakfast or should we bring it up to you?"

Seeing on her cell that it was already two hours past her normal waking time, Tess answered, "Be down in a minute."

As she reached to pull back the covers, a burning pain shot down her left arm. For a bullet wound that was not life threatening, it still hurt like hell.

Planning to return to the Executive Mansion in Albany after the Kingston signing event to join her husband and two teenage daughters, the discovery of Thatcher and Helms amplified the uncertainty around her own security force. It was on Albert's advice they go to the Garrison farm, guarded by Martin and a contingency of her trusted FBI agents. The decision to put her life in the hands of Martin and Albert had proven to be a wise one.

* * *

"Good morning," Tess said as she entered the large country kitchen.

Other than an agent posted outside each exterior window, the home had a wonderful sense of normalcy to it, and the brick fireplace blazing in the kitchen made her think of a Norman Rockwell painting.

Will, Martin, and Albert sat around a large oak table eating pancakes. Annah was tending the griddle on the antique O'Keefe and Merritt stove, turning out another short stack.

"Hope you like blueberries and maple syrup," Annah said smiling at Tess.

"I do! And thanks for the use of your lovely robe and pajamas."

"I'd be happy to have a set made for you. They're made of silk from my native Kerala."

"That's very sweet of you," Tess said taking the chair next to Will. "I'd love that."

The small talk was therapeutic. She needed a break from the world of politics, at least for this morning.

"I understand you are putting together another exhibit at the Brooklyn Museum," she said turning to Will.

"Yes, on the Dutch colonial printing company of my Gerritsen ancestors, including a cache of important historic records we found right here in our old barn.

"I'll be at the opening. You can be sure of that," she said with a sincere display of fearlessness.

The back door to the kitchen opened and Kari walked in with an armful of firewood. He carefully added several small logs to the blaze.

"Governor, I want you to meet our friend and caretaker of the farm, Kariwase. His friends call him Kari."

"A pleasure to meet you. Call me Tess," she said offering her hand.

"I am happy to see you up and around. It is our good fortune that you have survived this ordeal."

"Thank you, but something tells me it's not over yet."

Annah set a plate of pancakes in front of Kari.

Tess turned her attention back to Will.

"You acted so quickly," Tess said, "it was as if you had a premonition."

"Thanks to a vision I had, I recognized the time and place as the rifle scope caught a beam of sunlight."

"That was some vision," Tess said, reaching out and touching his arm.

Will urged Kari to explain the cleansing ceremony at the sweat lodge, and the powerful artifacts found in the brass box.

"This was not a coincidence. The ancestors spoke to Will."

Chapter 48

Front Page Worldwide

Before Martin cleared the governor to leave for Albany, Will flipped through the news channel. The assassination attempt and Governor Hendricken's new legislation eliminating religious tax deductions, were headline news across America, and the leading story in major news outlets around the world.

The religious extremists were already promising a holy war, predictably before reading or having any understanding of the new law. The fact that everyone's spiritual beliefs would now carry equal weight under the law seemed to have escaped commentators that relied on sensationalism over substance, particularly those on the ultra-right media.

Many established faith-based institutions insisted the law would bring about the end of organized religion, while conveniently omitting their own record of a continual decline in membership, a reduction verified to be more than ten percent in the last two decades.

One commentator managed to mention the contrasting growth in the number of the non-church goers who strongly identified themselves simply as *spiritual,* but not inclined to be part of any particular group. The question the governor insisted that the media ask was, *"Are the spiritual beliefs and practices of these independents any less worthy in the eyes of the law?"*

* * *

Martin followed Tess out into the cold Autumn wind that began to blow in the predawn hours, leaving the landscape with a heavy dusting of frost. Reassuring her that both she and Albert would join her in a couple of days, she watched as Governor Hendriksen left for Albany with a full FBI tactical team escort.

Turning back toward the farmhouse, Martin's mind went into overdrive. What she needed at the moment was a long sit down with Albert to work out their strategy going forward. Things were moving fast and they couldn't afford any missteps.

Within minutes they had gathered in the living room. Coffee in hand, they sat in comfy chairs by the crackling fire and went over every detail, with Will and Annah hanging on every word. There was no need to keep anything from them. At this point the two of them knew almost as much as they did.

"So, you are certain Thatcher was a patsy?" Martin asked Albert.

"I'm certain the autopsy will show a striking similarity to Sofiya's staged heart attack. They think it worked once, so why not do it again. When I interview Thatcher's girlfriend at the AG's office, I'll have a better understanding of his state of mind, and see what she thinks of the lone gunman theory being thrown around."

"You were wise to keep the findings of Sofiya's murder from the governor's security people," Martin said as she reached over and took Albert's hand.

"Meaning Thatcher and Helms?" Albert laughed.

"Right, with security like that, who needs the FBI?"

"So, what's next?" Annah asked.

"Exactly my question," Martin said, nodding her head toward Albert.

"Right. We know Strong was connected to Drexler by way of the shooting in Tarrytown, and we know both were paid through the same bank in Cyprus."

"As well as Drexler's connection to Thatcher through Sparky's burner phone analysis around the time of the bombing," Martin added.

"Then Thatcher to Helms by the burner we grabbed in Beacon," Will said over his shoulder as he rearranged logs in the fireplace.

"Correct," Albert agreed, "and we know Strong's connection to Darcy Wells.

"And now, Sharky has confirmed that Sydney's assailant was Helms, the man in Will's drawing," Martin said, nodding her agreement.

"Holy crap," Annah blurted out. "This thing fans out like the Nile Delta."

Albert chuckled at her comparison. "Yes, it does, but we still don't know who's behind it all. Assuming Thatcher was a patsy, the only person higher up in this pyramid, due to his Cyprus bank connection, is Grimes. I'm going to take a closer look into his private club. I can only imagine he has powerful allies among the Originalist Confederation, or ORCs, as I like to call them.

Guys like Strong and Drexler are just the foot soldiers of their seditious conspiracy. Strong knows at least one more ORC. We need to bring him in, but if we do it too soon, he will likely tip off his boss."

No one spoke for several minutes as they watched the flames sizzle and dance in the old stone fireplace. Martin, who had been analyzing the whole tangled mess, finally broke the silence.

"I've been thinking about Rybak. He clearly knew the players in the first assassination attempt through Sofiya and Caslav, which led him to Drexler, and Grimes as well, I imagine. On top of that, he managed to come into possession of some old KGB dirt on Grimes."

"Russian mafia?" Will asked.

"Likely," Albert answered.

Annah stood up and headed to the kitchen to warm up her coffee.

Stopping in the doorway, she turned around and looked at her three friends.

"So, if Rybak was able to track down one of the bosses on the next level up, so can we. Right?"

* * *

The convertible top was up but the cold was getting to Annah, being a warm-blooded Keralan. The Beetle's heater never seemed to work right. She turned up her coat collar to fend off the draft.

"The trip up to Kingston and the Garrison Farm wasn't as restful as I hoped it would be," Annah said, warming the mood with a little satire.

Her sly sense of humor gave Will a good laugh as he merged lanes on a section of the freeway under repair.

"Prospect Park will be beautiful, full of trees still in full autumn color," Will said, after successfully dealing with a second lane closure.

"I'm actually looking forward to being back in the archeology lab with you, helping wrap up the Gerritsen Print Shop exhibit."

"The report I received this morning from the exhibit designer said the fabrication phase was nearly completed and ready for installation, and the audio-visual content is under final review. So, we should be able to do our overall review in the next week or so, and hopefully, open the exhibit to the public before the holidays."

"That's fantastic, Will. Are we planning another reception and ribbon cutting?" Annah paused, realizing her question had unintentionally spooked both of them.

"We should, but…" Will paused as he made another last-minute lane change onto the Verrazzano Narrows Bridge approach to Brooklyn.

"It's your call, sweetheart."

Will adored Annah, this woman who had completely won his heart. In spite of the headless guy and the shooting, he actually felt things were getting brighter in his life. Something from his visitation at the sweatlodge had stuck with him.

Chapter 49

Tugging at Threads

She picked up her desk phone in her Brooklyn office.

"Ms. Shrader, there's an Everett Pendrake here to see you. He works for the governor."

"Show him to my office," she said, straightening her blouse and jacket. She was always conscientious about her looks, but since Dell Thatcher had been found dead, she'd been a bit disheveled and hung over.

A tall and distinguished gentleman walked into her office, in the carefree guise of the governor's biographer, and introduced himself with his usual English charm.

"Please sit Mr. Pendrake."

"Call me Everett."

"What can I do for you?" she asked.

"First, I must confess. I am Governor Hendriksen's personal biographer. I'm doing some background research on the assassination attempts on her."

Albert's trained eye watched as Margo's back noticeably stiffened at the word assassination.

He continued. "I'm interested in the reaction of staff in offices slightly removed from her inner circle, such as yourself."

"What sort of reaction?"

"Well, the obvious. Reaction to the news of a high-level department head going psycho and taking a shot at the governor with his sniper rifle."

"I was horrified, of course."

"Not saddened?"

"I'm sorry. I don't understand."

"Weren't you saddened by the death of a coworker?"

"I wouldn't call him a coworker. We both simply work for the State of New York."

Albert paused, feigning a search for his next words.

"My apologies. I meant coworkers in the sense of the meetings you had in the governor's limousine.

The blood drained from Shrader's face.

"No need to deny it. I'm good at research," Everett said, looking like a cat with a mouse.

Unmasked, she snapped back, "Who are you and what do you want?"

"What I want is to expose you for being a neo-Nazi and an adulterer, and perhaps, link you to the assassination attempt on the Governor. This is going to be one of the most sordid and sinister chapters in her biography."

"You're not a writer."

"It doesn't matter what I am. They are going to bring you in for your association with Thatcher."

She settled back in her chair, and crossed her long legs seductively. "I sense you are looking to make a deal."

"Is that what worked on Thatcher?" he replied like a parent disappointed in their wayward teenage daughter.

"Look, this is what I need to know before you get into even deeper trouble. Was Thatcher a crazed lone gunman, or were you in on the plot as well? And remember this before you answer. I know about your white supremacist comrades. Based on your philosophy of hatred, do you think any court will doubt that you were part of a conspiracy to commit murder, perhaps of one of its ring leaders?"

"I had nothing to do with it. Sure, we went for a drive in the governor's limo, but we did it for the thrill, like stupid high school kids. As to Dell Thatcher, he's being framed. There's no way he did the shooting. In the end he was just another weak man."

"My advice is to start looking for a new job. This might not go public, but there is no way on Earth you should remain in a position of public trust or law enforcement. *Without Fear, Favor, or Prejudice.* Stay where I can find you and don't mention our meeting or the limo records go straight to the press.

* * *

Martin found Annah's inference about Rybak being a possible back door into the ORCs dark world intriguing. If she was able to apprehend him, he might trade information for the right deal. Only problem was, with at least two murder raps hanging over his head, Rybak would likely fight to the death, getting her no closer to the ORCs.

Then it struck her. She could send him a message through a third party offering to set up a meeting and make some kind of deal. Someone must know how to get in touch with him.

"Of course," she said aloud to an empty room. "Caslav."

Before asking for help from Albert's man in Dubrovnik, she had some questions for her friend and old academy classmate Erin McEvers in DC, recently transferred to the new FBI illegal arms trafficking strike force.

"Johanna, it's been a while," Erin said, pleased to see her face on the phone.

"We'll have to get together to catch up one of these days, but right now I'm looking for help with a Serbian arms dealer."

"Serbian? You know I'll do what I can. What's going on?"

"I'm dealing with the conspiracy to assassinate Governor Hendriksen. I'm on special assignment to protect her and find the perpetrators. We think a Serbian by the name of Caslav Nedic has a nephew living in Brooklyn. Rybak Sadouski may be able to lead us to the higher ups in the assassination plot. We believe the same group made both attempts."

"Both?"

"We think the bomb that killed Senator Torres was meant for Hendriksen."

"So where do I fit in?"

"I need to get a message to Rybak. We are willing to make a deal if he leads us to the ringleader, and the only way I think we can do that is to deliver it through his Uncle Caslav. I'm betting on them still being in contact."

"So, you want us to get the message to Nedic discretely, without an ensuing gun battle?"

"That's it in a nutshell. I'll send you the exact message on your private phone."

"You do know nothing is really private anymore. Did I just agree to do this?"

"Well, you didn't say no." Martin laughed and hung up.

* * *

Albert's phone buzzed. It was Martin but he couldn't answer at the moment. He was in the private apartment of Burle Strong searching through his chest of drawers in the bedroom.

The apartment was freakishly decorated, with circus paraphernalia lying about or hanging on the walls. Strong's particular fascination seemed to be with tattooed big top performers, including the infamous tattooed lady of Barnum and Bailey fame.

One large replica of a nineteenth century circus poster featured a tattooed strongman in the foreground. Taking a second look, Albert laughed when he recognized Burle Strong's face photoshopped onto the strongman. The photo manipulation was up to his spy standards.

The rear door from the kitchen creaked open. Albert froze. He didn't expect Strong to enter his flat through his escape route in the back. He retrieved his pistol from his shoulder holster and flipped off the safety.

Repositioning himself in the living room, Albert waited for a sound or any indication of movement, but there was none. Quiet as a cat, he slipped into the hallway leading to the kitchen, ready to dive into the open bedroom or bath across the hall.

Creeping closer to the kitchen, he stopped and held his breath. A man was talking softly to someone on his phone.

There was something familiar about the voice, and as he moved closer, he was finally able to distinguish it.

"Sharky, fancy meeting you here."

Agent Obsharski jumped. "You just scared the shit out of me!"

Astonished by the coincidental encounter, Albert asked, "How is it you're here? Now?"

"After Strong's burner went silent, the judge finally granted us a search warrant to look for phones. What about you?"

"First of all, I'm not really here. Secondly, I'm looking for phones."

"We found that Grimes made calls to the same number from his burner as Strong had. We think he may be another of your ORCs with the obvious Tolkien reference."

"You can't blame me, it's a British thing. And the part of Cornwall I come from bears a striking resemblance to Bag End."

"Okay, Gandalf," Sharky teased. "Let's check the place out for phones and then get the hell out of here. I'll signal my backup outside that I have friendly company."

"You check the kitchen and living room, and I'll check the bedroom and bath. But don't leave a trace of our being here," Albert said, heading back down the hall.

"Roger, Albert." An instant later Sharky thought he heard a chuckle.

Albert went back and finished searching the dresser and closet. It was in the vest pocket of a three-piece pin stripped suit that Albert's search paid off. He found a thin, minimally equipped prepaid burner phone, with only a few recent calls in the call log. He snapped off several pictures of the phone numbers, including that of the burner itself, and texted them to Sharky.

They both left together out the back door.

* * *

It had been a long day and Martin was headed for her favorite Indian restaurant to meet up with Albert. A bit early, she decided to fill the empty time with a Flying Horse lager and papadum.

Mildly surprised, she found Albert waiting for her at their favorite table. As Martin took her seat, the waitress arrived with papadum and two bottles of Flying Horse.

"You really know how to treat a girl."

Albert rose to his feet, kissed her warmly on the side of her face, stealing a quick nibble on her ear. Always a gentleman, he pulled out her chair and adjusted it forward before she sat.

"Have you already ordered for me?"

"I have not, other than the vegetable pakora and samosas. I would not presume to go any further with your main course."

"I already need a to-go box and I haven't taken a bite," she said with a carefree chuckle.

They both had curry, hers shrimp and his fish, while sipping the ice-cold Indian beer that was always perfect with hot spicy food. The waitress packed up their leftovers with two orders of rice pudding, and they walked out into the clear and chilly October night holding hands like young lovers. They felt young when they were with each other, and to anyone watching, there was no doubt about them being lovers.

* * *

Albert walked to the kitchen to refill their waters. Martin followed close behind, pulling her robe closed over her naked body and securing the sash belt. But the thin cotton cloth left little to the imagination, and after a refreshing drink they were back in bed.

"You're such a sweet man," she whispered in his ear before rolling out of bed. "I'm heading for the shower. Want to join me?"

"Right behind you."

As Albert started for the bathroom, Martin's cell buzzed. He glanced at the phone but the caller ID didn't recognize the number.

The bathroom was already steamy by the time Albert stepped into the shower.

"A text just came in on your phone from an unrecognized caller."

"Probably spam."

"I don't think so. It just had a time of day and a location."

* * *

The air was crisp and clear with a steady breeze off the ocean as she walked onto a deserted boardwalk. Coney Island was a ghost town in the off-season, particularly on weekday mornings. Other than random bikers and joggers, a few lost tourists, and some small cafes, the boards were mostly abandoned.

Martin had arrived early. Being at the site of not one, but two assassination attempts in as many months, she was braced for anything. Intending to get a lay of the land and look for anything suspicious before the agreed upon meeting time, the sight of two girls flying their custom-made kites on the beach was a welcome dose of normality. She took a deep, welcome breath of fresh air into her lungs.

The café where she was to meet Rybak was obscured by a construction trailer, parked in front of a shop under renovation a few doors down. It seemed out of place so she approached with caution. She could feel eyes scrutinize her every move as she walked past.

Rounding the end of the trailer, the café came into full view. Half a dozen outdoor tables painted in bright rainbow colors lined the sidewalk. A man with dark sunglasses and a ball cap pulled down far enough to darken his face, sat at a light blue one.

Before she could step forward, a man who had come out of the back door of the trailer appeared on her right.

With a hint of a Russian accent, he whispered "In here."

As she followed him into the trailer, a woman similar in size and coloring walked over to the blue table and took a seat. From a distance, the two could easily be mistaken for Rybak and herself.

"Follow me," he said, as they walked through the trailer and out the front door, directly into the shop that was in the midst of a major renovation.

The only construction going on at the moment was a drywall crew working in a storage room. Overhearing one of them, it sounded like he was speaking some European dialect, possibly Albanian. Hurrying to the rear service entry, he ushered her out the door and into a limousine idling at the curb.

"Ingenious precautions. You must be Rybak."

"Yes, Rybak. And you are Agent Martin."

"I am, and I can assure you I wasn't followed."

"I know. We've verified that."

"We?

"You didn't say to come alone," Rybak said with a snicker.

"Nor did you. However, I'm the one in need of your help. Wouldn't it be crazy to scare you away?"

"It would be unless your sole motive was to catch me. But I did some research on you, and I believe it is more important for you to get the big guys than to catch me at this time."

Martin was so immersed in their discussion she hadn't noticed the limousine slowly moving down the service alley until in turned onto a beach access street heading away from the shore.

"Where are we going?"

"Just around the block, to a place where there are no security cameras. I am very impressed. You are a fearless woman to meet like this."

"Okay, no bullshit. In exchange for helping me catch the head of this assassination pyramid, I can call off the dogs in Brooklyn temporarily, and offer you safe passage out of the US to a country of your choice.

"The alternative is staying here and constantly looking over your shoulder until the FBI grabs you and tries you for murder and terrorism. Or the bad guys track you down and you disappear the hard way."

"What can I do to help?" Rybak asked in an obliging tone.

"First you can tell me how you found the link between Sofiya and Drexler, and then Drexler and Grimes."

Martin knew there was a risk throwing out assumptions that might not be true, but the look on Rybak's face told her she was on the mark.

"Drexler was a cold-blooded killer. I did everyone a favor. That is, of course, if I actually did it."

Rybak let his eyes wander to her breasts as his face broke into an insincere smile.

"Don't get cute. This isn't going to work if you're not straight with me," she said with steel in her voice.

"Okay, okay. I knew of Drexler only through Sofiya's telling. She and I had a little side business. And believe me, I had no involvement with either attempt on the governor."

"So, Senator Torres was not the target?"

"Hell no, that was a major screwup. I think that's why Drexler had Sofiya murdered."

"Yes, we figured that out," Martin said. "How did Sofiya get paid?"

He shrugged. "Maybe Drexler. Maybe one of his comrades."

"And what about Drexler's relationship with Thatcher," Martin pressed.

"I don't know, probably the money guy. I can check with my sources."

"Then tell me why you killed Drexler."

"It's simple. Someone dear to Sofiya wanted revenge."

"And Grimes?

"Grimes was a pig. He could have been Drexler's superior."

"OK," Martin replied. "Did you have some help?"

Rybak nodded. "From some family connections to the old Russian KGB."

"Well, that explains the pictures and documents left at the scene of the murder, doesn't it?" Martin asked without asking.

"Yes. Pretty bold of the killer, wouldn't you say?"

"Enough. How much higher does this go?"

"Still waiting for confirmation, but I am certain the inner circle lies within the walls of that exclusive club of confederates, or whoever the fuck they are. I just need to know which one's next."

"Absolutely no more killing while we're working this out," Martin said sternly. "There's enough crap coming down already. You need to inform me as soon as you identify any of his coconspirators. We need to take the top guy alive."

"Okay. Deal. I tell you."

Chapter 50

Got Your Number

After Sharky checked the phone log on Strong's burner against his master list of suspicious calls on the growing web connected to this case, he sent the analysis to Albert.

Sharky had confirmed calls from Strong to the burner found on the dead body of Grimes, and calls to Strong from a yet unknown third caller, a number that also showed up on Grimes' burner.

A closed three-cornered circuit between burners always spelled conspiracy in Albert's book. He used his spy craft to triangulate the location of the mysterious third burner, and wasn't surprised when it turned out to be the Originalist Confederation headquarters in downtown Manhattan.

* * *

A distinguished British gentleman presented himself at the reception desk as a representative from the Reform UK Party.

"I'm here to see Gaston Grimes," he said tipping his hat. "He said if I had a little time to spare on my next visit to New York, I should drop in on him."

He watched as the receptionist's face went pale before asking, "Did you have an appointment?"

"No, I tried to reach him on his cell but I couldn't get an answer. I'm certain I called the right number."

"And your name?"

"Oh yes, Everett Pendrake."

"Mister Pendrake, let me find someone who can help you," she said, rising from her seat and disappearing through the doors into the private offices of the Confederation.

Albert maintained his cool outer demeanor, but was gleefully entertaining the possibility that one of the big fish would actually come out to give him the bad news about Grimes.

While waiting for her to reappear, he studied the art on the walls. Old, classic, and probably very expensive. One of the paintings was an American version of a foxhunt, the fox handler and horse attendants all black men. Another was a family having a holiday get-together around a bountiful buffet in front of a large blazing fireplace. Strangely, the men had colorful jackets and ties while the women wore drab colored clothing, their hair covered in white cloth bonnets.

The receptionist found Pendrake studying the painting when she returned and said, "It's called *Thanksgiving in New England*."

"Really? Where are the Native Americans?"

* * *

The receptionist picked up her desk phone on the first ring. Looking over at Pendrake, she said in a cool, professional voice, "Someone will see you now."

"This way," she said as she rose from her desk and walked toward a pair of heavy wooden doors. He followed her down a wide hallway and into a wood paneled executive office.

"Please have a seat," she said pointing to one of the plush side chairs. "Mr. Clay Daggert will be with you shortly."

Clay Daggert, now that was a name Albert had not yet heard.

While he waited, he studied another large painting on the wall behind the desk. The inside of a seventeenth century Puritan church, a lone woman wearing a white bonnet knelt before an altar with her head bowed. Albert resisted rolling his eyes.

"Clay Daggert," the man announced as he entered. "I understand you are here to see Gaston Grimes. What is your business with him?"

"That is a matter I'd prefer to keep between Gaston and myself."

Not pleased with his evasive response, Daggert decided to cut to the chase and get rid of this Pendrake guy.

"I'm afraid Grimes was murdered a few days ago."

"Murdered? Oh my, I just spoke to him last week."

"Spoke about what?"

"Our mutual shared interest in bringing conservative Christian values back to the forefront of government and a rapidly declining society."

"Is that the work of your Reform UK political party?"

"Essentially, yes."

"We may be able to help each other. Leave your card and I'll contact you when the time is right."

"Right for what?"

"To align our forces. Anything else?"

Rising, Pendrake held out his hand. "I'm very glad to have made your acquaintance, and I'm certain we'll meet again when the time is right."

Daggert had no idea it would be sooner rather than later.

* * *

Martin was riding with Sharky following pings from Strong's new burner when her phone buzzed.

"Who do I have the pleasure of speaking to, Albert or Everett?" she asked playfully, immediately more cheerful knowing one of them was on the other end of the line.

"I'm on my way to Brooklyn Heights to check on Will and Annah and have some sushi."

"Any luck downtown at ORC central?"

"I think so. When I asked for Grimes, I got one Clay Daggert instead. He's my current frontrunner for the next rung up their bloody ladder. He has all the charm of a murderous religious zealot."

"Clay Daggers doesn't sound that scary."

"It's Daggert. With a T."

"Now *that's* scary. We'll have our team tear into Daggert's history, financials, and close associates."

"I think you're going to find that he and his ORC buddies have embedded a bunch of their far-right cronies on high courts across the country. Do I hear traffic noise in the background?"

"Yep. Sharky and I are tailing Strong at the moment."

"Two thoughts on Strong. I don't want to speak to him until we've confirmed his superiors. And when we finally grab him, he's treated like a terrorist and kept in isolation."

"We're on the same page. By the way, we expect to get approval from the judge to wiretap his burner today."

"Good news. By the way, I also think Strong was the triggerman in Kingston."

"We've come to the same conclusion. Sharky discovered that before the ORCs, he worked security for a travelling circus where he came under suspicion of running a small smuggling ring. Before that he was a SWAT sniper for the Detroit PD, booted off the force for failing a second drug test while still on probation for the first."

"A SWAT sniper. That's really creepy," Albert said. "He must have lured Thatcher to the roof and killed him before assembling the gun he'd stashed behind the chimney, taking the shot with Thatcher's own rifle."

"Sounds right, and matches the facts. Give my love to Will and Annah. Wait a minute. Are those snowflakes I'm seeing?"

* * *

In a moment of paranoia, Rybak began to entertain the idea that Martin had no intention of letting him go. He needed some insurance and began digging into her background.

It appeared they first crossed paths the night of the first assassination attempt. Both Martin and his dear friend Sofiya were at the opening of the museum exhibit in Brooklyn.

It turned out that Martin's association with the governor began after the museum bombing, so he began to dig for answers as to why she was there.

He found that Martin had been instrumental in clearing the names of Will Garrison and Annah Devar in a murder case that took place in the museum. The online news articles he found also mentioned a shootout in DC at the American Bible Museum earlier that year. Apparently, several important stolen archeological artifacts were recovered and returned to the care of Garrison and Devar at the Brooklyn Museum.

There were too many connections between the two of them to ignore. Reviewing all of the articles once again, the clincher for him was an article in the *Daily Freeman*, the local paper in Kingston who cited both Martin and Garrison in an article about the second assassination attempt on Tess Hendricksen. While nothing in the article pointed to a relationship, a few of their responses told another story.

Garrison was more to Martin than just a suspect or victim. Somewhere there was a relationship. He didn't believe in coincidences.

Chapter 51

Brookly Museum

Among the print shop records from the Garrison barn, there were several boxes from the time period after the British takeover, and not directly relevant to the New Netherlands time period of the exhibit. Theron had just completed his initial translation of those later documents when Will and Annah showed up at the lab.

"Good to see you both," he said, beaming with excitement. "I've got some things to share with you."

The big grin that spread across Will's face invited Theron to continue.

"It seems as though your people migrated to Kingston from Manhattan in 1728, and set up a print shop in the old town. Although a fairly small city, it was a thriving center of agriculture and industry, trading both up and down river with Albany and New York City.

"Some of those records date as late as the American Revolution, in the early days when Kingston played an important role. After the British routed George Washington's Continental Army in Manhattan, and occupied New York City with a division of seasoned troops, Kingston became the de facto capital of the rebel colony."

"You've got my attention," Will interjected. "Please continue."

"In the midst of this bloody conflict, a convention of representatives summoned their courage and met in Kingston in 1777, signing the first constitution of the newly declared State of New York.

"In the Old Senate House!" Annah's voice reflected her surprise.

"Exactly."

"We were just there! In the same room where the constitution was signed. Unfortunately, an assassin took a shot at the governor while we were in it."

"Good Lord. I'm glad you both made it through unharmed."

Theron was able to remain solemn for a few moments before his excitement got the best of him.

"Anyway, it turns out that more than half of the representatives at the constitutional signing still spoke Dutch, and because of that, a duplicate transcript of the minutes was also written in the colonial Dutch dialect of the time.

"Daniel Gerritsen, your ancestor, played a critical role in printing the records of those meetings in Dutch, while most of the documents in English have gone missing over the last two and a half centuries."

"And we have those?" Will asked leaning closer.

"All of them, right over here," Theron said, leading the way to the long, standing height table in the center of the room where his finished work was neatly stacked in piles.

They scanned the stacks of historical documents for several minutes before one heading in particular caught Will's attention. In bold letters, it read *Liberty of Conscience.*

* * *

Rybak waited in the shadows of the small park across Washington Avenue for nearly an hour, waiting for Garrison and Devar to emerge from the museum. A simple call to the front desk in the museum business office was all it took to confirm they were there.

A cold front was moving through the city and winter was making an early appearance. Large flakes of snow began falling as he discreetly followed them up Washington into the Prospect Heights neighborhood.

He huddled close to a doorway as he waited for them to exit a take away sushi bar. There must have been a line because it taxed his remaining patience. They finally emerged with their dinners and briskly continued up Washington, disappearing around the corner on Saint Marks Avenue.

The weather front was coming off the sea, and the snow flurries soon turned into a heavy snowfall. Rybak shortened the distance, following closer than he normally would in order to keep them in sight.

A few blocks down, the couple climbed the steps of a front stoop. The woman shook the snow off her jacket while the man fumbled for the front door key. Affectionately, the woman turned and brushed the snow from his shoulders, kissing him on the cheek before he followed her inside.

Conditions were worsening, giving Rybak an advantage. The snow flurry would be a distraction from him picking the front door lock, and if a cop happened to drive by, they wouldn't even notice him through the blur of white.

* * *

Albert drove the last mile to Will and Annah's city apartment in a swirling blizzard. Will hadn't answered his call, which was typical, so there was no sense trying again. Anyway, he was too busy navigating the storm to make another call.

The lights were on in their Saint Marks Avenue flat as he squeezed into a space just big enough for his 1962 MGA Deluxe Roadster.

He pulled on his gloves and hat before stepping into the street. The temperature was plummeting, and although the snow was melting as it hit the asphalt, it was already sticking to the sidewalk and porch steps.

Focused on the slippery stairs, he carefully made his way up their front stoop. Seeing a faint set of large footprints positioned under the door latch made him pause for a moment before noticing something else that put him on high alert.

The door was unlatched and left ajar.

He drew out his pistol and cautiously entered.

Wanting his presence known, he called out, "Will, Annah, anyone home?"

The only thing he heard in reply was the muffled silence of the falling snow.

Albert moved swiftly, his fluid catlike movements the result of years in the field, where survival often depended on it.

Making his way through the compact apartment, the view from the kitchen doorway only added to the mystery. Containers filled with sushi, rice, miso, and seaweed salad sat unopened on the counter. Two small cups of sake sat untouched on the small wooden table, as if waiting for someone to discover them.

There was no sign of a struggle. Either there was a sudden emergency, or someone got the drop on them. Will had a loose relationship with his phone, particularly answering it, but Albert knew he would have called if there had been an emergency or they needed help.

His gut feeling told him their disappearance had something to do with the ORCs and the governor, but he was having a hard time seeing a connection. He punched the call button underneath the image of Martin laughing. He needed her and her team's help immediately.

Chapter 52

Fair and Equal Treatment

A judge at the Albany County Supreme Court in New York State, Judicial District 3, upheld the new tax legislation, agreeing with Tess Hendriksen's basic argument of *Fair and Equal Treatment Regardless of Spiritual Beliefs*.

The ruling was clear and straightforward, but the conservative element of the New York State High Court of Appeals agreed to hear the challenge being made by the minority party of the state legislature.

Governor Hendriksen believed she had the stronger argument, and history would prove her right. With a rapidly declining membership in religious organizations, and the equally rapid increase in independent and alternative spiritual beliefs, the time for cleaning up this vestige of state sponsored religion had come.

The storm was picking up intensity as a plow heaped snow along the side of the long driveway to the executive mansion. Tess wrapped her scarf tightly around her neck and turned up the collar of her winter coat as she walked out into the bitterly cold night and stood under the protection of the porte cochere.

Dylan, the temporary limousine driver on loan from the FBI, maneuvered through the icy streets of Albany as the snow outpaced the plows. A ten-minute drive turned into a thirty-minute ordeal before Tess was safely delivered to the office of the Attorney General Nette Bergen.

Shortly before the snow began to fall, word came down from the Court of Appeals that they would hear the case challenge. In spite of the bitter weather, a bizarre mix of diehard media personnel and rabid protesters began to materialize around the state capital building in front of the entry to the Offices of the Attorney General. What had been a green lawn the previous day was now transforming into an impressionistic winter night scene filled with ghoulish masks and shadowy snowmen.

Tess's ire rose when she recognized several of the custom death masks she had seen on the night of the museum bombing. Fear was irrational, so she did her best to shrug it off, but like the snow now falling, the stress was mounting faster than she could shake it. She was grateful for the support of Martin and her FBI team as she searched for a new security chief. She was looking for someone capable of rebuilding her security detail into a stronger and more professional division, and hoping Martin might want the job.

As required by state law, Bergen had been notified of the constitutional challenge to the tax reform law late that afternoon. And although the court had agreed to hear the challenge more quickly than Tess had expected, she and Nette had already been making contingency plans for that possibility. Tess wanted to fine tune their defense strategy immediately, snow or no snow, to make sure their case was fresh and in line with the latest relevant legal arguments around the country.

The FBI staff backed the crowd away from the entry, pushing their tape line perimeter out to the edge of the sidewalk. This expanded security buffer raised shrill cries of injustice by the protestors, followed by a flurry of snowballs thrown at the agents.

* * *

"Allow me to take your coat Madame Governor," the Attorney General said, formally greeting her in the reception area.

A designated camera woman from the AP took candid shots from across the room. She had discovered early in her career that the more images she captured without interfering, the more natural her subjects tended to be, although politicians were usually pretty good actors when cameras were present.

"Thank you. It's so nice and warm in here."

"You're in luck. This part of the original building has one of those old steam heated radiators. This way to my office, Governor Hendricksen."

"Please, call me Tess. We've been friends a lot longer than I've been governor. I haven't forgotten that I worked for you when I was just out of law school."

"Shortly after I had become a junior partner at the firm. That goes back a way."

"I admired you then. I still do."

They walked up the formal staircase to the second floor and into Nette's office.

"Shall we take it from the top, Tess?

"Please. Let's start with our foundational principle, *Freedom of Conscience*."

"The first legal document establishing this freedom in the New Netherlands was the Vlissingen Charter of 1645. Vlissingen, which was later called Flushing by the English, placed at the heart of its founding charter the laws of tolerance that had been established in the Dutch homeland regarding matters of personal conscience. We will project the following definitive phrase from that document on the big screen during this part of our argument, along with the signature of approval by the Director-General of the New Netherlands - Willem Kieft."

We do give and Graunt, unto the said Patentees, and to have and Enjoy the Liberty of Conscience...

"Our second principal was contained in the Flushing Remonstrance, a letter of protest written in direct response to the tyranny of Pieter

Stuyvesant, and his intention to enforce a single state religion," Tess said.

"That's correct. Stuyvesant was on a campaign against anyone who dared to openly espouse beliefs other than those of his church. He exercised his authoritarian rule, harassing and punishing people of beliefs that did not align with his. But his utter cruelty toward Quakers on Long Island was a step too far for the citizens of Flushing to ignore.

"They submitted the Flushing Remonstrant to Stuyvesant, a document that cited and stressed the relevance of the clause in the original village charter. Stuyvesant considered their submittal an act of treason, and ignored it after punishing several of its leaders.

"But a few years later, a Quaker man from Flushing refused to back down and held meetings at his home. Stuyvesant imprisoned him for months, where he was treated harshly. The man appealed his case to the high courts in the Netherlands and they agreed with the Flushing Remonstrance. Religious tolerance was amended into the laws of the New Netherlands, and Stuyvesant was forced to abide by them," Nette concluded.

"So, what do you plan to put up on the screen during that segment?" Tess prodded.

"We'll figure it out. Maybe that famous etched print of a Quaker being hung in Boston during this same time period."

"That could work," Tess said, nodding her head.

"The last two pillars supporting our position are in regards to the transfer of these rights to future government. This first occurred when the Dutch surrendered the New Netherlands to the British. And from the peace negotiations arose a document known as the *Articles of Capitulation* in which all of those newly acquired rights were guaranteed to the citizens. The first governor of the colony of New York was the British fleet commander who agreed to the terms of surrender and lived to honor them."

Tess gathered a thought, and spoke, "That weaves the foundational clause from the Flushing Charter into the legal fabric of the State by an official act of the first British colonial governor."

"Well said. Essentially, these rights passed into British common law in New York by his action."

"A strong case so far. Where's the weakness?"

Nette was silent for a moment. "It gets a bit trickier from there. As you well know, the next transfer of those rights is from the colony to Statehood, at the signing in the Old Senate House."

"That's correct. I thought it was clear cut, with legal scholars and the high court judges agreeing that the founding fathers of the newly constituted State of New York incorporated colonial common law in the state's jurisprudence."

"I agree that it's our argument, and a fairly strong one based on relevant case law."

"But?" Tess asked, feeling the chink in their armor being exposed. She often imagined these feelings to be a kind of intuition that gave her an edge in the courtroom as a prosecutor, and of late in politics. It was also possible it was simply some kind of low-grade paranoia.

"The representatives at the constitutional meeting certainly implied that the colonial law was accepted as the basis of law, of course after striking out any references to the king, crown, monarchy, or royalty. But after fire swept through an old section of the archives, many of the original handwritten transcripts of constitutional debates and discussions were lost. This happened long before cameras."

"So, what *do* you think they can claim?" Tess asked, her voice revealing the worry she had been carrying.

"Tess, that's what we're working on. One of the opposition's strategies will likely be to poke holes in the argument, claim it was never the founder's intention to incorporate all of the colonial precedent. Their lawyers will demand that we produce physical evidence that specifically supports our contention, knowing those documents were destroyed by fire."

Chapter 53

Down On the Waterfront

Martin had finally received the text she'd been expecting. The snow was still falling as she exited the parking garage. Against the backdrop of night, the large flakes glowed like luminescent stars as they danced in the beam of her headlights. The streetlights and colorful signs of shops and restaurants along the boulevard cast a soft glow around the edges of darkness.

She wanted to stop the car and catch a snowflake on her tongue, but there was no time for kid stuff. She was taking a risky gamble, and not thrilled about meeting late at night in a snowstorm. But if it paid off as she hoped, the new information from Rybak could help expose the ringleaders of the whole assassination enterprise.

This political violence needed to be put down. While she knew Rybak was responsible for several of the murders, his victims wouldn't have thought twice about killing him. Between the Russians executed in Brighton Beach, the Palestinian fall guy who was the bomber, Senator Torres and the limo driver, she had a total body count of twelve. A deal that sent Rybak far away would be in the public interest.

* * *

Annah struggled to open her eyes. Seeing an unfamiliar ceiling, she closed them again and fought to remember what had happened. Bits and pieces floated by, walking up the steps to their apartment, laughing at one of Will's silly jokes as she opened boxes of take out.

Will! Annah's eyes flew open and she searched the dark room for him. It was then she realized her arms were tied behind her back and her legs bound with some kind of rope. In a panic, she managed to sit upright and quickly scanned the room. She was on board a boat large enough to have at least one private cabin. The only light came from a cheap nightlight plugged into an electrical outlet, and for a brief moment, the headlights of a boat returning from the open sea created an orb of white sparkles outside the porthole window.

The sound of the boat faded, and she heard something move on her right. Turning, she saw a dark form on the floor about five feet away.

"Will? Will, is that you?"

Relief washed over her as she heard his voice. "Annah. Are you okay?" followed by "Shit! My hands and feet are bound."

"Mine too. I think we may have been drugged."

"Who's the guy that snatched us? Do you know where the hell we are?"

Annah's recollection was still vague, but the face of the stranger was vivid. "I'm not sure what happened, but I know I'd never seen the man before. I'm pretty sure we're on a boat.

"I have a few disjointed memories. I think we may have been in the back of an SUV. I remember seeing a sign, Gearson Creek, or something like that."

"Gerritsen Creek," Will said as he tried to scoot closer to Annah. "It's actually the name of a narrow lagoon between Sheepshead Bay and Gerritsen Beach."

"Seriously. Your family has a bay *and* a beach town named after them?"

"I suppose they could have been my relatives," Will said, now almost next to her.

"Impressive. But I'd be more impressed if you got us out of here. At least the generator is running and the heater is on, or we'd most certainly freeze to death."

"That means he wants us alive. We're hostages."

"I know, Will, but check out this cabin. It spans from side to side, with portholes on both sides," Annah observed. "The long sleek proportion suggests it may be a sailing yacht."

"See if you can untie me. I'll take a look and see if I can figure out where we are. Maybe we'll get lucky and find a way out."

Annah wormed her way closer, and as it often did when she was under stress, her sense of humor surfaced. "This reminds me of a nicer version of the delivery van we were kidnapped in last year."

"Very funny. Try my hands first."

Annah tugged, pushed, wiggled and pulled at the knot, but it wouldn't budge.

"This guy ties knots like he's spent time on the water," Annah growled.

"Why don't you try my ankles? If that works, I might find something to help loosen the rest of the knots, or maybe cut the cords."

Annah twisted around until her hands could feel his ankle bonds. Her focused pushing and pulling finally began to loosen the knot.

* * *

Albert rang Martin's cell and it went directly to voicemail. He decided a short text would work, figuring that she was in the middle of something important.

He wasn't thrilled about her plan to meet Rybak alone, but he trusted her judgement. He did, however, put a tracking device on her car in case he needed to find her in an emergency.

The disappearance of Will and Annah was now bumping up against that emergency threshold.

His text was straight to the point; *Will and Annah missing. Looks like foul play.*

* * *

A powerful supercell was bringing in an unexpected amount of snow and frigid air from the east, as it continued to gain strength from the moisture rising from a relatively warmer sea.

The snowplows and frontend loaders in south Brooklyn were barely keeping up with the snowfall. They were dumping their loads into large transport trucks, which were then unloaded at one of the ten snow melting facilities in the borough. Each site was quickly becoming a massive mountain of snow.

The closer Martin got to the waterfront, the deeper the accumulation was on the streets. She strategically arrived early, pulling off down the street from a large rusted boat repair shop and storage barn, located on the western waterfront of Gerritsen Creek in the Sheepshead Bay neighborhood.

 With pistol drawn, she circled the perimeter of the enormous shed. Drawing on her tactical training, she was dressed in white from her hooded coat to her weather tight overalls, all but invisible as she surveilled the site. Martin didn't want any surprises.

There was a faint glow coming from a frosty window in one of the back offices and she assumed Rybak was already waiting. As agreed, she came prepared to give him the plane tickets and traveling credentials he would need to return to Serbia, the land he'd left as a teenager.

Her instructions from Rybak were clear. Bang hard on the front coiling door, wait ten seconds, and bang three more times. Almost through with her walkaround, she discovered a small window on the side toward a wooded patch near the end of the lagoon. It looked like the vestige of an office that had been torn down decades before, and now a convenient view into the central core of the huge tin shed. The space was filled with all types of watercraft, the majority rigged for sailing and large enough to have cabins below.

In the stillness of the thick snow cover, Martin heard a slight screech, a sound that made her think of opening rusted steel hinges. She made a false trail leading into the woods, then carefully doubled back in her own footsteps. Making her way to the rear of the barn, she crouched down and waited.

Cautiously peeking around the corner, she spotted a man significantly larger than Rybak, standing at the false diversion trail she had just made into the woods. Appearing to ponder his next move, he turned abruptly and went back around to the front entry door.

Martin backtracked to the small window and watched as Rybak unlocked the door and let him in. They clearly knew each other, likely making him a partner in the murder for hire business.

The man soon left and turned toward the bay. Once again, she made her way around the shed and watched as he crossed the marina's private boat launch and walked onto the dock. After shaking snow off the cover of a small runabout, he launched from the dock using only the electric trolling motor. In eerie silence, he and the boat disappeared into the lacelike curtain of snow.

She considered calling Albert for backup, but with the big guy gone so quickly, and the timing of his arrival, it now seemed more like a coincidence than a setup.

As she approached the front entry, her cell vibrated. Pausing, she pulled it out of the deep pocket of her thermal jacket and read the brief text from Albert. Will and Annah were in trouble.

Sending a quick reply, Martin tucked the phone back into her pocket, and as instructed, banged loudly once on the metal coiling door, waited ten seconds, then banged three more times. The sound would have carried a long way in normal weather, but the heavy snow devoured it. It was plenty loud inside, however, and Rybak soon appeared at the door as if he didn't have a care in the world.

* * *

Albert wasn't going to sit around while three of the people most dear to him were in jeopardy. An expert in the art of stealth, he pulled on a reversible rain coat over his ski wear, white side out. Then donning his gray woolen beanie and winter boots, he went back out into the bleak frozen night and jumped into his all-wheel drive Land Rover, still warm from his earlier drive.

He followed the blip of the tracker he'd put on Martin's car through Brooklyn, heading for Sheepshead Bay. Traffic was light as people across the city opted to stay in the warmth of their homes. The hour was late, and other than the methodical movements of snow plows and loaders, the streets were empty. It was a sight not often seen in Brooklyn at any hour.

He'd received a cursory text reply from Martin. *Boat repair barn, Knapp Street, Gerritsen Creek waterfront.*

He spotted her car a block and a half away from a large barn-like shed clad with severely rusted corrugated metal panels. He followed Martin's footsteps, which had already been reduced to snow-filled dimples in the pristine white blanket covering the roadside.

* * *

"This better be good," Martin said, brushing snow off her jacket.

The place smelled of oil and gasoline, with a hint of seaweed. Rybak had set up a folding chair on each side of a beat-up steel table.

"We will put our guns and documents on the table first. Then we sit down with hands above the table."

"Like in the movies." Martin said.

"Yes, movies."

They mirrored each other's movement, carefully laying their pistols on the table. Martin slowly unzipped her coat and retrieved a large envelope, laying it down beside her pistol. Rybak followed suit.

Martin was still processing the news about Will and Annah's

disappearance as she stood across the cold metal table from Ryback. Could he actually be that stupid? Her experience had proven that most criminals expected everyone else to be as sneaky and manipulative as they were, so it was quite possible he may have succumbed to paranoia. She needed to proceed with caution. The safety of her friends was her first priority.

"We look in the envelopes?"

"That's why we're here," Martin countered.

They exchanged envelopes and began sorting their contents.

Martin laid out dossiers of three individuals. The first she knew as Burle Strong, the man Albert strongly suspected of being the actual trigger man for the second attempt on the governor. An FSB document confirmed that he was not only getting paid from the same Cyprus bank account as Drexler, he also received payments from the Oklahoma bank Grimes was deeply involved with.

Grimes had personally authorized the payments to Drexler and Strong. As the director of the board of the very same Cyprus bank, his dividends were in the neighborhood of a million dollars a month. A separate document identified him as a leader of the *Stop Tess Hendricksen* political action committee that had recently spent millions in dark money to derail the new tax law.

The third man had a resume that revealed similar unhealthy and highly illegal proclivities, oddly similar to Grimes.

An arriving text vibrated in Martin's pocket. Putting up her hands, she said, "You mind if I answer this? I'm worried about my friends."

"Give me your phone. I will make sure you are not signaling FBI friends."

She carefully reached into her pocket and handed the phone across the table. Rybak scanned the message and broke into a broad smile. He handed it back to her. The message was simple.

Strong found dead. Speargun bolt through the heart.

Martin put her phone back into her pocket and looked past Ryback's left shoulder. A row of spearguns hung next to the scuba gear near the office.

* * *

It took a while, but Annah finally managed to untie Will's hands. It wasn't long before both of them were free.

"We need to get off this boat," Annah said, scoping out the cabin for anything that might help their escape.

"I can barely make out the shoreline through the snow," Will said as he went from porthole to porthole. "It appears to be several hundred feet off starboard, far too risky to swim in these conditions."

The cabin door was locked from the outside. They methodically searched the dark cabin for keys, or something they could use to pick the lock, with no luck. Frustrated, Will moved to plan B and slammed into the door with his full weight. On the third attempt, the jamb split and the door swung free.

The air was frigid as they climbed the stairs. Wearing only the jeans and oversized sweater she'd had on when they'd been abducted, Annah was shivering uncontrollably by the time they made it to the cockpit. The wheel and throttle were covered with snow. Will brushed it away with bare hands as he checked to see if there was a key in the ignition. He groaned in frustration.

"Will this help?" Annah handed him a fluorescent yellow floating key ring with a single key attached.

"Where did you find it?"

"In the emergency first aid kit with this," holding the object in her hand.

"Is that a flare gun?"

"Looks like it."

"Careful. That might be our last resort."

Will inserted the key. Turning it to the right, the dashboard lit up. Another quarter turn and the large inboard motor came to life.

"We need to raise the anchor before I try to engage the propellers."

"Over here," Annah said. "These look like the controls for the anchor deployment motors."

Annah pushed one of the levers to the up position. The boat groaned and lunged forward as the motor began reeling in the forward anchor.

"Now raise the stern anchor," Will urged, turning toward Annah. "We need to hurry. I'm afraid the sound of the motor will attract attention."

Annah pushed the stern lever up. Turning to give Will a thumbs up, she saw the dark form of a very large man materialize behind Will. Before she could warn him, the man slammed into Will's side. Caught by surprise, Will was somehow able to grab the man's arm as he was falling, and pulled him off balance. They tumbled onto the snow-covered deck that was quickly turning to ice as the temperature dropped even further.

Stunned, Annah was immobilized for an instant before her instincts kicked in. As the men struggled to get purchase on the slippery deck, she engaged the props and pushed the throttle to full forward. The yacht lurched forward, sending both men tumbling toward the transom as the boat picked up speed.

Annah took the wheel and steered the craft toward land, heading for what appeared to be a stretch of shoreline clear of trees.

* * *

Martin pressed Rybak about the death of Strong. "Did you do this?"

"Me? No. Perhaps a gift from a distant admirer," Rybak said as he scrutinized the airline ticket and travel documents in his envelope.

At a crossroad, she knew her choices. Accept his gift or get aggressive.

"And my friends? Where the fuck are they?"

The neutral mask on Rybak's face turned ugly as he jumped up and put his hands on the edge of the table. He was leaning toward Martin when a loud screeching sound broke the silence, followed by an ear-splitting crash. Martin watched in disbelief as the entire bow of a sixty-foot sailing yacht crashed through the huge doors on the boat launch side of the barn.

Holding tightly onto the wheel, the collision knocked Annah off her feet, inadvertently firing the flare gun. The red ball of fire careened off the wall like a bank shot in a game of pool and came directly at the table in the center of the room.

Martin and Rybak dove for cover, overturning the table on their way down. She grabbed Rybak's ankle as he scrambled to reach one of the pistols now on the floor.

Albert, who had been outside waiting for the right moment to intervene, broke through the door with his weapon drawn. In all of his years of service, he hadn't seen anything like what laid before him. More than half of a large yacht laid seriously askew on the shop floor, surrounded by large pieces of twisted metal from the siding of the old shed wall.

He watched as Will dropped from the front bow rail. The second his feet hit the floor a rough looking burly man appeared at the rail above him. Will dove for cover as the man took aim at his back.

Two shots rang out in rapid succession.

Albert ran toward Will through a wall of dark smoke. The flare had started a fire in the degreasing area, igniting an old wooden workbench, with cans of flammable solvents stored dangerously close to the flames. He spotted Will crouched beneath the port bow a few feet away from the large man lying face down in his own blood.

Annah made her way to the low side of the leaning sailboat deck, and scrambled down behind a small boat and trailer that had been flipped onto its side. With the fire growing in intensity, she crept toward the front exit on her hands and knees, trying to stay below the billowing fumes.

Rybak broke Martin's grip and lunged for the gun as Annah emerged from the smoke. Raising his arm, he took aim. In an instant, Martin leapt over the overturned table and tackled Annah to the floor. The gun blast rattled the metal siding as the bullet struck Martin in the back.

Rybak spun toward the exit and was greeted by Albert's fist. Kicking the gun away, Albert had the assassin handcuffed before he knew what had hit him.

Rushing through the increasingly dense smoke, Albert's heart sank. Will and Annah knelt beside Martin, who was lying prone on the cold cement floor.

As he closed the gap between them, he heard Martin groan as she reached for her back. Will gave him a quick thumbs up.

"That's my girl, wearing your vest under that snow suit," Albert said as he helped her sit up. "We need to get out of here before those acetylene tanks blow."

"We can't go without Rybak's documents."

Annah quickly gathered the files that were strewn across the floor and followed Will and Martin out of the barn. Albert brought up the rear, his gun firmly in Rybak's side.

They sprinted away from the building headed for the cover of a deep snow drift when the barn blew up. There was no going back to recover the body of the burly man Will last saw lying dead in a pool of blood congealing on the cold concrete floor.

Chapter 54

Court of Appeals - Albany, New York

The chief justice gaveled the Court of Appeals into session as the sun finally broke through. The light reflecting off the fresh blanket of snow made it unusually bright inside the packed courtroom.

The emergency session opened with a brief statement by Chief Justice Mulder, followed by the opening statement of the opposition lawyers representing a coalition that opposed the Freedom of Conscience Act.

Carson Frick, the lead lawyer and proud associate member of the Originalist Confederation, focused on the issue of hard evidence.

"Your Honor, our case is quite simple. The defense has no physical evidence supporting their *theory* of the founders' intent, yet we are asked to believe that the founding fathers of our great state held that any individual, no matter how degenerate or uneducated, should be held in the same esteem as those practicing the traditional religions in New York at the time of our first constitution."

Aware he had the majority of the bench leaning into his words, he pressed his point.

"Certainly, something of this importance would have been recorded in the minutes of their debates. Other than third party opinions that are no more than hearsay, we demand to see physical proof."

Nette Bergen abruptly rose to her feet. "May we approach, your honors?

"You may."

Walking quickly to the bench, Nette argued her point. "The opposition well knows that the physical documents they are demanding were lost in a tragic fire at the capital before the age of photographs and copiers. The surviving firsthand accounts of the founders' intentions contained in our brief are at minimum circumstantial evidence, and should be admissible."

"You will have an opportunity to defend your position and challenge their statements and witnesses. The plaintiffs may continue with their argument."

For the better part of the next hour, the opposition lawyers presented a picturesque vision of rural life during the time of the American Revolution, a society guided by the tenets of well-established churches.

The governor's defense team objected to these nostalgic references insisting they were not relevant to the case at hand. But the lure of a pure and pastoral America was being used like a shiny object hypnotists dangle before their subjects. Nette was not convinced the justices were immune to this type of seductive nostalgia. She had practiced law long enough to know that, while enrobed, judges could be tempted to consider themselves keepers of the moral code, or shepherds helping the masses determine right from wrong.

* * *

Nette led the legal defense by presenting an unbroken chain of case law and precedent going all the way back to the Dutch colony. Her strongest physical evidence was an authenticated duplicate of the Articles of Capitulation agreed upon by both the Dutch and British commanders at the time of the New Netherlands surrender. Article Eight was of specific relevance, and read:

> *The Dutch here shall enjoy the Liberty of their Consciences*
> *in Divine Worship and Church Discipline.*

311

Tess believed that this document alone proved their case, but Nette cautioned that the plaintiffs would continue to argue that this was a treaty provision later superseded by the first state constitution.

Tess leaned closer to Nette, and whispered, "I've been watching the body language behind the bench. None of these justices want their legacy to be linked to the undoing of religion, or worse yet, working for the devil."

"You *are* aware how treacherous these waters are to navigate," Nette replied in a low voice.

"I am. But we can counter that argument by making it crystal clear that the healthy spiritual diversity we have today in New York is one of our strengths as a people. Old laws that favor one religious group or sect over an individual's own unique and personal spirituality can no longer be justified, and must therefore be eliminated. There will be no state sponsored church as long as I am governor."

Nette nodded as Tess continued.

"I'm afraid the case may be slipping away. Not because we are wrong, but because of social inertia, conventional opinion, and old reactionary thinking set in a mythical version of America that simply..." Tess was interrupted by the buzz of an incoming text.

New physical evidence, be there soon. Stall if you must.

* * *

The storm clouds were finally lifting above JFK International as Martin and Albert arrived at the FBI aircraft hangar and evidence warehouse just off the main cargo loop. Several private jets and transport planes stood ready on the runway access lane. A sleek new Airbus ACH 145 was fueled up and waiting for them on the FBI's private helipad.

After being escorted to their Brooklyn apartment by two of Martin's agents, Will and Annah arrived at the helipad, dressed in warm clothes and clutching the relevant portions of the original Gerritsen print shop documents.

"Climb in! We're cleared to take off," the pilot yelled over the sound of a jet taxiing toward the runway.

"We're waiting for two more," Martin shouted back as she stood on the tarmac next to the sleek new helicopter.

Sharky arrived a few minutes later with Kai Theron. Informed that he had been called as a witness in the high court in Albany, Kai had quickly gathered his translation files of the State constitutional convention minutes before following Sharky to his idling car.

Martin greeted them as they piled out of the car and quickly led them across the tarmac. The last to enter, she gave the pilot a thumbs up and joined the others who were already strapped into their seats.

With the new evidence from Rybak confirmed, Martin had secured an arrest warrant for one Clay Daggert, and ordered her taskforce to take him into custody. She had just received confirmation by text that the arrest had been made at his Manhattan office. She was anxious to deliver the promised new evidence to the governor, and serve a second arrest warrant in person, once they landed in Albany.

The turbines began to whine and the rotors to turn as the copilot secured the door behind her. She scanned the passengers to make sure they had secured their seat restraints and donned their headsets before taking her own seat in the cockpit. Within minutes, they were rising above Jamaica Bay with Flushing and the East River coming into view on the horizon.

As they flew over the Spuyten Duyvil and the heart of what had been Colen Donck, Will wondered what Adriaen van der Donck might have thought about this current expression of New York which had grown from the seeds of tolerance and self-governance that he'd planted so long before.

And now Will and his companions were flying toward Albany to defend the Freedom of Conscience that the Yonker had inspired in Flushing and elsewhere across the New Netherlands. He was so engrossed in his musings about their historic mission, he hadn't noticed that his fear of flying had all but vanished.

Their flight north took them directly over Kingston. Studying the landforms and development patterns as Will was prone to do, he spotted the old Stockade District and Senate House. The western horizon beyond the city was dominated by the Catskill Mountains. He could make out the reflective surface of the Ashokan Reservoir near the Garrison Farm.

It was beyond coincidence that the old print shop documents discovered in his family barn came to light at the precise time they could lend relevant evidence to support the governor's case. Will had experienced a benevolent force acting through the veil of time before, and could feel it's presence again, much as he and Annah had during their escapades in Palmyra not long ago.

Will was pulled from his reflections when the Airbus dropped into its descent over the capital district in downtown Albany. The high courtroom windows began to shake as the large shadow of the helicopter passed overhead.

In spite of the frigid air and heavy snow cover, the crowd gathering around the courthouse had grown into a large assemblage of media, citizens waving homemade signs supporting Governor Hendricksen, and their counterparts, many wearing death masks and black cloaks. The appearance of the helicopter drew them like a magnet, almost as if the FBI helicopter had some important bearing on the trial.

The pilot knew the area well, and carefully veered away from the approaching crowd, setting the helicopter down on the snow-covered lawn of Academy Park across the street from the Court of Appeals.

* * *

With the court in recess, Judge Bragg returned to his chambers where he received a call on his private cell from the senior partner of the law firm that represented the Originalists Confederation.

"Byron, thank God you answered your phone. Clay Daggert has been taken into custody by agents of the FBI's assassination taskforce."

Bragg was silent for a beat before he replied, "Clay? That's terrible!"

"It gets worse. Your name is listed beside his on the arrest warrant."

"What? Why on earth would they arrest me?"

"My question exactly."

His face was ashen as he ended the call and laid his cell on the edge of his desk. An uncontrollable panic overtook him and he frantically began to stuff sensitive documents into his briefcase.

Pulling on his coat, he scanned his office one last time. Remembering the gift Grimes had given him when he was appointed to the high court, he opened the bottom drawer of his desk and slipped it into the pocket of his overcoat.

Turning up his collar, he headed for the exit.

* * *

The helicopter doors slid open and the crowd, that moments before was headed toward them, suddenly did an about face and ran toward the side doors of the courthouse.

As Martin stepped out of the Airbus, she heard people shouting *Judge Bragg* as the unruly crowd ran across the snowy lawn.

Pushing their way through the wall of reporters, Sharky positioned himself on the sidewalk leading to the judge's parking lot as Martin made it to the bottom of the broad granite staircase outside the courthouse moments before Bragg.

In a panic, the judge didn't notice her in the crowd until he was almost at the landing. Martin's eyes locked on him as she held up her badge, and for a fleeting moment, she felt pity for him.

"Byron Bragg, you are under arrest for sexual conduct with minors aboard a United States flagged ship, and conspiracy to commit an act of terrorism."

Bragg froze for a split second. Confused, he took a few steps toward the parking lot, then stopped abruptly when he saw Sharky blocking his way.

Martin was close enough to see the fear in his eyes. Realizing he had become a cornered animal, she made eye contact with Sharky and nodded. On her signal, he took a few steps toward the judge.

Catching Sharky's movement in his peripheral vision, Bragg reached into his coat pocket and pulled out a gold-plated pistol. The gift from Grimes.

"Everyone back!"

He swung the pistol wildly in the direction of the reporters. Someone screamed, and the crowd broke into chaos. While some ran, others kept their live cameras and microphones trained on the judge.

Bragg was distracted by the movement of the crowd, allowing Sharky to make his way over the low wall that ran along the side of the staircase and position himself behind him on the steps. Martin kept her gun trained on his chest.

Seeing there was no escape, Bragg spun around and headed up the stairs toward the side door. He made it up two steps before he saw Sharky.

Without hesitation, Bragg raised the pistol to his head.

The crack of the gunshot echoed off the old stone walls of the courthouse, as his last moments were streamed across the world.

* * *

Bragg's suicide and the ensuing commotion at the courthouse delayed the resumption of the trial until the following morning. Chief Justice Mulder knew she had to restore order.

"Bring the Defendants and their new witnesses to my chambers," she ordered her bailiff. "I want to see this new evidence for myself before I resume these proceedings."

So directed, the group followed the bailiff through security and down a wide, lovingly preserved neo-classical corridor detailed in black and white marble.

Crossing a centrally located lounge area, they entered the first office suite on the right, following the bailiff through the tall wooden door inset with obscure glass.

The office suite was spacious. A large and ornate wooden desk was positioned by the window, surrounded by several modern work stations. Justice Mulder sat behind the desk, flanked by her clerk and transcriptionist. Five chairs had been arranged in front of her desk, and they took their seats.

"What is the nature of this new evidence?"

Nette introduced the team and did a quick summary of their facts. Will began by verifying the provenance of his family print shop, and the recent discovery of the historic equipment and original transcripts found in the boxes of old business files. He described in detail how the storage room in the family barn was scientifically recorded and its contents meticulously catalogued before being moved to the Brooklyn Museum for conservation.

Annah picked up where Will left off, describing how she had performed the conservation work and authenticated the paper documents, scientifically establishing the age and origin of the ink, type face, and paper. Her analysis proved the records to be genuine, and appropriate to the time of the American Revolution, and to the location of Kingston where the state constitution was debated and written.

Kai Theron then walked the judge through his translation of the papers in question, and the particulars of the Dutch dialect spoken at the time they were allegedly written. He stated with absolute certainty that the dialect and language of the written transcripts matched perfectly.

"My staff has verified your credentials. You have an exemplary reputation, Doctor Theron, therefore we allow your testimony. Please tell us what these Dutch minutes tell us that is relevant to your defense."

Theron handed the judge and her clerk copies of the translated minutes.

"The relevant documents are dated April eighteenth and nineteenth, in the year of seventeen hundred and seventy-seven, putting it precisely in the center of our dating range for the paper. What caught our attention was a section entitled *Discussions Regarding Liberty of Conscience*. It soon became clear that we had discovered the original minutes from the state constitutional convention. It made perfect sense they were written in Dutch, considering that half of the delegates still spoke Dutch."

The judge paused to organize her next question.

"Did they express their views regarding the relationship between the state and religion?"

"Your honor, we've concluded that these minutes are a complete record of the discussions held at that first convention. A great deal of attention was paid to the matter of Liberty of Conscience which was clearly focused on protecting the rights of individual citizens to practice their beliefs, whether based on a recognized religion, their own practice of spirituality, or whether they held any beliefs at all.

"You can read here on page one where they specifically warned against the government showing any religious bias, or establishing laws that allowed favoritism to one sect over everyone else."

* * *

Judge Mulder called the court back into session. After reviewing copies of the new evidence, they were polled for further questions of the defense, but had none.

She turned to the lead opposition lawyer who had also reviewed the Dutch records. "Now that we have the physical proof you've been demanding, where does that leave your central argument, in fact your only argument?"

Carson Frick, the lawyer for the ORCs, struggled to find a plausible counter argument.

"We request a recess your honor, to digest this new evidence."

"Denied. You came to this court with an argument that has been proven to be meritless."

Calling for a vote from the other justices, there was unanimous agreement.

"I hereby declare your appeal denied. This case is dismissed."

The strike of her gavel echoed through the courtroom.

Chapter 55

Garrison Farm – Esopus Creek

"Good idea taking a moonlight walk on the river trail," Annah said as she exhaled a thick cloud of steam.

"You warm enough?" Will asked, reaching over and turning up her collar.

"All but the tip of my nose, but the Irish Cream in my coffee is helping a lot," she said before taking another sip from her thermos bottle.

The moon was at its zenith, painting the scattered patches of snow beneath the leafless trees in its blue white glow. Other than the distinct sound of the partially frozen ground crunching beneath their feet, the woods were totally silent.

"It felt good to get out of the city after opening the Colonial Dutch Print Shop exhibit," Will said, leading the way forward on the path.

"I'm impressed with the governor's courage. After two attempts on her life, she didn't hesitate to attend the opening, or to push ahead with her reforms."

"And the world hasn't come to an end as her detractors predicted."

"Not yet, but the ORCs and madmen like them are always looking for something to blame the end of the world on," Will said over his shoulder. "Good idea about the Irish Cream," he added, taking another swig of his coffee.

The sound of the river broke through the silence as the trail wound down the wooded slope. Ahead of them, the river came into view, looking like a ribbon of polished silver as the moonlight shimmered over the surface of the water.

"Show me the place where you found the brass box. I'm guessing it's not far from here."

"You're right, it's just up ahead," Will answered.

The moon was bright and it lit the path, making it easy for him to find his way back to the place by the river bank where he'd found the box.

Nearing the bank, Will was startled to hear the sound of a horse whinnying in the clearing. Following the sound, he turned to his right.

"Mary Lou, what are you doing here?" Will said, equally pleased and puzzled, wondering how she had gotten out of the barn.

"Nice to see you Mary Lou," Annah said, taking her presence in stride. She stood next to the gentle horse and stroked her forehead with her gloved hand.

Mary Lou snorted, instantly creating a cloud of vapor that hovered in the air as she struck her hoof on the ground.

"What is it girl?" Will asked.

Scanning the clearing, Will realized Mary Lou was standing in front of the same tree where they had found the brass box. Striking the ground again, he focused on the area close to her hoof.

Something small and round protruded from the frosty loam in front of her, illuminated by the moonlight.

He knelt down and used his pocket knife to free the object from the frozen earth. Holding it in his open palms, he gazed into a perfectly spherical iridescent crystal that radiated an etheric blue light.

Drawn deeper into the sphere, he recognized the stylized hand, the symbol of the Yamin, the Right Hand Path of old. The hand appeared to be hovering at the center of the celestial orb.

Will stood up and held out his hand so Annah could see what Mary Lou had led them to. As their eyes met, a strange vibration began to come from the crystal.

* * *

Will opened his eyes to find Annah sitting beside him on the edge of the bed, holding out his cell phone.

"Sweetie, you may want to read this text. It's from Bene Rivkin at the British Museum."

The mystical moonlit vision still swam in his head as he took the phone from Annah's hand.

How quick can you get to London? Found new evidence about the Well of Records.

The End

Characters
(Seventeenth Century)

Adriaen van der Donck (Jonk Heer): lawyer, naturalist, explorer, champion of liberty

Agatha van Bergen: mother of Adriaen van der Donck; settler in New Amsterdam

Aghar (Agheroense): Mohawk interpreter/diplomat; friend of Adriaen van der Donck

Annekan van Beyeran: wife of Tobias Feake; widow of Daniel Patrick

Arent van Curler: Rensselaer's nephew; Director of Rensselaerswyck

Cornelius Melyn: Dutch settler of Staten Island; ally of Adriaen van der Donck

Cornelis van Tienhoven: corrupt second in command to Kieft and Stuyvesant

Eduard Hart: town clerk of Vlissingen (Flushing); signer of the Flushing Remonstrance

Elias Doughtie: brother of Mary Doughtie; brother-in-law of Adriaen van der Donck

Hannah Feake: sibling first cousin of Tobias Feake; early Quaker in New Netherlands

Hendrick van Dyck: started a war by shooting a Munsee woman stealing peaches

Hugo van der Groot (Grotius): Dutch lawyer; father of international law

John Bowne: husband of Hannah Feake; early Quaker in Flushing, New Netherlands

Katonuk: sagamore of Siwanoy village near the white plains

Manetuwak: Siwanoy name for Tienhoven, meaning the "Devil"

Mary Doughtie: wife of Adriaen van der Donck; daughter of Francis Doughtie

Michiel Janszen: Dutch settler of Rensselaerswyck, ally of Adriaen van der Donck

Oakwari: Mohawk sachem; grandfather of Agheroense; reader of dreams

Oratam: great sachem of the Hackensack Lenape; buried in the Sicomac

Pieter Stuyvesant: Director General of New Netherlands; surrendered to the British

Reverend Francis Doughtie: father of Mary and Elias Doughtie; unorthodox views

Richard Nicholls: captured New Amsterdam, first British governor of New York

Robert Hodgson: immigrant tortured by Director Stuyvesant for practicing Quakerism

Roger Williams: founder of the Providence Colony; advocate of religious freedom

Sarah O'Neal: wife of Elias Doughtie

Seconeok: Mohican sachem in the Catskills; friend of Agheroense

Sicomac: Lenape for "Happy Hunting Grounds" or "Resting Place for the Departed"

Tobias Feake: English settler; coastal trader; schout (sheriff) of Vlissingen (Flushing)

Wilden: Dutch name for the indigenous people of the New Netherlands

Willem Blauvelt: Dutch pirate and privateer in the service of New Netherlands

Killian van Rensselaer: Dutch merchant who founded the colony of Rensselaerswyck

Willem Kieft: Director General of New Netherland; started war with the Wilden

Characters

(Present Day)

Albert Harwick: retired MI6 agent; lifelong friends of Will Garrison's family

Anika Spaulding: mother of the deceased Riley Spalding, Will's former girlfriend

Annah Devar: Indian archeologist from Kerala; partner of Will Garrison

Bass Drexler: covert operative of Gaston Grimes and the ORCs

Beatrix de Boer: Director of Brooklyn Museum

Burle Strong: covert operative of Clay Daggert and the ORCs

Byron Bragg: corrupt judge on New York's highest court; member of the ORCs

Caslav Nedic: explosives and weapons smuggler; love interest of Sofiya Balashov

Clay Daggert: senior member of the Originalist Confederation (ORCs)

Clovis Helms: covert operative of Del Thatcher; member of governor's security detail

Darcy Wells: wife of Hollis Marsh; member of governor's planning group

Del Thatcher: compromised head of governor's security; controlled by Byron Bragg

Everett Pendrake: alias of Albert Harwick; ghost writer for Governor Hendriksen

Hollis Marsh: compromised mechanic on Governor Hendriksen's limousine

Gaston Grimes: senior member of the Originalist Confederation (ORCs)

Johanna Martin: Special Agent, FBI Brooklyn; assigned to Governor's security detail

Kai Theron: South African translation expert of colonial Dutch dialects

Kariwase (Kari): Mohawk caretaker of the Garrison farm; friend of Will and Annah

Nette Bergen: Attorney General of the State of New York

Rybak Sadouski: enforcer for Sofiya Balashov; nephew of Caslav Nedic

Senator Torres: United States Senator from the State of New York

Sofiya Balashov: bombing facilitator on first assassination attempt on the governor

Sydney Rogers: graduate intern in the Brooklyn Museum

Sharky: Special Agent Obsharski, FBI Brooklyn; assigned to Governor's security detail

Tess Hendriksen: governor of the State of New York

Thomma Devar: brother of Annah Devar; archeologist killed by Taliban in Afghanistan

Will Garrison: American paleographer and philologist; partner of Annah Devar

Other Books by Curt Ench

Secret of the Fire Temple
(The Translation Trilogy - Book 1)

ISBN 979-8-9873782-1-2 (e-book)

ISBN 979-8-9873782-2-9 (paperback)

Return of the Mystic
(The Translation Trilogy - Book 2)

ISBN 979-8-9873782-4-3 (e-book)

ISBN 979-8-9873782-5-0 (paperback)

Lady of the Lake
(The Translation Trilogy - Book 3)

ISBN 979-8-9873782-7-4 (e-book)

ISBN 979-8-9873782-8-1 (paperback)

Visit our website at curtench.com

Bio

Curt Ench is the author of *The Devar-Garrison Historical Mystery Series* in which he explores the inescapable and sometimes magical connections between the past and the present.

Influenced as a young child by his parent's quest for both scientific and spiritual knowledge, and their trail blazing exploration of Western and Eastern philosophies, he has maintained a lifelong pursuit of understanding the cultures and beliefs of others, and find the common ground we all share. With a true love of storytelling, *The Devar-Garrison Historical Mystery Series* is the culmination of that quest.

The first novels of the series are collectively known as The Translation Trilogy, in which Curt explores the watershed events at the turn of the first century that still bear heavily on our current civilization. The issues of tolerance and empathy are at the heart of these stories.

In his latest novel, *The Yonker - Lost Treasure of Esopus Creek*, he traces the origins of American liberty and religious tolerance back to their seventeenth century Dutch roots in the bustling port city of New Amsterdam and the nearby village of Flushing. It was in Flushing that freedom of conscience, a newly adopted liberty in the Dutch homeland, was passed on to its offspring colony, where it ultimately became a fundamental part of American law. And although the authoritarian directors of the West India Company tried to extinguish its essence, much of it has survived into our modern era.

Curt's intention is to create a series that brings light important historical events in ways that people find relevant to their current lives, and honors those who practice tolerance and seek justice, both now and in the distant past. He holds in the highest regard those who had the courage and conviction to risk everything in order to replace cruelty with compassion, prejudice with acceptance, and deceit with honesty.